Douglas Lindsay was born in Scotland in 1964. He
wrote this book while living in Senegal, one of ever
dwindling number of countries in the world never to
have beaten Scotland at football.

Belgrade
19ᵗʰ Nov 04

To Polly & Steve,

Thanks for a lovely visit.
Jessica and I had a ball. Hopefully
some time we can return in the summer, and
watch the Red Sox beat the Yankees on a
warm, sunny evening!

Hope you enjoy the ethnic
literature.

D

Also by Douglas Lindsay:

The Cutting Edge of Barney Thomson

A Prayer For Barney Thomson

Barney Thomson & The Face of Death

The King Was In His Counting House

THE
LONG MIDNIGHT
OF BARNEY THOMSON

DOUGLAS LINDSAY

This edition published in Great Britain in 2003 by
Long Midnight Publishing
Suite 433
24 Station Square
Inverness IV1 1LD
e-mail: info@barney-thomson.com

First published (0 7499 3087 X) in 1999
by Piatkus Books
Reprinted 2000

www.barney-thomson.com

A catalogue record for this book is available
from the British Library

ISBN 0 9541387 1 6

Printed and bound in Great Britain by
Mckays of Chatham plc, Chatham, Kent

For Kathryn

Contents

Prologue

Breasts.

The body of the young woman lies on the kitchen table. The face, azurean white in the melancholic repose of death; the eyes, open and stark, staring blankly into whatever world of demons she has ventured; the body, lying to attention, as if on parade; and then the breasts. Small, firm, strangely upstanding, in the pale fluorescent light of the kitchen.

What will happen if they are removed, now that the girl has been dead for over three hours? Will they fold into some amorphous mass, losing their singular beauty, or will they remain firm and shapely, their allure and elegance preserved?

The killer looks over the rest of the body. Until now the victims have all been men. In death their bodies are always brutal and ugly, repugnant flesh on the cusp of decay. But this girl, with her smooth, ghostly complexion, the neat, silvicultural thatch of thin blonde hair nestling snugly between her thighs, and her beautiful breasts, is so much more. It will almost be a shame to cleave into the luxurious pale skin.

Perhaps it would be simpler to send off an ear or a hand. A bland statement of release to the dear departed's family. A pleasant reminder of their daughter. Something for them to cherish in future years.

A delightful surprise, this girl, when a man had been expected. Ian, she had said her name was. A final, pointless, damning lie. And the poor girl had been so disappointing in death. It is always the most sumptuous part of it, that horrified look on the face as they watch the cut-throat razor descend with elegant panache to proffered neck. But this one. This girl. She had hardly looked interested. She might have been being offered a cigarette.

Drugs probably. That would have been it. So high on drugs she would hardly have noticed. That's the trouble with people today – the great bane of our times – no one has any standards any more.

It is time. And it has to be the breasts. It's so much more artistic. The killer smiles – ever the slave to the aesthetic – and, firmly clutching the right breast, pierces the skin with the eight-inch butcher's knife.

Chapter 1

The English Are Bastards

There's nowhere worse than Glasgow on a freezing cold, dank, sodden day in March, especially when your car is in the garage undergoing repairs costing twice NASA's annual budget, and you are obliged to spend your day cutting hair. Greasy hair; pungent hair; hair riddled with insects; hair which cries out to be fashioned into a work of art, when the customer won't allow; hair which requires the use of a chainsaw, an implement long ago outlawed in barber shops. Hair of all sorts – vile, messy, contemptible.

Barney Thomson, barber, scowls. They're all bastards, every one of them that comes into the shop. And if, on occasion, some leave feeling like their head has just been raped, then they deserve it.

As he stands at the kerb waiting to cross the road for the final struggle up the hill, a passing van, hugging the pavement, sends a panoramic rainbow of water over his trousers and jacket. He has no time to move before the rear wheels kick up that little extra which propels some more into his face.

He watches it speed off, thinks of raising his fist, but sodden apathy gets the better of him. There's no point. Hunches his shoulders even further, trudges across the road, imagines the van driver having a heart attack, dying at the wheel.

Sure, it rains everywhere in Scotland, he thinks, one foot plodding relentlessly in front of the other. It's one of the things that defines it as a place. But there's no other city as dour as Glasgow in the rain. Edinburgh – the rain just makes the castle look even more dramatic. Same for Stirling. Perth, a land of kings, glorious in all weather. Dundee, Aberdeen – they're on the east coast, so if it wasn't raining then they wouldn't look natural.

It's just Glasgow. In the sun it looks good, and in the rain it's terrible. An awful place to be.

He thinks he should leave. Agnes doesn't want to go, but then he doesn't have to take her with him. He could open up his own shop in one of the small towns up north. Fort William, Oban, Ullapool, wherever. Just away from here, and all these bloody miserable people. Like himself, the most miserable of the lot.

Two small children, duffel-coated against the rain, school bags plastered onto their backs, gallons of molten snot careering down their faces, scuttle past him on their way to some pre-school turpitude, and he does his best to embrace them with a scowl.

Thinks of children. The barber's nightmare. He hates the lot of them, with their mothers looking at every snip of the hair, and talking all the time, telling you what to do. And the kids sitting on the chair, kicking their feet up and down, making noises, incapable of keeping still. You spend twenty minutes just dying to give them a clip round the ear. But your hands are tied. Mothers should have to cut the hair of their own children until they are eighteen, he thinks, and the only smile of the day comes to his lips as he does so.

He's nearly there, the long trudge almost over. Imagines himself to have been on a long trek across the Arctic. In euphonious celebration of his achievement, the rain increases its intensity so that it bounces off the pavement. He hurries the last hundred yards to the shop, but it's to no avail, and by the time he arrives his jacket has given up the ghost, his clothes are sticking to his skin like an over-reliant child, and his carefully nurtured bouffant hair has plummeted into a watery abyss. Neither of the others has yet arrived, and so he has to stand for another minute in the rain, fumbling to get the keys from his pocket, before he can escape the downpour.

In the grey early morning the shop is cold and lonely, and his heart sinks further at the thought of the day ahead. He should have become an astronaut when he'd had the chance.

The television mutters in the corner. Wullie Henderson looks up from the *Daily Record* to watch the action from the previous day's English football. Aston Villa versus Derby County. Dire stuff, but football is football, and he's reached the end of the sports pages.

They are filled with the usual things. Football, football, football, and an enlarged section on the England cricket team's latest Test defeat. The size of the report is always directly proportional to the size of the defeat, he reflects, as the ball flies into the net from twenty-five yards, sparking a minor, but nevertheless engaging, pitch invasion.

He looks back and rereads the article on whether Rangers are about to sign Alessandro del Piero for £30 million, in an effort to still be participating in Europe come September, then folds the paper and lays it on the table. Takes a cursory glance at the front-page headline. 'The English Are Bastards'. Par for the course, he thinks, as he tucks into his final piece of toast and marmalade. Beneath that story is a follow-up report concerning the latest murder in the city. The most recent in a series of grotesque killings, the work of one man, or so the police believe, which has been dominating the news for a couple of months. The English must really be bastards to keep that off the headline.

'Ye'll be late. It's nearly five to,' says his wife, not bothering to raise her eyes from the *Daily Express*.

Wullie Henderson looks at the television. They've moved on to women's golf. Time to go. Looks at his wife. Thinks of the girl he met on Friday night in the Montrose, wonders if she'll be there again this Friday. Doesn't do any harm to think, though he knows that he'd do more than think if he got the chance.

'Aye, Ah suppose ye're right.'

He stands up, pulls at his jeans, is satisfied that he's

beginning to lose some weight, then turns to walk out of the back door.

'Here you! You put a jaicket on, or ye'll catch your death oot there, so ye will. It's bucketin' doon oot there, so it is.'

'Ah've got one in the motor, and Ah'll be parking right ootside the shop anyway. Keep yer knickers on, wumin.'

'Aye, well, away ye go,' she says to his back, and with a final grunt thrown over his shoulder, he's gone. Moira Henderson looks up from the paper to see the door close, wonders whether to have another piece of toast.

The rain is hammering down as he steps out of the door, and he runs to his car and jumps in. A month ago he would have been expecting trouble getting his car started in this weather, but now, as he sits in his new Peugeot 305, his mind is more on how all this rain will affect the chances of the Rangers–Motherwell game going ahead the following night.

The car starts like a dream and he sets out on the five-minute drive to the shop. It's not too far, but there are several strategically placed traffic lights, specifically positioned to hold him up in the morning, and he wonders to whom he can complain on the council.

By the time he pulls up outside the shop, the torrent of rain has eased, and he leaves his jacket in the car as he steps out. There's a light on, which means that one of the others has already arrived. Probably Barney. Chris would be late again. He's always late on Monday mornings, and Wullie knows he'll have to have a word with him about it. Some day.

He opens the door and walks in. The little bell rings above his head, and Barney looks up from his seat where he is reading the *Herald*.

'Barney, how ye doin'?'

'Hello, Wullie. No' so bad, no' so bad.'

'Good weekend?' asks Wullie, walking into the shop, and experiencing the sinking feeling that he always feels first thing on a Monday.

'Aye, it was awright, Ah suppose. You?'

'Aye, aye, fine.' He looks around the drab surroundings of the small shop which has been his workplace for over ten years. Was any weekend which just led back to this place really fine?

'Nightmare weather,' says Barney. 'Ah got bloody soaked when Ah came in.'

'Aye, terrible,' says Wullie. Stands in the middle of the shop looking at Barney, then realises he has nothing else to say to him. The same brief conversation every Monday morning, with seasonal variations, and then they would hardly talk to one another for the rest of the week. No point in telling Barney about the girl in the Montrose.

They stare blankly for a few seconds, then with a nod Barney looks back at his paper, Wullie goes about his business.

Chris Porter stirs, his head encased in a pillow. His girl-friend has been sacked from her job as a Formula One driver by Tom Jones, the team owner, and he is in the middle of head-butting the Welshman, when he wakes up. He smiles sleepily.

That had been a good dream. He would have to tell Helen later.

He rolls over and his eyes flicker open long enough to glance at the clock. Five past eight. It doesn't register, and he closes his eyes again, tries to slide back into the dream from which he has just come.

Shite. He opens his eyes, bolts upright. Shite. He's slept through the alarm again. The usual Monday morning event. Shite. Looks at the clock again to make sure he isn't rushing unnecessarily, then leaps out of bed and into the bathroom.

It's not that he ever does anything particular on a Sunday night, he reflects, as he washes all the parts of his body that seem appropriate, randomly spraying water over the floor as he does so. It's just a natural aversion to Monday mornings. He knows it's a good thing that it's Wullie who's in charge and not Barney, or he would have been in trouble a long time ago.

He dresses with unnecessary flourish and flies into the kitchen, debating whether to accept the fact he is late and be even later by having cereal. Finding the fridge uncontaminated by milk, his mind is made up for him, and he speeds to the front door and down the stairs with a sigh and an empty stomach.

He is still driving the same old Escort which his dad bought for him in his last year at school, and after spluttering a little in the rain, it kicks into action and he sets out on the ten-minute drive to the shop, wondering if this is going to be the morning when he finally gets his backside kicked for being late.

He arrives at twenty-five past eight, finds a heaven-sent parking space right outside the shop, runs in. Barney and Wullie look at him from empty chairs. There are no customers in yet. A little prayer answered.

Wullie looks at his watch, shakes his head. 'Whit time dae ye call this, Porter?'

Chris looks around the empty shop, slightly annoyed that he is out of breath after a ten-yard run from his car. 'The time before any customers have come in yet?'

Wullie raises an eyebrow. 'Aye, it's quiet now, but ye should have seen the first twenty minutes o' the day. Heavin', so it was. That no' right, Barney?'

Barney shrugs, grunts, goes back to reading his paper.

'Willnae happen again, Wullie,' says Chris, taking off his jacket and assuming his position.

'Aye, an' youse lot are gonnae win the Cup this year.'

Chris smiles. 'Hey, we beat Stirling Albion three–nothin' on Saturday.'

'Yoo hoo!' says Wullie, raising his arms in celebration.

'Aye, ye can laugh now, but ye better hope youse lot don't get us in the Cup or ye're in trouble.'

Wullie laughs again, and stands up as the first customer of the day, his hair matted with rain, his face an atlas of misery, comes through the door to the melodic tinkle of the bell.

'Aye, Ah'm shittin' ma pants, Chris. It's no' as if ye're gonnae get past Aberdeen in the quarter-final, is it, Big Man?'

'You wait an' see.'

Barney watches them out of the corner of his eye. Football, football. It's all they ever talk about. It would be so beautiful one day to shut them up. What damage he could do with a pair of scissors. With a shake of the head, and further malicious reflections upon dark deeds, he returns to the gardening page.

Chapter 2

Customers Must Have Hair

It is going badly. Exceptionally badly. There are voyages of the *Titanic* which have gone better than this. Barney catches the eye of the customer in the mirror, and does his best not to convey what he knows and what the victim has yet to realise. Sometimes the first haircut of the day can be catastrophic. A headlong rush to do good, which turns to bloody disaster. James IV at Flodden, the Charge of the Light Brigade, the Zulus at Rorke's Drift. It won't start out that way, but somewhere along the line it becomes a horror story. Grown men weep.

He surveys his handiwork, and realises the damage being cleaved by his own scissors. The man has asked for a straightforward short back and sides, a Frank Sinatra '62, but things have rollercoasted out of hand.

As he ensures that he avoids the gaze of his customer, he considers the two options open to barbers in such circumstances. One – keep cutting until all is recovered, and the hair looks fairly even. Unfortunately, this usually leaves the victim looking like a US marine, and if it so happens that he thinks like a US marine, you're in trouble. Two – cover his head in water, pretend your hairdryer isn't working, and let the full devastation be revealed to him later on when he is sitting at work, his hair has dried, and his colleagues are having a field day. It is a lucky man who, under such circumstances, has a job which requires headwear.

The man who sits before him is of considerable stature. Seven feet tall, thinks Barney. Giant Kills Barber in Revenge Attack. Barney sees the headline. Option one is not viable. It must be number two, with the expectation that such a large man is unlikely to even ask for the hairdryer, in case anyone else in the shop might equate wanting your hair dried artificially with a desire to sleep with other men.

Intricate and subtle are the politics of the barber shop.

He hesitates, but the decision is made. Imagining himself to be Clint Eastwood, he fixes a firm look in his eye and sets about his work with as much conviction as he can muster. It's the only way.

Ten minutes later he breathes a sigh of relief as the slaughtered head retreats from the shop, the victim still unaware of the full horror which has been visited upon him, and curious as to why Barney has deposited a jug of water over his head. Barney makes a mental note, to add to the list, to be certain to avoid the bloke in the street for the next few weeks.

He turns his attention to the waiting area. One man awaits, but he recognises him as one of Wullie's regulars, so he nods a slightly resentful acknowledgement and goes about sweeping up the debris from the previous customer – noticing in the process that a disproportionate amount of it lies on the right-hand side.

As he sweeps, he casts a wearied glance over his two colleagues, busy doing that barber thing, cutting hair while talking drivel to the eager listeners beneath them. Chris discusses the likelihood of truth in the rumour that Marilyn Monroe had forty-three abortions; Wullie grandstands on the rights of man, as opposed to the rights of women, one of his common topics, to which Barney hates to listen. The words drift across the short distance of the shop, and no matter how much he tries to switch off, the sound is always there, eating away at him. Like a disease. Yes, that's it, he thinks, a disease.

'Naw, naw, ye see, Ah hate that,' Wullie says to a young

lad. 'A' this garbage aboot girls maturin' faster than boys. Ah'm tellin' ye, it's a load o' bollocks, so it is.'

'Ye think so, Wullie?' says the boy, bright-eyed, acne-blighted face, teeth yellowed by illicit teenage cigarettes.

Wullie smiles. There's nothing a barber likes better than some eager sponge who shows interest in everything he says. 'Aye, of course it is. Think aboot it. The thing people equate most wi' maturity is sense o' humour. That no' right? One person's humour is another's schoolboy immaturity. Benny Hill, John Cleese, Tommy Cooper. For everyone that thinks they're funny, there's some eejit who thinks they belong in the classroom.'

'Ah hate Benny Hill,' says the boy.

Wullie nods. 'Exactly. But he's the most famous British guy in America. Ye know,' he says, adding edge to the voice, 'that he ran for President against Ronald Reagan in 1980 and won nearly twenty per cent o' the vote.'

The lad looks impressed, nods his head. Wullie continues before anyone can object, while deploying evasionary scissor tactics to avoid cutting off the boy's ear.

'So that's the thing aboot comedy, and whit happens is that these young birds lose their sense o' humour when they reach puberty, and boys don't, so they all think they're mair mature than us. But they're no'. They've just forgotten how tae laugh, that's a'.'

The lad's eyes are opened. Such an expression must Saint Paul have worn on the road to Damascus. 'Jings, Ah never thought of it like that, Wullie.'

Wullie nods, executes a neat manoeuvre around the left ear.

'Thing is, ye cannae really blame these birds for losing their sense o' humour, can ye? Ah mean, if Ah'd had a pint o' blood bucketing oot o' me once a month since Ah wis twelve, Ah expect Ah'd have lost ma sense o' humour a long time ago as well.'

The lad is impressed with Wullie's sensitivity for the female condition. 'Here, you're no' one of these new men, are you, Wullie?' he says. Wullie smiles, polishes off the left ear with a Calvinistic lack of flourish.

Barney rolls his eyes, shakes his head and goes back to his sweeping, an act in which he is deliberate and slow, as he is in everything he does. He has never had the knack of talking drivel to complete strangers, and it irks him. Certainly, he can talk about the weather with the best of them, or can cast an opinion on the repeated episode of *Inspector Morse* shown the night before – although the opinion usually belongs to someone else – but when it comes to uncompromising asinine bollocks, he just doesn't have it. He has been cutting hair for over twenty years, and yet, in this respect, he remains an amateur. Still, on this imagined Day of Days, he has something up his sleeve. Today is the day when he gets his certificate in Drivel.

The door to the shop opens, accompanied by a gay tinkle from the bell. It is a Sad Man. Barney groans. It is ever his fate to get such customers. The 'few pathetic strands of hair' brigade. Men for whom hair is something which happens to other people. Men who grow a few strands of hair to a length of several metres, then wrap it tenuously around their scalps. Wonder if people notice.

The Sad Man looks at the solitaire in the queue who gestures that he waits for Wullie, then walks towards Barney. Barney ushers him into the chair, runs a discreet and well-trained eye over his baldy napper, encloses him in the confines of the cape.

'What will it be then, sir?'

'A short back an' sides'll be just fine, Big Man.'

A short back and sides. What a joke. Barney looks at his hair, and dreams of being able to cut it off at its roots. He lifts a pair of scissors, and they itch in his fingers. Twitch, twitch, twitch, eager to cut. Has to control the muscles in his fingers, the thoughts in his head. He sighs, puts the scissors back on the worktop and lifts a comb. Might as well do as he is bid. As usual. One day he will have his revenge on all these bastards.

He combs the hair several different ways, examines his options. He isn't a fast worker, but he could have this hair cut and the guy out of the shop in under a minute. But they never appreciate that, these Sad Men, so he knows to spin it out for at least twenty. Make him think he has a decent head of hair on him. A dream-maker, that's what he is. Feels like Steven Spielberg as he ponders the tools of his trade. Scissors, brushes, combs and razors, before deciding on an electric razor. Might as well pretend he has to shave the back of the neck and round the ears.

On a normal head of hair that would be good for at least five minutes per ear. He was told at barber school that he would resent ears at first, so much would they get in the way, but in time that resentment would pass, and he would come to love and cherish the ears, like you do any other more straightforward part of the head. However, it has never happened for Barney. His resentment of ears goes beyond rational thought, and he knows he will never be cured of it. And as always, even though there is little to be done with this Sad Man, he gets himself into a tangle of arms and legs as he attempts to negotiate the elaborate folds of skin and cartilage.

However, ten minutes into the cut things are going smoothly. He is making it look as if he has much work to do, the Sad Man seems happy, and there has been minimal conversation. Barney looks around the rest of the shop. Chris is temporarily unemployed and reading the paper, Wullie has just finished telling his next customer of Florence Nightingale's screaming lesbian tendencies.

He smiles. Now might just be the time to drop his bombshell, show the others he can compete on level ground. Show them that when it comes to talking shite he is right up there with the two of them.

He has no interest in football. He hates it with something approaching passion, if so dour a man can feel passion for anything. Grown men as little boys. A war substitute. But even though he knows nothing of football, he has done something grand. This weekend he has looked at the league tables. He now has a little knowledge.

'Hey, any o' youse ever read these lonely hearts messages?' says Chris from the bench, the paper rustling in his hands.

Barney turns round quickly, nearly depriving the Sad Man of his right ear. God, don't they ever shut up? Shakes his head.

'Listen tae this. "Single wummin, late thirties. Interestin' looks. Likes gardenin', books and quiet nights. Seeks Marty Feldman lookalike." ' He laughs, is joined by Wullie and his customer. 'Interestin' looks. Bloody hell, she must be a stankmonster if that's the best she can dae.'

'Ugly bird, left on the shelf, mair like,' says Wullie.

'And these guys are just as bad,' says Chris. ' "Forty-six-year-old aesthete . . ." Whit's an aesthete again?'

'I think it's someone who changes his Y-fronts twice a day,' says Wullie.

'They probably meant athlete. It'll be a printin' error,' says Wullie's customer.

'Aye, right,' says Chris. ' "Forty-six-year-old athlete seeks attractive wummin in early twenties." Bloody hell, Ah bet he does. "For long walks, gin and tonic as the sun goes down, Corelli's Concerto Grosso in G Minor, Wordsworth and Keats, 16th-century Renaissance architecture." ' Shakes his head. 'If ye ask me this guy's a wank.'

'Whit are ye sayin'?' says Wullie. 'Ye don't like Corelli?'

'No' sure,' says Chris. 'Wis he the one who played centre half for Juventus that the Rangers tried tae sign?'

'Very funny.'

Chris laughs, returns to reading the paper. Barney simmers. Waits to see if he'll say something else. Thinks: Just shut up for five seconds. Gets ready to talk his own bit of drivel. Opens his mouth, smiles.

'Listen tae this one,' says Chris, laughing. ' "Mature wummin, mid-80s, lookin' for love. Skilled in Eastern love-makin'. Seeks man in 20s/30s for nights o' passion. Nae cranks." Mid-eighties! Can ye believe it? Whit twenty-year-old mug is gonnae hook up wi' a bird that's old enough tae be his granny?'

'There's some strange folk out there,' says Wullie. 'Bet she gets loads o' replies. Good luck tae the auld cow.'

'Eastern lovemakin'?' says Wullie's customer. 'Ye think that means she's shagged someone in the back o' a motor in Edinburgh?'

The others laugh, Barney fumes. Annoyed at himself for listening. Mid-eighties. Incredible. Could be his own mother. Shivers at the thought.

Silence again. This time he'll seize the moment. Fixes a smile, teeth show.

'Whit dae ye make o' those Rangers, eh?' he says to the Sad Man, slightly louder than is necessary. He casts an eye over the rest of the shop to see the reaction he has elicited. Chris is laughing at the paper, ignores him.

Wullie glances over, but no more. He looks back to the customer.

Sad Man shrugs. 'What about them?' he says. 'Don't really follow it masel'.' He catches Barney's eye in the mirror, and looks convincingly back. He is lying. He has been a season-ticket holder at Ibrox for over seventeen years, but he is aware of Barney's deficiencies when it comes to fascinating discourse, and no more wants to enter into conversation with him than he would want to smother him in strawberry jelly and lick it off.

Barney thinks about this. He has little reply, as he is already almost at the cusp of his knowledge, so he lurches into his usual silence. All that waiting, for nothing. Feeling spurned, he hurries through the rest of the haircut, managing to stop himself cleaving off several feet of hair emanating from behind the right ear.

Five minutes later, the Sad Man hands over his cash, an extra fifty pence in the price. Satisfied that he needed the haircut he has just received, and that no one will realise he only has hair growing out of two per cent of his scalp, he walks out into the light drizzle of morning feeling like Robert Redford.

Barney watches him go, shaking his head with every step. If he ever got to run the shop he would have a sign put in the window. 'Customers Must Have Hair.' He sneers, looks at the waiting area. The next customer up, he shuffles his razors, and contemplates whether or not to mention the fact that he knows Rangers are five points clear at the top of the league.

The day drags on, following its usual course. Barney only cuts about half the amount of hair as the other two, partly because he is a lot slower, partly because few people seek him out in particular ahead of the others. It isn't until late in the afternoon that he feels able to broach the subject of football again, and with an almost mathematical inevitability he is caught with his pants down.

It is a big bloke, a labourer from a site down by the Clyde. He is wearing a Scotland top, making Barney feel confident in starting a football conversation. Once again he bides his time, then chooses his moment with a flourish, foot firmly in mouth, when all else in the shop is quiet.

'Whit dae ye make o' those Rangers, eh?' he says, not quite as cocksure as before, but still with the semblance of a glint in the eye, a smile on the lips.

'Whit about them?' growls the Scotland strip.

Displaying the kind of blinkered enthusiasm which allowed Custer to stop for a picnic at the Little Big Horn, Barney fails to spot the warning signs.

'Five points clear at the top o' the league. Some team, eh?'

The Scotland strip grunts. 'They're shite. Lost their last three games now. Pile of pish, so they are.'

Barney is given pause, but he bravely determines to battle on, like the German tanks in the Ardennes, until he runs out of fuel.

'Aye, but ye know, five points clear at the top of the league. Can't be bad, eh?'

'They're still shite. They're only five points clear at the top o' the league because everywan else is even mair shite than them.' He looks at Barney. This man eats babies. 'Whit dae you know aboot fitba' anyway?' he says, the finger pointed in accusation, voice growling.

Barney swallows, scissors tremble in his hands. Unable to think of an answer, he quickly resumes some gentle snipping, a layer of tension now descended on his area of the shop. For once he does not dither over a haircut, and while ensuring that he does not make a hash of it, he sends Scotland strip packing as quickly as possible. He leaves with a grunt and all his change in his pocket.

As the door closes behind him, and Barney breathes a sigh of relief, Wullie laughs and speaks to him for the first time since six minutes past eight that morning.

'If ye're gonnae tell someone how good the Rangers are, try no' tae tell a Celtic fan next time, eh, Barney? We don't want a riot in here.'

He laughs again and is joined by everyone else in the shop. Barney, suitably embarrassed, retreats to the hiding place that is his natural reserve, and plots his usual schemes of revenge.

Bastards. They're all bastards.

He looks out of the window at the massive figure retreating into the distance, and dreams of him falling into a manhole, breaking his neck. The rain thunders down

17

with ever greater ferocity. The skies are dark; occasional cruel streaks of lightning rend the clouds. The streetlights are already on, fighting a losing battle against the gloom. Barney bends low over his brush, sweeping with slow deliberate strokes, and thinks of dark deeds. Deeds to match the weather. Deeds which fate will force his hand to commit within the week.

Chapter 3

The Lure of the Flashing Blue Light

It rains all the way home. It always rains all the way home when Barney has to walk back from the shop. A phone call to the garage at four o'clock had produced the usual mutterings about a 'big job', and an estimated time of readiness of some time the following morning – and so he had stepped out into the raging torrent without even making the effort to cover up. Head bowed, spirit broken, besieged by ill-humour.

He lives in a top-floor flat in a tenement at the university end of Partick, one of the old houses, with huge rooms, and ceilings higher and more ornate than the Sistine Chapel. The kind of place which years ago had fostered a warm community spirit, but no longer in such times as these. Barney views all those around him with varying degrees of contempt and suspicion – his neighbours are no different.

He hangs his soaking jacket on the hook behind the door, trudges wearily into the kitchen. Agnes is making an uninteresting dinner, with one eye glued to a prosaic Australian soap opera on the portable television. As Barney clumps in, Charlene is having a fight with Emma's sister's ex-boyfriend's girlfriend Sheila, who is pregnant by Adam's gay lover Chip.

'Good day at work, dear?' she asks, her eyes never leaving the television.

He grunts, takes a glass from a cupboard, goes to the fridge, pours himself some wine from a carton. Chilean Sauvignon blanc, flinty with a hint of apple; good length; full-breasted; serve with fish or chicken, or perfect as a light appetiser. He takes a long and loud slurp and belches. Puts the back of his hand to his mouth in some affectation of manners, then points at nothing in particular.

'You know what really pisses me off?' He looks at her expectantly, assuming her interest, although long years should have told him to expect otherwise.

'What, dear?' she says eventually.

'It pisses me off, all these bastards' – he waves his hand – ''scuse the French, who come in there every day and insist on one o' they two wee shits cuttin' their hair.' The voice rises a fraction in agitation. 'Ah mean, dae these people, these dumb bastards, actually think that Wullie or Chris is gonnae gie them a better haircut than Ah am, eh? Eh?' He stabs his finger in the air, unintentionally pronging a passing fly.

'Yes, dear,' she says. Troy has finally told Charlene that Cleopatra is pregnant by Julian.

'Exactly. Ah mean,' he goes on, slight bubbles of froth beginning to appear at the side of his mouth, a string of spit suspended between top and bottom lip, 'how long have these two been cuttin' hair? Five, maybe six years. Awright, maybe ten years wi' Wullie. So what? Look at me. Twenty years Ah've been cuttin' hair,' he says, scything the air with his hand in time with each syllable, 'and Ah'm bloody good at it, am Ah no'?'

'Yes, dear.'

'Bloody right Ah am. And look at those two useless bastards. They couldnae cut the hair aff a . . . aff a . . .' He searches the air for a suitable analogy, finding it as Charlene slaps Tony in the face and tells him that there is no way that she and Beatrice are half-sisters. ' . . . They couldnae cut the hair aff a drugged mammoth. No they couldn't. Bloody useless the pair of them. Ye know what they dae?'

'Yes, dear?' She isn't listening, but the tone of his voice

20

has wormed its way into her subconscious so she knows to sound inquisitive.

'Ah'll tell ye. They just bloody talk about fitba' a' day. As if it's important. Who gies a shite about fitba'. It's a lot o' pish. Or that Wullie just stands there and comes out wi' a' sorts of garbage. Did you know,' he begins, attempting an impersonation of Wullie, and missing by several kilometres, 'that Cary bleedin' Grant had an affair wi' Randolph Scott. Big bloody deal! As if anybody's gonnae believe that shite. Ah mean,' he says, rising to his subject, while his voice descends to Churchillian depths, 'Ah mean, look at a' that's goin' on in the world. The country's goin' down the toilet. There's wars, and strikes and death.' He clutches the breast of his shirt with his right hand. 'Whit's happenin' tae the Health Service? Transport? Eh? Whit about that stuff? There's some bloody nutter runnin' about Glasgow slashin' folk an' cuttin' them up. Whit about that? Whit's the bloody polis daein' about that? An' whit dae they talk about? Fitba'!'

'Yes, dear.' Charlene is now convinced that Troy and Beatrice are having an affair and that Bethlehem isn't her brother, while some savoury pancakes which Agnes magicked from the freezer twenty minutes earlier quietly burn on the stove.

Shaking his head and grumbling in a low voice, Barney polishes off the glass of wine, and begins pouring himself another.

'Where's ma dinner?'

'Programme'll be finished in a couple of minutes, dear.' Has Bill really lost his voice, or is he just doing it so that Charles won't realise that Emma still loves Tom?

Barney grunts loudly, wanders off into the sitting room. He flicks on the television, finds the snooker on BBC2 and within five minutes is sound asleep.

The rain strikes relentlessly against the window of the dingy little office. Detective Chief Inspector Robert Holdall stares gloomily at the water cascading from the gutters outside and wonders what other disasters can befall him this day. As he has occasion to do most days, he tries to remember what it was that made him want to be a policeman in the first place. Action, adventure, glamour,

21

women. Obviously it was none of those, so what had it been? A vague desire to fight the forces of evil? Something like that. He has had the thought in the past that it was because of the sixties *Batman* TV series, and has spent much time since persuading himself that it wasn't that at all. That would be just too sad. Thwack! Biff! Blam! Love your tights . . .

The lure of the flashing blue light, that was all. Just the lure of the flashing blue light. He could be driving an ambulance.

There is a knock at his door, and a young constable walks into his office. Not long removed from school, the dregs of adolescent acne still clinging wildly to his face, barnacles to a boat. He closes the door behind him and stands before Holdall, nervously awaiting the invitation to talk.

'Yes, Constable, you have something for me?'

'Yes, sir. The results from the lab are negative, sir.'

Bugger.

Why are you thinking bugger, Holdall? Of course the results are negative. You're not dealing with an amateur here. You're dealing with some bloody bastard who knows what he's doing. And who's taking the piss out of you something rotten.

'All right, Montgomery.' Wonders as he says it if this really is Constable Montgomery. 'Will you ask MacPherson to come in here, please?'

The constable nods and disappears back through the door, leaving a trace of Clearasil in the air. Holdall leans back in his chair, puts his hands behind his head, his feet up on the desk. Where do they stand?

Five murders. No corpses, just body parts mailed through the post to the victim's family. Never anything from the package to help them trace the killer. Always postmarked from a different town in Scotland; always some bloody note sent to the police at the same time, each one more laden with mockery than the one before. When he catches the guy, which he is sure he will do, before going through the formalities of making the arrest, he is going to kick his head in.

The door opens and Detective Sergeant MacPherson walks into the room. He is a big man, who has in his time

22

played full back for West of Scotland, but after being sent off for the eleventh time, has decided to save his brutality for the job.

Holdall looks at him as he walks into the room. He likes him, enjoys the barbarian pleasure of working with him. It makes him feel safer, if nothing else. And for all his brawn and thuggery, he is a good man. Intelligent with it, perhaps.

'Take a seat, Sergeant. I won't keep you long. I presume you'll be wanting to get home.'

MacPherson shrugs his giant shoulders. 'There's some fitba' Ah wouldnae mind watchin'. It's no' that important.'

'That English Premier league stuff?'

'Aye.'

'Don't know how you can be bothered with it. Seems like a load of shite to me.'

He looks away from MacPherson, takes his feet off the desk and swivels round, so that he is side on to the other man. MacPherson knows what is coming, sits and waits patiently for it. Another examination of the facts. Another run-through of the salient information. Another drive down the road to nowhere. They are in exactly the same place as they have been since the first murder, and all there is for them to do is talk. However, he understands Holdall's need to do it.

'Roberts tell ye about the lab report?' says MacPherson.

Roberts! Bugger. That was it. Who was Montgomery? Feels a slight redness in his face as he remembers. WPC Eileen Montgomery.

'Aye, aye, he did,' says Holdall, and shakes his head. Puts his hands down, clasps them on his stomach. Feels like he should be giving some leadership to the investigation, but the tank is empty. He has no ideas.

'Where does it leave us, Sergeant? Where are we at?'

MacPherson considers.

'We're in a pile o' shite,' he says.

Holdall smiles. That was just about right.

MacPherson continues his résumé of events.

'We're nowhere. We've got some heid-the-ba' runnin' around Glasgow committin' indiscriminate murder, then visitin' other parts o' Scotland tae send back a slice o' body. Nae connection between the victims, other than that

23

they've a' been men. Don't know if there's any significance tae that. Certainly doesn't appear to be a gay thing, and hard tae imagine a woman doing a' this stuff. But ye never know, cannae rule it out. No' these days. Anyway, nothin' tae link the places the body parts have been getting sent back fi' . . .'

'Which have been?'

'Pitlochry, Edinburgh, Kingussie, Largs and Aberdeen. We've checked out hotel guest lists in they places for the nights that the packages were posted, but there hasnae been anyone who stayed in mair than one o' them. We've spoken tae everyone fi' Glasgow who stayed o'ernight in these towns on the relevant dates, but they a' had their reason for bein' there, and there was nothin' suspicious. There've been a few people that we cannae trace, and it could be that he left false names and addresses, but it could also mean nothing at a'. There's nae reason why someone couldnae have got the train tae any one o' they places and back again in the same day.'

Holdall nods his head, grunts.

'That's about it, isn't it, MacPherson? Everywhere he goes is on a main rail route, so we can maybe assume that he's been taking the train. So that narrows it down.'

'Sir?'

'All we have to do is arrest everyone in Glasgow who doesn't have a car.'

MacPherson smiles, nods. The idea appeals. Too bad it isn't practical.

'Anything else, Sergeant?'

MacPherson marshals his thoughts, then continues in his low voice.

'There's nae connection wi' the body parts that he's sendin' back. So far we've had an ear, a right hand, a right hand and left foot the gither, a left leg, and then on Friday we had a heid.'

Holdall shakes his head, still unable to comprehend the awfulness of the crime. Killing someone, beheading them, and then mailing the head back to the family, when they'd probably still been under the impression that the bloke had run away to Blackpool for a few days. Can't think about it too closely. You couldn't do that on this job and stay sane.

24

'This is a sick bastard we're dealing with, Sergeant, a sick bastard.'

MacPherson nods, continues talking.

'So far we've nae idea what he's doin' wi' the remainder o' the bodies. Certainly, if he's got rid o' them, we don't know where.' He pauses, thinks for a second or two. 'Ah don't think there's anythin' else, sir.'

Holdall shakes his head, staring wearily at the ground.

'No, Sergeant, you're right. There isn't, is there? We've got some sick bastard carving up the citizens of Glasgow, they're expecting us to do something about it, and we haven't got the faintest idea what that is.'

For a fleeting second MacPherson feels pity for him. He knows he takes his cases personally. But it's all part of the job, and Holdall has been doing it long enough to accept it. The weight of expectation. They all have to live with it.

Holdall turns round in his chair, places his hands decisively on the desk, looks MacPherson firmly in the eye.

'There's nothing else for it, Sergeant. Take the list off our computers of everyone in Glasgow who owns a car, and then arrest everyone else.'

MacPherson raises his eyebrows, but rises from his seat to start the task. The look on Holdall's face tells him he's joking. Of course he is. If they did this they would have to arrest too many councillors currently off the roads on drink-driving charges. The stink would be unbelievable.

The two men smile at each other, and with a wave of the hand Holdall dismisses the sergeant from his office.

'Have a good evening, Sergeant. Who's playing?'

MacPherson thinks about it then shrugs his shoulders. 'Who cares? Fitba's fitba', in't it no', sir?' He turns and walks slowly from the office.

Holdall nods. 'You can't say fairer than that,' he says to the empty room. He looks out at the Gothic darkness of early evening, the rain now hammering against the window. Allows his chin to slump into the palm of his hand. 'Fuck,' he says softly, before rising slowly from the chair.

Chapter 4

Death Row

Barney looks on proudly as his finest haircut of the month walks from the shop. The lad had wanted his hair cut by Chris, but there had been too many people in the queue ahead of him, forcing him to settle on Barney. And he has shown him what real barbery is all about. The haircut has been a peach. A non-technical short back and sides job, low difficulty certainly, but executed with beautiful panache nonetheless. Even and neat on the top, tapered to geometric perfection around the ears and the back of the neck. Barbery at its finest, he thinks to himself, from one of the best exponents of the art in the West of Scotland.

He glances at the other two to see if they've noticed, but Chris is too busy discussing the on-going plight of Partick Thistle, while Wullie is contemplating the exact nature of the relationship between Laurence Olivier and Danny Kaye. Barney shrugs. If they are too busy discussing trivialities to notice real genius, then that's their problem.

He turns and surveys the shop, feeling good about himself. A warm glow. Like the pilot who lands the plane in a storm without a bump, or the teacher who discovers the one pupil in a thousand who understands triple differentiation, the barber who carries out the perfect haircut has reason to be proud.

It is a small shop. A row of four chairs along one side next to the great bank of mirrors, and a long cushioned bench along the other, upon which the customers await their fate. Wullie works the chair nearest the window, Chris is next to him, then there lies an empty chair, occasionally filled on busy Saturdays by a young girl they get to moonlight from an expensive hairdresser's in Kelvinside. At the back of the shop, working the fourth chair, is Barney, and he resents it. Behind him, making the room into a slight L-shape, is a small alcove, where there is a fifth seat, a seat which hasn't been worked since the great hair rush of the late seventies, when every man in Britain had wanted a perm, so that they could look as much of an idiot as everyone else. It is some surprise to Barney that he has not been relegated all the way back there.

There was a time when he'd had possession of the coveted window seat – for some fifteen years in fact – but he was ousted late one Friday afternoon in a bloodless coup. Wullie had been after the chair for some time and, using the fact that his father owned the shop to his advantage, executed a manoeuvre that relegated Barney to the back of the room. It was the talk of the shop for some time – the talk of hushed voices – but gradually the affair quietened down, as Wullie knew it would, and they settled back into a steady routine.

However, it had widened the gap between Barney and the other two men. They share no interests whatsoever, and consequently no conversation. And they share very few customers, most of them preferring to go to the younger men. Barney is left with a few old boys whose hair he has been cutting for years, a few men who don't care, and the odd stray first-timers who don't know any better.

He looks over the queue of ten people cramped onto the seat, and realises there are none who fit any of the required categories. They will all be waiting for one of the other two – one of the other two bastards. However, he still has the post-dream-haircut glow about him. Surely some of them will have surveyed the majesty of the hair on the bloke who has just left. Surely brilliance such as that will not go unrewarded.

He looks at the row of men, each with their private thoughts about the ordeal which awaits them. A mini-Death Row. Some sit with anticipatory relish, some are nervous, some are angry, present only on the instructions of their wives. Or mothers.

'Who's next?' says Barney, with the confident air of a fighter who takes on all comers.

Like a row of disciples denying all knowledge of Jesus under the scrutiny of an unpleasant centurion, most of the ten stare blankly ahead, ignoring him as best they can. The two or three nearest him feel obliged to shake their heads, although only one of them can do it while looking him in the eye. Barney gives them an incredulous stare, but since they're all ignoring him, it is wasted. A change in strategy is required.

It is frequently effective for the unemployed barber to remorselessly select individuals who may well crack under the pressure of personal attention. Another useful lesson from barber school, which Barney has never forgotten.

'You, my good man,' he says, pointing to the chap at the head of the queue, 'come on.'

He has chosen unwisely, however, for this is not a man to be browbeaten. He looks Barney in the eye, unconcerned about such things as direct appeals.

'It's awright, mate, Ah'm gonnae wait for Chris, thanks.'

Beaten, but not yet bloodied, Barney nods. 'Fair enough.' He points to the next in line. 'You then, my man, on ye come.'

The man shuffles his feet, remembers the words of his wife as he left the house – 'Here, you, mind an' git a good bloody haircut, and dinnae let that auld bastard cut yer hair, 'cause ye know whit he did the last time, and if you come hame and ye huvnae goat yer hair cut an' Ah fun oot ye've spent the money doon the boozer, yer a dead man, James McGlinshey' – and lamely shakes his head.

Barney rolls his eyes, grits his teeth, looks like he's going to punch someone. Does his best to remember the lessons he has learned in years past, keeps his cool. Perseverance, that's what's needed. Someone will eventually crack. He just has to make sure it isn't him.

He gestures to the next chap, who noiselessly gestures towards Chris. Barney grits his teeth again. He isn't coping with this at all well. One more. He'll try one more.

'Here, you, what about you?' he says to the next in line, his temper beginning to spill over.

The man ignores the tone of his voice. 'No thanks, mate, I'm just going to wait for Wullie, if that's all right.'

The final straw, settling gently on the camel's back. Forgetting everything he learned at barber school, Barney cracks.

'Naw, it bloody well isnae awright.' He stares angrily up and down the row of embarrassed faces. 'Not one o' ye, eh? Not one o' ye are willin' tae get your hair cut by me? Am Ah that bad?' He points towards the closed door. 'Did yese no' see that haircut Ah just did? Bloody stoatir, so it wis. And you're all gonnae wait for these two,' he says, sneering. 'It's half past three the now. If yese a' wait for them, some of yese arnae gonnae get your haircut at a'. Ah've just pulled aff one o' the finest haircuts this shop's seen in months, and yet youse a' just sit there like bloody sheep.' He stares them up and down. 'Well?'

He is aware of the beating of his heart, the redness in his face. Begins to feel a bit of an idiot, but something drives him on. He searches for the one who looks the most sheepish, the most likely to crack under pressure.

'You!' he says, pointing. The chap turns reluctantly to look at him. 'Aye, you, young man. How about you?'

It is a lad of about seventeen, and with pleasure, Barney realises that he is about to give in. He will have his chance to show the rest of these bastards what a decent haircut looks like.

'Look, Barney, if they all want tae wait for Chris or me, then that's fine. You cannae have a go at the customers. Someone else will come in shortly.'

Slowly, Barney turns and looks over at the window. Wullie stands wagging a pair of scissors in Barney's direction. Barney stares back. His heart beats a little faster.

The bastard. The total bastard. That he should humiliate Barney in front of all these customers.

He stands with his feet spread. An aggressive stance, almost ready for a fight. Wullie is having none of it. He murmurs something to his customer, and takes a few paces over towards Barney. He speaks in a quiet voice, but it is a small enough shop that there is no way that anyone will miss what is said. At the last second, and with a fine sense of diplomacy, Chris turns on his hairdryer to create some background noise.

'Look, Barney, don't think that Ah'm embarrassin' you in front of the customers. Ye're embarrassin' yourself. And them. If they don't want tae come tae you, it's nae bother. Just leave them tae it, awright?'

Barney grumbles something about it being not all right, without having the guts to really say it.

'Ah'll talk tae ye about it later, Barney, if that's awright wi' you.'

Barney stares at Wullie, the anger boiling up inside him, but contained for all that. He nods a bitter nod, sits down in his chair, roughly picks up the paper, and makes no attempt to read it.

The moment has passed, but tension still hangs thick in the air. Barney looks at his paper for a few seconds, then turns the corner down and glances menacingly over it at the row of men sitting trying to ignore him.

It is the first time that he has felt so humiliated since the window-seat débâcle, and while he had eventually let that one pass, there is no way he is going to let Wullie talk to him like that in front of all these bloody goons.

Chris silences his hairdryer – much to the relief of the man at the other end of the warm blast; homosexual, but still firmly in the closet – and then the only sound in the shop is the quiet snip of two pairs of scissors going about their business. Finally, the man at the whim of Wullie's hand asks him if he has read the gossip about some film star whom Barney has never even heard of, and slowly the shop returns to normal. The quiet hum of pointless chatter, interspersed with electric razors and the gentle flop of hair to the floor.

Then, with the elegant timing of a Victorian watch, the door to the shop swings open. Ten pairs of eyes look expectantly. The possibility that here might be someone to assuage their guilt. It is a man in his late twenties, unaware of the cauldron into which he has just walked. Quietly he closes the door, takes his place at the end of the queue.

Barney lays down the paper, stands up, brushes down the seat, lifts up the cape, looks the man in the eye. He doesn't immediately recognise him. A good sign.

'All right then, my good man. All these others are waitin', so you're next in line.'

Unaware of the expectations weighted upon his shoulders, the man does not even hesitate.

'That's OK, mate, I'm just going to wait for Wullie.'

Barney stands, cape in hand, a bullfighter without a bull. He stays calm. Bites his tongue, although the sight of Wullie staring at him out of the corner of his eye does nought but increase the desire to explode. He places the cape back over the chair, deliberately picks up the paper, and once again sits down. Just before his backside hits the seat, he pauses, looks once more at the customer.

'Are you sure now, my friend? There's a long queue.'

The man nods. 'Aye, I'm all right, mate, thanks. There's no rush.'

'Very well.'

Barney slumps into the seat, seething quietly within. He hates all these bloody customers. Who do they think they are anyway? Complete bastards the lot of them. But no matter how much he hates them, it does not tie the shoelaces of how much he hates Wullie and Chris. Those smug bastards. He will have his revenge.

He doesn't know how, but somehow he will. He is sure of it. He looks along the shop at Wullie, and then past him out of the window. It is a dark day, the rain falling in a steady drizzle, as it has done all afternoon. Doleful figures pass by, hunched against the wind and rain, unaware of the injustices within the shop which they scuttle past. But some day they will find out. Some day, everyone will know about what goes on in the shop. Some day soon.

Robert Holdall slumps into his seat with the enthusiasm of one settling into the electric chair. Another press conference. The Chief Superintendent is forcing them on him almost daily. He would like to argue that they are stopping him from doing his job, but he has so little to go on that the only thing that they are getting in the way of is his afternoon tea and sandwich.

31

He is accompanied as usual by the burly press officer, a woman of quite considerable stature, who exercises an amount of control over the press that no man has ever managed. And as Holdall readies himself to read his prepared statement, she silences the packed room with a couple of dramatic waves of her right arm. This is a woman who eats large mechanical farm implements for breakfast.

Holdall stares gloomily at the words written down in front of him. God, it's short. Of course it is. They have nothing to say to these people. What can he tell them? That they're thinking of arresting everyone in Glasgow who doesn't own a car? Of course not. And so he has written down three sentences of total vacuity. A nothing statement, forced on him by a bloody-minded boss. He'd like to see him sit there and read out this garbage.

He finishes staring at it, looks up at the collected press. Aw, shite, he thinks. There are more than usual. Maybe a few up from England. He makes the decision quickly, and without any prior thought. Bugger it, he thinks, give them something a bit more solid than this piece of vacuous garbage.

Clearing his throat and pretending to read from the paper in front of him, he begins in his low, serious press voice.

'Ladies and gentlemen. I shall be necessarily brief today, which I am sure you will understand when you hear what I have to say.' He pauses briefly. Shit. What is he going to say exactly? Clears his throat again, takes a drink from the glass of water at his right hand. Jumps into the blazing inferno, eyes open. 'Late last night, officers from this station came into possession of a valuable piece of evidence, the exact nature of which I am not yet at liberty to divulge. It has given us a very definite direction of inquiry which we are now pursuing with all possible vigour.' Not bad, he thinks. Optimistic, but vague. Don't blow it. 'Given the nature of this new information, we are hopeful of a major development in this investigation, some time in the next forty-eight to seventy-two hours.' Christ, what are you saying? You idiot. Shut up, and don't say any more. 'I am afraid that I am unable to disclose any more information at this time, but you can be assured that when these anticipated further developments have taken place, you will be notified in the usual manner.'

He closes his mouth, blinks, looks up. A brief second, and the room has erupted in a cacophony of noise. He sits looking like a stuffed fish, while Sergeant Mahoney does her best to calm the crowd. Eventually, and with much difficulty, the room has returned to rest, and the sergeant points a yellowed finger at a man with his arm raised, near the front of the crowd.

'Bill Glasson, *Evening Post*,' he says, a look of surprise upon his face. It's the first time he's been picked out at a press conference in fourteen years, and he has no idea what question to ask. He knows they're not going to get anything more out of the guy, but they are obliged to shout at him. It's their job. When the tumult erupted he had been asking what the inspector had had for breakfast that morning, just so he could add to the clamour. A new question is needed, however.

'So,' he says, thinking frantically, 'you say you have some idea who the killer is. Do you know exactly who the killer is?'

Holdall shakes his head. What a crap question, he thinks. He could have sworn that before this bloke was asking him something about breakfast.

'I'm sorry, but I'm not at liberty to discuss any information other than that which I have just given to you.'

When it becomes obvious that he isn't going to say any more on the matter, the clamour immediately starts up again, and after a minute or two, is quietened down. Bugger this, thinks Holdall. What's the point? If I go on with this, I'll just end up saying something even more stupid than I already have done.

He mutters quietly to the sergeant that he will only take one more question, and when she announces this to the crowd, there is an even more extravagant clamour, and frantic waving of hands. She selects the most innocent-looking one, a young blond-haired woman sitting in the centre of the room.

'Greta Burridge, the *Mail*.' Greta Burridge swallows. Third day on the job. She has her question to ask, however. 'So, Inspector Holdall, does this mean that the rumours that you intend to arrest everyone in Glasgow who doesn't own a car are unfounded?'

Holdall sits at his desk, his head firmly buried in his hands. He still hasn't come to terms with what an idiot he has been. Looks at his watch. Another forty minutes, and then he will have a meeting with the Chief Superintendent. He is going to have to explain himself. As always, he can't help thinking of the time he was dragged to the headmaster's office when he was fourteen, after exploding a small bomb in the music teacher's sandwich box.

And he hadn't had an explanation for that either.

Chapter 5

Faith and Puberty Have It Out with Bliss

The rain streams against the windows. The old wooden frames rattle in the wind, the curtains blow in the chill draught which forces its way into the room. Ghosts and shadows. Outside, the night is cold and bleak and dark, to match Barney's mood as he sits at the dinner table. He pushes the food around his plate, every so often stabbing randomly at a pea or a piece of meat pie, imagining that it is Wullie or Chris. All the while Agnes looks over his shoulder at the television, engrossed in a particularly awful Australian soap opera, taped from earlier in the afternoon. The food grows cold on their plates, as Dr Morrison tells Nurse Bartlett that she will never be able to have children, as a result of the barbecue incident at Tom and Diane's engagement party, and Barney holds forth on what he intends to do to take his revenge upon his colleagues.

'Ah'm gonnae get they bastards if it's the last thing Ah dae. Ah mean it.'

'Yes, dear.' Agnes's mind is on other things.

'Ah mean, who the hell dae they think they are, eh?' He stabs a finger at her. 'Ah'll tell ye. Naeb'dy, that's who they are. They're naeb'dy. And Ah'm bloody well gonnae get them.'

'Yes, dear.'

There is a mad glint in Barney's eye. The possibilities are endless, the bounds for doing evil and taking his revenge unfettered, limited only by his imagination – a very tight limit, as it happens. He has been thinking it over since the afternoon's humiliation, and the more he dwells upon it, the more he likes the idea of murder.

Murder! Why not? They deserve it. You should never humiliate your colleagues in front of the customers. Isn't that one of the first things they teach you in barber school? But these young ones today. They never even bother with any sort of hairdressing education. Five years of high school learning sociology and taking drugs, and they think they know everything. They lift a pair of scissors and start cutting hair as if they're preparing a bowl of breakfast cereal. It just isn't that simple. It's a skill which needs to be nurtured and cultivated. Like brain surgery, or astrophysics.

The trouble is that they're all bastards, every one of them. Not just Wullie and Chris, but every other cretin who ever lifted a pair of scissors in anger. But not for much longer. It's payback time.

'Whit dae ye think? Stabbin'? Shootin'? Poison even?'

'Yes, dear,' she says, absent-mindedly nodding.

He brightens up. Poison. Brilliant. Agnes was good for bouncing ideas off sometimes. 'Aye, ye're right. Poison's the thing. Ah don't know anythin' about it, but Ah'm sure Ah can find out. Ah'm sure Ah can. Whit dae ye think?'

'Yes, dear.'

'Aye, Ah expect Ah can. It shouldnae be too difficult.' Murderous plans race through his mind, a manic smile slowly wanders across his lips. 'One o' they slow-acting ones, so Ah can stick it in their coffee durin' the day, and they willnae die until much later.' He rubs his hands together. 'Brilliant idea. Bloody brilliant.'

There is some illuminated corner of his mind telling him that he isn't being serious. Not murder. Surely not murder. But it is good to think about it for a while. Thinking about it isn't the same as doing it.

'Yes, dear,' says Agnes. Is Doreen really a lesbian or is she just pretending she loves Epiphany so she can get close to Dr Morrison without Blaize becoming suspicious?

Without any further stabs of conscience, Barney tucks into his pie, chips and peas, all the time plotting his wild revenge. It is sad that it has to come to this, he thinks, but they've brought it upon themselves. Particularly that bastard Wullie.

Another thought occurs. Perhaps he could poison some of those bloody customers as well. They were asking for it, most of them. He gets carried away for a second on a rollercoaster of genocide. Calms down. He's Barney Thomson, barber, not Barney Pot, deranged dictator. Still, the thought is there, if it ever becomes necessary. A lot of them deserve it, that's for sure.

His mind begins to wander to a grand vision where he is in the shop with two other barbers, neither of whom anyone will go to, while there sits a great queue of people all waiting for him to cut their hair. He would take three-quarters of an hour over every haircut, and annoy as many of them as possible. Heaven.

He is reluctantly hauled from his dreams by the ringing of the telephone. He stops, a forkful of chips poised on the cusp of his mouth, looks at Agnes. Her eyes remain glued to the television, oblivious to the clatter of the phone. He points the chipped fork.

'You gonnae get that, hen?'

She scowls, answers without removing her eyes from the television. 'Ah cannae. Faith and Puberty are about tae have it out wi' Bliss.'

Executing his trademark eye-rolling and head-shaking routine, he envelops the chips in his mouth, tosses the fork onto the plate, stands up to get the phone, hoping it will be a wrong number.

'Whit?'

'Hello, Barney, it's me.'

Breathes a sigh of relief. It is one of the few people from whom he doesn't mind receiving a call – his drinking and dominoes partner, Bill Taylor. This will be a call to arms.

'Oh, hello, Bill, how ye doin'?'

'No' so bad, no' so bad. And you?'

'Oh, cannae complain, cannae complain.'

They discuss trivialities for a few minutes, such as Bill's brother Eric having told his girlfriend Yvonne that he

37

loves Fiona. Finally, however, Bill gets to the main item on the agenda.

'Fancy goin' out for a few pints the night?' he says.

'Oh, Ah don't know, mate. Ah always go tae see my mother on a Tuesday night, ye know. She'd be a bit upset if Ah didnae go. Ye know whit they're like, eh?'

'Well, how about a couple o' pints before ye go? Ah'll meet you doon the boozer aboot half seven, eh?'

'Aye, awright, that shouldnae be too bad. Can't stay too long though, eh?'

'Aye, aye.'

Barney says his goodbyes, trudges back into the sitting room. Tries to ignore the television while he polishes off his dinner, then slumps into the armchair and falls asleep. He dreams of poison and of long prison sentences and of chain gangs and electric chairs, and then he awakes with a start at just about the time he needs to.

As he leaves the house to go to the pub, the aftermath of dinner remains where it has been for over an hour, while Chastity and Hope attempt to bundle Mercury into the boot of a car, in what he assumes to be an entirely different soap opera from the one he suffered earlier.

'Ah'm goin' tae the boozer, then ma mother's. Awright?'

'Yes, dear.'

'Ah'll be back aboot ten.'

'Yes, dear.'

He waits for some more reaction, waits in vain. Walks out, slamming the door as he goes.

'Aye, well, that's a' very well,' says Bill Taylor, brandishing his pint, 'but who is tae categorise depth? Eh? Everyone is capable o' depth. Nietzsche said, "Some men consider wimmin tae be deep. This is untrue. Wimmin are no' even shallow." Well, tae me that's a load o' crap. Now, Ah'm nae feminist or nothin', Ah'm sure you'll understand, but Ah've got tae say, that even wimmin can say stuff that's deep too. Most o' whit they say's crap now, but it disnae mean they can't come out wi' somethin' intelligent every now and again.'

Barney nods in agreement. 'Ah never realised that ye were a student o' Nietzsche?'

Bill grunts, buries his hand in a bowl of peanuts. 'Ah

widnae go that far. Obviously Ah've studied a' the great philosophers, but Ah'm definitely no' a fan o' Nietzsche.'

'Me neither. Typical bloody German. Spent his life writin' about some kind o' master race, tae which he presumably considered himself tae belong, and then he went aff his napper, reverted tae childhood, and spent the last ten years o' his life in an asylum, playing wi' Lego and Scalextric, and pretending tae be a cowboy. Tae be perfectly honest, they nineteenth-century German philosophers get on ma tits.'

Barney wonders about himself sometimes. Why is it that when he sits over a pint and a game of dominoes in the pub he can talk pish with the best of them, but when the chips are down, and he really needs to, there is nothing there? Like the guy who can hole a putt from any part of the green, until someone offers him a fiver to do it.

'My friend, my friend, my friend,' Bill says, his mouth full of peanuts, 'ye dinnae need tae tell me aboot German philosophy. Ah'm as aware as anybody else o' the failings o' German philosophy. An' let's face it, when it comes down tae it, a' German philosophy amounts tae is "if in doubt, invade it". Aye, that's it in a nutshell, so it is.'

'Well, well, Bill, Ah never thought Ah'd hear ye talk like that. Certainly Germany was guilty of horrendous imperialism during the first half o' the twentieth century, but that's no' necessarily indicative of the past two hundred years.'

Barney executes a swift manoeuvre with a double four, lifts his pint.

'Is it no'? Is it no'? That's a load o' shite, so it is, and Ah don't think ye can just dismiss fifty years as no' indicative. Especially when it is,' says Bill.

Barney pauses to take another sip of beer, studies the state of their game of dominoes. It is turning into a bloody tussle, good-natured but life-threatening. He is about to make his next move and expand his thoughts on German imperialism when he pauses briefly to listen to what two young women are saying as they walk past their table.

' . . . no, no, that's no' right, Senga, so it's no'. Ah'm telling ye, Neptune's the planet that's the furthest fi' the sun at the moment. Awright, Pluto's further away maist o' the time, but Neptune has a circular orbit, while Pluto has an elliptical one, so that for some years at a time, Pluto's orbit takes it nearer tae the sun than Neptune. And that's the case at the . . .'

The voice is lost in the noise of the bar as they move away. Barney and Bill look at each other with eyebrows raised.

'Unusual tae find,' says Barney, 'a wummin with so much as an elementary grasp o' astronomy.'

Bill raises his finger, waves it from side to side. 'As a matter o' fact, Ah wis discussing the other day wi' this girl in my work called Loella, the exact . . .'

'You have a girl in your work called Loella?' asks Barney, with some surprise.

'Aye, aye Ah dae.'

'Oh.'

'And as Ah wis sayin', Loella and I were talking about anti-particles. Ah wis under the impression that a photon had a separate anti-particle, but she says that two gamma rays can combine tae produce a particle-anti-particle pair, and thus the photon is its own anti-particle.'

Barney considers this, while keeping one half of his brain on the game.

'So, whit your sayin' is that the anti-particle o' an electron is a positron, which has the same mass as the electron, but is positively charged?'

Bill thinks about this, slips a two/three neatly into the game. 'Aye, aye, Ah believe so.'

'And a wummin called Loella told you this?'

'Aye, she did.'

The two men jointly shake their heads at the astonishing sagacity displayed by the occasional woman, then return with greater concentration to the game.

They both try to remember what they had been talking about before the interruption, but the subject of German imperialism has escaped them, and Bill is forced to bring up more mundane matters.

'So, how's that barber's shop of yours doing, eh, Barney?' he says, surveying the intricate scene before him, and wondering if he is going to be able to get rid of his double six before it is too late.

Barney shakes his head, rolls his eyes. 'Ye don't want tae know, my friend, you do not want tae know.'

'Is there any trouble?' asks Bill, concern in the voice, although this is principally because he finds himself looking at a mass of twos, threes and fours on the table, and sixes and fives in his hand.

Barney shakes his head, rolls his eyes. 'Ach, it's they two bastards, Wullie and Chris. Ah don't know who they think they are. Keep taking a' my customers. It's gettin' to be a joke.'

Bill nods. In the past, he has been on the receiving end of one of Barney's one-hour-fifteen-minute 'Towering Inferno' haircuts, and in the end was forced to move from the area to avoid subjecting himself to the fickle fate of his friend's scissors. He well understands those in the shop who flock to the other two.

'They're good barbers, Barney.'

Barney stops what he is doing, the words cutting to his very core. Drops his dominoes, places his hands decisively on the table. Fire glints in his eye. A green glint.

'And Ah'm no', is that whit yer saying, Bill? Eh?'

Bill quickly raises his hands in a placatory gesture. 'No, no, Barney, Ah didnae mean it that way, ye know Ah didnae.'

Barney shakes his head. 'Like hell ye didnae. Et tu, Bluto?' he says, getting within inches of quoting Shakespeare.

'Look, Barney, calm down, Ah didnae mean anythin'. Now pick up yer dominoes and get on wi' the game, will ye no'?'

With a grunt, a scowl, a noisy suck of his teeth, Barney slowly lifts his weapons of war and, unhappy that Bill has seen what he holds in his hands, resumes playing.

The game continues for another couple of minutes, before Bill feels confident enough to reintroduce the subject. The quiet chatter of the pub continues around them, broken only by the occasional ejaculation of outrage.

'So, whit's the problem wi' the two o' them, then, Barney?'

Barney grumbles. 'Ach, Ah don't know, Bill. They're

41

just makin' my life a misery. They're two smug bastards the pair o' them. Gettin' on my tits, so they are.'

Barney is distracted, makes a bad play. Doesn't notice, but Bill is watching closely. Bill the Cat. Suddenly, given the opening, he begins to play dynamite dominoes, a man at the pinnacle of his form, making great sweeping moves of brio and verve, which Barney wrongly attributes to him having had a glimpse of his hand.

'So what are you gonnae dae about it?' says Bill, after administering the coup de grâce.

Barney, vanquished in the game, lays down his weapons, places his hands on the table. Looks Bill square in the eye. They have been friends a long time, been through a lot. The Vietnam War, the Falklands conflict, the miners' strike of '83. Not that they'd been to any of them, but they had watched a lot of them on television together. And so Barney feels able to confide the worst excesses of his imagination to Bill.

He leans forward conspiratorially across the table. This is it – a moment to test the bond to its fullest.

'How long have we been friends, Bill?' he asks, voice hushed.

Bill shrugs. 'Oh, Ah don't know. A long time, Barney.' His too is the voice of a conspirator, although he is unaware of why he is whispering.

Barney inches ever closer towards him, his chin ever nearer the table.

'Barney?' asks Bill, before he can say anything else.

'What?'

'Ye're no' gonnae kiss me, are ye?'

Barney shakes his head, rolls his eyes. 'Don't be a bloody mug, ya eejit. Now listen up.' He pauses, hesitating momentarily before the pounce. 'Tell me, Bill, dae ye know anythin' about poison?'

'Poison? Ye mean like for rats, that kind o' thing?'

'Aye,' says Barney, thinking that rats are exactly what it's for.

'Oh, Ah don't know . . .' says Bill, and then as his rapier mind begins to kick in, and he sees the direction in which Barney is heading, he sits up straight. Looks into the eyes of his friend. 'Ye don't mean . . .?'

'Aye.'

42

'Ye've got rats in the shop?'

Barney tuts loudly, goes through his head-shaking routine, slightly lifts his jaw from two inches above the table.

'Naw, naw. It's no' rats Ah want tae poison.' Takes a suspicious look around about him to see if anyone is listening. 'Well, it is rats, but the human kind.'

This takes a minute or two to hit Bill, and when it does it is like an electric shock. As the realisation strikes him there comes a great crash of thunder outside and the windows of the pub shake with the rain and the wind. He stands up quickly, pushing the table away from him, almost sending the drinks to a watery and crashing grave.

This momentarily dramatic display attracts the attention of the rest of the bar, who have, up until now, been sedately watching snooker on the TV. Barney panics, fearing his plan will be discovered before he has even begun its formulation.

'Sit down, Bill, sit down, for God's sake.'

Bill looks down at him, horror etched upon his face for a few seconds, then slowly lowers himself back into the seat. The two men stare at each other, trying to determine exactly what the other is thinking, trying to decide how they can continue the discussion. Bill is clearly not going to be impressed with Barney's idea. Barney wonders if he can talk him into it.

'Look,' he says eventually, attempting to sound hard and businesslike, although Bill knows he is soft, soft as a pillow, 'Ah want tae know if ye can help me or no'.'

The look of horror on Bill's face increases tenfold. 'Commit murder? Is that it? Ye want me tae help ye commit murder?'

Barney looks anxiously around him to see how many people have noticed Bill's raised voice. Fortunately, the rest of the bar have returned to more mundane interests.

'Look, keep your voice down.'

Bill leans forward, once again regaining the mask of the grand conspirator. 'You cannae seriously be thinkin' o' killin' Chris and Wullie, can ye? They're good lads. For Christ's sake, man, Ah know Wullie's faither.'

Barney shakes his head. He has chosen the wrong man for advice.

43

'Huh! Good lads my backside. They'll get what's coming tae them.'

'But why?'

Barney thinks about this for a second or two. It is a reasonable enough question, demands a good answer. He fixes his gaze on Bill. 'Because they're asking for it.'

Bill shakes his head. 'Ye're no' makin' any sense, Barney, and whatever ye're planning, Ah don't want any part o' it, dae ye hear me? Keep me out o' it.'

He rises from the table again, starts to put on his coat. Barney feels chastened, looks up anxiously.

'Very well, Bill. Ah'm sorry ye feel that way,' is all he says.

Bill pulls on his cap, nods shortly to Barney as he makes to go.

'We never had this conversation, eh, Bill?' says Barney.

Bill looks him hard in the eye. Is there an implied threat in the voice? If he doesn't help him will he be included in Barney's murderous plans? Another possible victim? – although deep down he cannot believe that Barney is serious. Still waits for him to say that it's all a joke.

'Ah don't know about that, Barney, Ah really don't know,' he says. Their eyes battle with each other – two weak men – and then he turns and walks from the pub, out into the squalid storm of the night.

Chapter 6

Wine-Making

Holdall sits looking out of the window. Evening rain spatters against the glass, streetlights illuminate the rain in shades of grey and orange. There is a tangible silence in the room. The silence of a courtroom awaiting a verdict; the silence of a crowd awaiting a putt across the eighteenth green.

The Chief Superintendent reads the latest report on the serial killer investigation, fumbling noiselessly with a pipe. The only light in the room is from the small lamp on the desk, shining down onto the paper which the old man is reading. It casts strange shadows around the room; the old face looks sinister under its curious glare.

Chief Superintendent McMenemy has been on the force for longer than anyone knows, and his presence in the station goes beyond domination. 'M', they call him, and no one is quite sure whether it's a joke or not. There is no Moneypenny, no green baize on the door, but he is a considerable figure. A grumpy old man, much concerned with great matters of state. And perhaps his senior officers like the implication; if he is 'M', then they must be James Bond – although in fact, most of them are 003s, the men who mess up and die in the pre-credit sequence of the movie.

He puts the pipe to his mouth, sucks on it a couple of times while attacking it with a match, eventually manages to get it going. Tosses the box of matches casually onto the table, looks at Holdall. There is nothing to be read in those dark eyes – Holdall shifts uncomfortably in his seat. Long, unnerving silences, another of his trademarks.

Continues to suck quietly on his pipe, finally points it at Holdall.

'Well, one two seven, what have you got to say for yourself?'

Another one of his ridiculous pretensions, thinks Holdall. Referring to everyone on his staff by the last three digits of their staff number. Shows a decent memory, perhaps.

He tries to concentrate on the question. It is a good one. What does he have to say for himself exactly? He can't tell the truth – that he felt like a bloody idiot giving the press conference, and had made something up so that he wouldn't look stupid. Apart from anything else, it is destined to make him look even more stupid when they don't produce the promised serial killer, and he has to explain that one in a press conference.

He looks into the massive black holes of M's eyes, wonders what to say. M grunts, picks up the report so that he can toss it back onto the desk.

'You've got the whole of the country thinking we're just about to collar someone, when as far as I can see we're no nearer making an arrest than we were at the start. What in God's name were you thinking about, man?'

Holdall stares at the floor, tries to pull himself together. Be assertive, for God's sake. The one thing the old man hates is fumbling idiots. He straightens his shoulders, looks him in the eye. Tries to banish the picture of Mrs Holdall brandishing a frying pan, which has inexplicably just come into his head.

'I thought that maybe we should try and sound positive for once. We've spent two months now coming across as losers, sir. I thought it was about time people started thinking that we've got some balls about us. If we haven't come up with anything in the next few days, we'll have to say that our inquiries in this respect have come to a dead end. But at least we'll look as if we've got some spunk, and that we're putting something into this investigation. Certainly the shit'll be on our shoes the next time someone is murdered, but until then we have to look as if we're getting somewhere.

'We don't know anything about this killer, sir. Why he's doing it, what motivates him, none of that. It could be that he won't kill again. Who knows? Or it could be that we come up with a lead in the next few days. I thought it was about time that we showed some assertiveness.'

He stops, looks into the impassive face, the eyes which haven't moved from Holdall while he talked, the expression of stone. Now M turns his seat round so that it is facing towards the window, and he stares at the night sky, the dull orange reflection in the low clouds. His pipe has gone out, and he once more begins to fumble with the matches.

Holdall waits for the reaction. The fact that he hasn't immediately exploded is a good sign. He had half expected to be out of a job already.

Eventually, after several minutes of working the pipe, followed by ruminative smoking, he turns back to Holdall, holds him in his icy stare. He considers his words carefully; when he speaks, he speaks slowly.

'Well, I'm not sure about this, one two seven, and I'd rather you'd talked to me about it first. But on reflection, perhaps it wasn't too bad a strategy. Of course, if pieces of dismembered body start turning up in the post tomorrow morning, like confetti at a wedding, then we're in trouble.' He stops, points the pipe. 'You're in trouble.'

He swivels the chair back so that he is looking out of the window again, and Holdall is looking at the imperious profile. M toys with his pipe, tapping it on the desk.

'It might be a good idea if you came up with something solid in the next few days, one two seven.'

'Yes, sir.'

He adds nothing to that, and Holdall shifts uncomfortably in his seat, wondering if he has been dismissed. Never rise until you have been told, however, he says to himself.

Finally, M turns and stares at him. There's a look of surprise on his face due to the fact that Holdall is still there.

'That will be all, one two seven, thank you.'

* * *

Mrs Cemolina Thomson is eighty-five, lives alone in a twelfth-floor flat in Springburn. Smokes eighty cigarettes a day, an obscure brand she found during the war, containing more tar than the runways at Heathrow; spends her days watching quiz shows on television. Donald Thomson died when Barney was five years old, and ever since she has attempted to rule the lives of her children. Her eldest son has long since escaped her clutches, leaving Barney to face the brunt of her domineering personality. Her attitudes have not so much progressed with the century through which she has lived, as regressed to some time between the Dark Ages and the creation of the universe. A white, Protestant grandmother with a bad word for everybody.

Barney lets himself into the flat, is immediately struck by a smell so rancid it turns his stomach. His first grotesque thought: perhaps his mother has lain dead in the flat for some days, the smell her decomposing body. He steels himself for the stumble across her rotting flesh, but no, that won't be it. He knows it, as he talked to her the night before. Even his mother's crabbed body would not decompose so quickly – certainly not in the damp chill of Scotland in early March.

The first rooms off the hall are bedrooms, and he looks into those to see if she is there. However, as he nears the kitchen, he realises that this is where the smell most definitely emanates from. Quickens his pace, bursts through the door.

Cemolina stands stirring a huge pot of steaming red liquid, wearing an apron; curlers in her hair. He wonders whether the stench is coming from the pot or from the horrendous stuff women stick in their hair when they do a home perm. Decides it is too bad even for that. Must be the pot.

'Whit the hell are ye daein', Mum? That stuff smells bloody terrible.'

She turns her head, looks at him as if she had known he was standing there. Beads of sweat pepper her face at the effort she is making – haystacks on a ragged hillside. Her face is slightly flushed.

'Hello, Barnabas, how are ye? Nearly finished,' she says, turning back to her strange brew.

Visibly wincing, as he always does at the mention of his name, he walks over beside her, looks down into the pot. It is a deep red, thin liquid, bubbling slightly, close to the boil. Beside it, the stench is almost overwhelming, but Barney does not withdraw; the look of incredulity on his face holding him there as if it might be glue. Aghast.

'Whit on earth are ye making, Mum, for God's sake?'

'Whit does it look like?' she says. Sons should not use such a tone with their mothers.

He stares at it for a while, trying to work it out. Very thin strawberry jam? Jelly, several hours before it has set? Who knows? he thinks. Neither of them would smell like that.

'Ah honestly huvnae the faintest idea. Whit in God's name is it?'

She tuts loudly, bustles some more. 'It's wine, for God's sake, surely ye can see that?'

He stares at it – new understanding, even less comprehension. Maybe that explains the smell, but he knows nothing about wine-making.

'Is this how ye make wine?' he says.

She stops stirring, looks him hard in the eye, lips pursed, hands drawn to her hips. Nostrils flare. He knows the look, having suffered from it for over forty years, and prepares to make his retreat.

'Well, Ah dinnae know about anybody else, but it's how Ah make wine. Now away an' sit down, an' Ah'll be wi' ye in a few minutes.'

He nods meekly, makes his exit, closes the door behind him. Glad to escape the kitchen. Goes into the sitting room and opens up the windows, letting the cold, damp air into the house, clean and refreshing. Stands there for a couple of minutes breathing it in, trying to purge the stench of the kitchen, then withdraws into the room, sits down. Finds the snooker on BBC2, and settles back on the settee.

He doesn't have long to wait before his mother walks into the room, red-stained apron still wrapped around her, a bustle in her step. Tuts loudly when she sees the open windows, closes them noisily, then sits down to light herself a cigarette. Sucks in deeply, two long draws, and with a shock realises that there is snooker on television.

'For God's sake, what are ye watching this rubbish for? *Whose Pants!* is on the other channel,' she says, grabbing the remote control and changing it over.

Barney rolls his eyes, looks at his mother, thinks he might as well not be there. She sits engrossed in the television, while a variety of celebrity undergarments are brought on, and the contestants attempt to identify them from the stains. She has finished her second cigarette by the time the adverts arrive. Lowers the volume, turns to look at her boy.

'Whit are ye making wine for, Mum?'

She shrugs. Not all questions in life have answers, she thinks. 'Ah didnae have enough sugar tae make marmalade,' she says, and pulls hard on her newly lit cigarette. 'So, how are ye? You're lookin' a wee bitty fed up, are ye no'?'

He sits back, stares at the ceiling. Can he talk to his mother?

Probably not. He's never been able to before, so why should he suddenly be able to start now? Mothers aren't for talking to; they're for obeying and running after. At least, that's what his mother is for. Iron hand in iron glove.

'Ach, Ah'm just a bit cheesed aff at work an' a' that, ye know. It's nothin'.'

She draws heavily on the cigarette. 'Oh aye, whit's the problem?'

He tuts, shakes his head. 'Ach, it's they two that Ah work wi', they're really gettin' tae me. Keep taking a' my customers, so they dae. Pain in the arse, tae be quite frank.'

Now Cemolina shakes her head. Lips purse, eyes narrow. Sees conspiracy. Believes Elvis was abducted by aliens on the instructions of the FBI. 'It doesnae surprise me. Yon Chris Porter. He's a Fenian, is he no'? Cannae trust a bloody Tim, that's what Ah always say.'

Barney shakes his head. 'Naw, naw, Mum, the other yin's just as bad.'

She looks surprised. 'Wullie Henderson? He's a fine lad. Goes tae watch the Rangers every week, does he no'?'

Barney nods. Feels like he's in the lion's den. Even his mother puts great store by football. What is it about a group of men running around like five-year-olds? 'Maybe he does, Mum, but that's no' the point.'

'Oh, aye. Whit is the point, then?'

He shakes his head. 'Ah don't know. They take a' ma customers. Make me look bloody stupid in front o' everyone. They're a' laughin' at me.' Stops when he realises that he sounds like a stroppy child with a major huff on, lip petted, face scowling. Cemolina hasn't noticed. Either that, or she is used to seeing him like this.

'So, whit are ye gonnae dae about it, then?'

He stares at the floor, wonders what to say. Feels he has to obey the golden rule of not confessing murderous intent to your mother – not forgetting the Norman Bates Exception, when you and your mother are the same person – and his villainous ardour has been partly quashed by Bill's horrified reaction to his nefarious scheme. There is little point in talking to her about it. And who is he fooling anyway? He isn't about to kill anybody. He's Barney Thomson, sad pathetic barber from Partick. No killer he.

He shrugs his shoulders, mumbles something about there being nothing he can do. Sounds like a wee boy.

'Why don't you kill them?' she says, drawing hard on her cigarette, as far down as she can get it.

He stares at her, disbelief rampaging unchecked across his face. 'Whit did you say?'

'Kill them. Blow their heids off, if they're that much trouble tae ye. Yer old dad used tae say, "If someone's gettin' on yer tits, kill the bastard, an' they willnae get on yer tits any more".'

Barney looks at her. Staring at a new woman, someone he's never seen before. His mother. His own mother is advising him to kill Wullie and Chris. Stern council. She can't be serious, can she? Was that the kind of thing his father used to say? He remembers him as kind, gentle; distant memories; soft-focus, warm, sunny summer afternoons.

'Dae ye mean that?'

She shrugs, lights up another cigarette. 'Well, Ah don't

know if they were his exact words, it's been about forty years after a', but it wis something like that Ah'm sure.'

'Naw, naw, no' that. Dae ye really think that Ah should kill them? Really?'

'Of course Ah dae. If they're upsetting ye that much, do away wi' them. You've been in yon shop a lot longer than they two heid-the-ba's. Ye shouldnae let them push ye aboot. Blow their heids aff.'

A huge grin begins to spread itself across Barney's face. He has found a conspirator. A confidante in the most unlikely of places.

'Ah cannae believe ye're serious.'

'Why no'? They're bastards, are they no'? Ye says so yersel'. Especially yon Fenian, Porter.'

'Wullie's worse.'

She shakes her head, looks sad. 'Ah don't know. A good Protestant lad gone wrong.'

Barney looks upon his mother with wonder. That her mind is now undoubtedly caught in a tangled web of senility is completely lost upon him, so delighted is he to find an enthusiast. He is about to broach the subject of poison when she realises that the adverts have long since finished. Holds up her hand to stop him talking, returns her gaze to the television.

The presenter, an annoying curly-haired man with a thick Yorkshire accent, is holding up a gigantic pair of shorts, festooned with numerous revolting stains. A caption at the bottom of the screen gives a choice of four celebrities. The giggling girl – all lipstick and false breasts for her big TV appearance – partnered by Lionel Blair, presses the buzzer, giggles some more. 'Pavarotti!' she ejaculates, and with a 'Good guess, luv, but not correct this time. A big hand for that try, though, ladies and gentlemen' from the presenter, the audience erupts.

And so the show continues for another ten minutes, before with a 'Thanks for watching, tune in next week for some more pants!', the programme is finished. Cemolina lowers the volume once again, turns back to Barney, the look of the easily satisfied on her face. Barney has been staring blankly at the television, none of it registering, his face a study in concentration.

'So, ye're gonnae blow their heids aff?' she says. Her look gives a stamp of approval.

Barney strokes his chin in murderous contemplation. 'Actually, Ah wis, eh, thinkin' o' poison. Dae ye know anything aboot it?'

Cemolina grabs the arms of the chair, lifts herself up an inch or two. She is a small woman, but still she presents an imposing figure, especially to the weak son.

'Poison!' she shrieks. 'Poison, did Ah hear ye say?'

Barney flummoxes about in his seat for a second, a landed fish. Recovers his composure enough to speak, although not enough to stop himself looking like a flapping haddock.

'Whit's wrang wi' poison?'

She tut-tuts, shakes her head. 'It's womany for a start. Ye'd huv tae be a big jessie tae want tae poison somebody. Did Ah bring ye up as a girl? Well, did Ah?'

'No, Mum,' he says, sounding dangerously like a six-year-old caught with his finger in the jam jar.

'Naw, ye're right, Ah didnae. Act like a man, for pity's sake. Ye've got tae gie it laldy, Barney, none o' this poison keich. Blow their heids aff. Carpet the floor wi' their brains. Or get a hammer and smash their heids tae smithereens. That's whit tae dae. Beat them tae a pulp. That's whit yer faither would have done. Or kneecap them and . . .'

'Mum!' There is a growing look of incredulity on his face, horror in his voice. He has long known that everyone has their dark half, but he's never really thought that everyone included his own mother.

Cemolina looks aghast at her son, however. 'Ye want them deid, dae ye no'? Ye says so yersel', so whit are ye blethering aboot?'

'Aye, aye, Ah dae, but something simple. Ah don't like mess, ye know that.'

She screws up her face, waves a desultory hand. 'Well, Ah didnae think ye'd be that much o' a big poof. Ah just thought that if ye were gonnae dae it, ye might as well have some fun while ye're aboot it.'

Barney looks at his mother with some distaste. Maybe she is mad. But then, it was him who was thinking about killing them in the first place. She has merely added some enthusiasm to the project. If she's mad, then he isn't far behind.

'Ach, Ah don't know, Mother. Ah'll huv tae think aboot it. Ah certainly don't think that Ah could go beating anybody's heid tae a pulp.'

She scowls at him, turns her attention back to the television to see which quiz show will be on next.

'Ah can't believe ye're bein' such a big jessie. Yer faither would've been black affrontit, so he wid,' she says, turning the volume back up.

'Yes, Mum,' says Barney.

He can't do it. Not anything violent. He knows he can't. Perhaps, however, he can get someone else to do it for him. A hired hand. There's a thought. Strokes his chin, and as the opening strains of *Give Us a Disease* start up, sinks further into the soft folds of the settee, and loses himself in barbaric contemplations.

Chapter 7

A Pair of Breasts

Margaret MacDonald glances up at the television, which has been droning away in the background all morning. They are running over the previous night's football results. She raises her eyebrows. Rangers lost 2–0 at Motherwell. Typical. That was why Reginald was in such a foul mood when he came in last night. And still this morning. Stomping around like a baby who's been woken up too early, and then charging out the door without saying a word to her. God, men are so pathetic.

Her eyes remain on the television, but she isn't watching. She's thinking about Louise, as she has been for the past three days. It isn't like her to just vanish. Nearly twenty now, and there have been plenty of times in the past when she has gone off for the night without letting them know where she is. But three days . . .

She feels that nervous grip on her stomach, the tightening of the muscles, which she has been experiencing more and more often. Gulps down some tea, tries to put it out of her mind. It's not as if she doesn't have plenty of other things to think about.

The doorbell rings. She jumps. Looks round in shock, into the hall, can just make out the dark grey of a uniform through the frosted glass of the front door. Swallows hard to fight back the first tears of foreboding. It's the police. The police with news about Louise.

The doorbell rings again. Feeling the great weight rested upon her shoulders, she rises slowly from the table, inches her way towards the door. Whatever she is going to find out won't be true until she has opened that door and been informed. Her hand hovers over the key; she wishes she could suspend time; wishes she could stand there for ever, and never have to learn what she is about to be told.

She turns the key, slowly swings the door open, the first tears already beginning to roll down her face.

'Ye awright there, hen, ye're lookin' a bit upset?'

She starts to smile, and then a laugh comes bursting out of her mouth. A big, booming, guttural laugh which she has never heard herself make before. She puts her hand out, touches the arm of the postman.

'I'm sorry, Davey, it's nothing. I thought you were going to be someone else, that's all.'

'Christ, who were ye expectin' wi' a reaction like that? The Pope?'

She laughs again, and for the first time looks past him. It is a dark and murky morning, the rain falling in a relentless drizzle. The winds of the previous day have abated, but still it is horrible, as it has been for weeks.

'God, it's a foul morning to be out, is it not, Davey?'

The postman shrugs and smiles. 'Ah'm no' in it fur the weather, hen.' Rummages inside his bag, pulls out a small parcel. 'Anyway, Ah've got this for ye, an' a few letters. Ah'd better be goin'. Still got bloody miles tae dae yet.'

She takes the parcel and letters from him, looking through them to see if there is one with Louise's handwriting. Looks up to see Davey MacLean already walking down the road, hunched against the rain, the hood of his jacket drawn back over his head.

'Thanks, Davey. I'll see you later.' He responds with a cool hand lifted into the gloom, and – the Steven Seagal of his trade – goes about his business with a certain violent panache.

She closes the door, retreats into the kitchen, shivering at the cold weather. Drops the letters onto the table – nothing from Louise, fights the clawing disappointment – and studies the parcel. She isn't expecting anything, doesn't recognise the handwriting. Studies the postmark. Ayr. Ayr? Who does she know in Ayr?

Then suddenly it's there. A horrible sense of foreboding. A cold hand touching her neck, making the hairs rise; the chill grip on her heart. She lets the package fall from her fingers and land on the table. Her stomach tightens, she begins to feel sick. Walks slowly over to the drawer beside the sink and lifts out a pair of scissors. She starts back to the table, but suddenly the vomit rises in her throat, and she is bent over the sink, retching violently, as the tears begin to stream down her face.

Chapter 8

The Accidental Barber Surgeon

It comes sooner than Holdall could have feared. Every morning he sits in his office waiting for the phone to ring, the angry herald of more news of stray body parts popping through someone's letterbox. Every time the phone rings he assumes the worst, and given what he told the press the evening before, he is even more fearful this particular morning.

However, fate does not even bother to tease him. There is no endless stream of calls concerning more mundane matters, leading up to the dramatic one confirming his worst fears. The dreaded call arrives first, and within three minutes of him sitting at his desk.

A woman in Newton Mearns, a woman with a missing daughter, has received what appears to be two breasts, neatly packed into a small wooden box, that morning. It had been but the thought of two seconds for her to realise that they were more than likely the breasts of her daughter, and that if she is missing her breasts, it's a fair bet that she is in some degree of trouble. And so she had turned up on the doorstep of her local police station – hysterical, and who could deny her that – demanding to speak to the bloody idiot who'd been on television the previous night implying that the police had as good as got their man.

The policeman had done his best to calm her down, and then put the call through to Holdall to tell him the grim news. And to ask him what the hell he had meant when he had talked to the press the previous evening.

When the call comes down from McMenemy's office, Holdall is not the least surprised. Ill becomes those who are summonsed to that office two days running.

The rain is falling in a relentless drizzle against the window of the shop, the skies grey overhead, the clouds low. Every now and again someone bustles past the front, their collar pulled up against the cold wind, a dour expression welded to their face.

The shop is near deserted, as it has been most of the day. Wednesdays are usually slow, and with the cold and miserable weather, today has been even worse. Barney has had to do only two haircuts all day, both of which were ropey; one indeed so bad that he thinks it might lead to retribution. He hadn't liked the way the man had asked Wullie for Barney's address on his way out, and had been surprised that Wullie had claimed ignorance on the matter. Nevertheless, it is a day for keeping his head down.

At three o'clock Wullie offers Chris the chance to go home early, tells Barney that on the next quiet day he can take his turn of an early departure. After that there are only three more customers, all of whom want Wullie to cut their hair. Barney sits and reads a variety of newspapers, and finally gives in to the boredom and falls asleep, his dreams a web of exotica.

He wakes with a start to slightly raised voices, dragged from a screaming drop down a black, bottomless shaft. Wullie is discussing modern art with his last customer of a dreadful day. Barney stretches, yawns, squints at the clock. Two minutes past five. Time to go. Thank God for that.

He stands and stretches again, busying himself with clearing up, not something that will take very long. Takes his time, however, doing as many unnecessary things as possible, not wishing to leave before Wullie. He listens to the idle chatter from the end of the shop; is not impressed.

'Now sixteenth-century Italian art,' Wullie is saying, as he puts the finishing touches to a dramatic taper at the back of the man's neck, 'there's the thing. It's full o' big fat birds gettin' their kit aff. It disnae matter whit the paintin's about, in every one they always managed tae squeeze in about five or six huge birds, with bloody enormous tits, lying back and showin' their duffs.'

The customer nods his own appreciation of sixteenth-century Italian art as much as he can, given that there is a man with a razor at the back of his neck.

'Ah mean,' Wullie continues, after pausing to pull off some intricate piece of barbery, 'ye've got some paintin' o' a big battle scene or somethin', or a nativity scene for Christ's sake, and they'd still manage tae get in some great lump o' lard, bollock naked, legs a' o'er the place, dangling a pun o' grapes intae the gob o' another suitably compliant naked tart, wi' nipples like corks, and her lips pouting in a flagrantly pseudo-lesbian pose. Ah love it, so Ah dae. It's pure brilliant, so it is.'

'Even so,' says the customer, holding up his finger as Wullie produces a comb to administer the finishing touches, 'Ah still don't think it's a patch on modern art. That's got far more life and soul tae it than a bunch of birds wi' their kit aff.'

Wullie stops combing, looks at the man as if he's mad.

'Yer jokin'. Ah mean, fair enough, if they painted a bit o' paper completely orange, then put a red squiggle in the middle o' it, and called it "a boring lot o' crap that took me two minutes, and isnae worth spit", then that'd be fine. But they don't. They'll dae that, and then call it "Sunrise over Manhattan", or "Three Unconnected Doorways", or "Ah'm a pretentious wank, so you've got tae gie me a million quid", or some shite like that, and get paid millions for it. It's a piece o' bloody nonsense.'

'Naw, naw, ye've got it a' wrang. These things have got a depth and soul tae them, that a lot o' people cannae see. If ye cannae see whit an artist is sayin', then it's because ye're no' in tune wi' the guy. That's hardly his fault.'

60

Wullie shakes his head as he dusts off the back of the neck.

'Come off it. Any nutter can splash paint ontae somethin' and call it "Moon over Five Women wi' Hysterectomies" – Wullie is indeed a new man – 'or something like that. Jings, ma two-year-old niece could dae it, and Ah bet she widnae get two million quid.'

'Of course no',' says the man, as Wullie removes the cape from around his neck, hands him a towel to apply the finishing touches himself, 'and that's the point. If just any bastard does it, it doesnae mean anythin'. It's got nae meanin'. The artist, however, is expressin' himsel', is lettin' ye see whit's inside him. It means somethin' because it comes fi' within, fi' his soul. That's what gies it heart, and that's why people are willin' tae pay money for it. Artists bare themselves tae the public.'

Wullie thinks about this for a second or two. The man stands, brushes himself down.

'A fine defence o' modern art ye've constructed there,' says Wullie eventually.

'Aye, thanks,' says the customer, fishing in his pockets for the required cash.

'However, it's a complete load o' bollocks.'

The man shakes his head as he produces a five-pound note from his pocket.

'Ye're no' listening tae me, Wullie.' He pauses, stares at the ceiling, tries to think of how he can best get his point across. He is not used to such intellectual debate. Reaching for his jacket, he finds what he is looking for. 'Let's put it this way. If ye're watchin' fitba', right? Let's say some wee bloke playin' for Raith Rovers blooters the ba' fi' forty yards and it flies intae the net. Now, it may seem like a great goal, but let's face it, he probably meant tae pass it tae some eejit out on the wing and mishit it. Whatever, ye know he's bloody lucky. But if Brian Laudrup kicks the ball fi' forty yards and it flies intae the net, ye know he meant it. It's a thing of beauty. It's art. The execution and the outcome are the same, but the intentions were different. That's whit it's a' about. That's the difference.'

He stops on his way to the door, holds out his hands in a gesture of 'there you have it'. Wullie shakes his head.

'Are you sayin' that Brian Laudrup's the same as one o' they eejits who throws a bunch o' paint ontae a picture?'

The man shakes his head, laughs, waves a hand at Wullie.

'Ah'll never win. See ye next time, Wullie, eh. See ye, Barney.'

The barbers say their goodbyes, Barney with a grudge – bloody idiot, he thinks – then Wullie turns to start his final clearing up for the day, after fixing the closed sign on the door.

Still shaking his head at the discussion which has just finished, Barney completes the minutiae of clearing his things away. Now that Wullie has finished, he feels free to go. Modern art; naked Italian women; these people don't half talk some amount of shite.

'Can Ah have a word wi' ye, Barney?'

He looks up; Wullie walks towards him. Barney shrugs his acceptance, Wullie sits in the next seat up from his. The usually vacant chair. Barney looks into Wullie's eyes and sits down, feels a tingle at the bottom of his spine. It could be the label on his Marks and Spencer boxer shorts, but he has the feeling that it is something worse than that.

'What is it, Wullie?'

Wullie is staring at the floor. Looks awkward, like a seventeen-year-old boy not wanting to tell his father he's written off his new Frontera San Diego. He struggles with himself, then his eyes briefly flit onto Barney then away again, before he speaks.

'Em, this isnae very easy, Barney. Ah'm no' really sure how tae say this,' he says. Looks anywhere but into Barney's eyes. Barney stares at him, a look of incredulity formulating across his face. He can't be going to say what he thinks he is, can he?

'Em, Ah'm afraid we've hired a new barber, Barney. It's an old friend o' ma dad's who's just moved intae the area. Ye know, ma dad wants tae gie him a job and . . .'

Barney switches off, knowing what is coming. He can't believe it. Feels a strange twisting in his stomach, a pounding at the back of his head. Cold, wet hands. Thinks: The gutless, gutless coward, making himself out to be merely the messenger of his father's decision, rather than the instrument of it.

How the hell can they let him go? He's the only one in the place who can give a decent haircut. Certainly he's better than these two young idiots, surely everyone can see that? But of course, bloody Wullie will have been telling his father something completely different. Maybe his mother was right – poison wasn't good enough for him; not violent enough.

' . . . so, ye can work here for another month if ye like, or we'll understand if ye want tae leave now, and we'll keep your wages goin' for the rest o' the month. Ye don't have tae make any decision right now, but if ye could let us know in the next couple o' days, that'd be great.'

Not once has he been able to look Barney in the eye, and now he sits, an attempted look of consolation on his face, eyes rooted to the floor.

Barney is in a daze, a thousand different thoughts barging into each other in his head. Cannot believe it's happened, cannot believe that they have the nerve to do this to him. He is by far the most superior barber of the lot of them. This is ridiculous. His immediate thoughts are of violent retribution. Vicious, angry thoughts involving baseball bats, sledgehammers and pickaxes.

But he can't show his hand. Not yet. He has to be calm about it. If he is going to avenge this heinous crime, he has to be calculating and cold; has to pick his moment. Cool deliberation away from the scene of the crime is required. And as he sits staring angrily into Wullie's eyes, which remain Sellotaped to the floor, he decides that he will have to stay in the shop, however great the feeling of humiliation, however great his desire to leave.

'Ah'll stay for the month,' he says abruptly.

'What?'

Wullie looks up at him, for the first time, surprised. He hadn't expected an answer so quickly, hadn't expected the one he has been given, and moreover he had been thinking about the phone call to the shop that morning from Serena – the girl from the Montrose. Wondering if that's her real name, anticipating Friday night; vague intimations of guilt.

'Ah'll stay for the month.'

Wullie stares briefly at the floor again. Thinks: Shit. He and his father had assumed that Barney would just take his leave. Hadn't reckoned on an awkward month with Barney still in the shop. He looks up.

'Awright, that'll be great. Ye're sure now?'

'Aye,' says Barney, almost spitting the word out. Manages to contain his wrath. Fingernails dig into palms. Wrath would have to be for later.

'Right, then. That's great, Barney. Ah'll let my dad know.'

That's great, is it? You've just stabbed me up the backside with a red-hot poker, and you think it's great because I accept it. Fucking bastard. Thinks it, doesn't say it.

Wullie attempts another look of consolation, succeeds only in an almost tortoise-like grimace. Goes about his business.

Barney stands up to clear away a couple of things which don't need clearing away. Doesn't want to storm out of the shop immediately, knowing his presence will unsettle Wullie. Doesn't want him to be at ease any earlier than he should be. Although, should he ever be at ease?

As he lifts an unnecessary pair of scissors from his workplace, he realises his hands are shaking. Shit. Doesn't want Wullie to see what effect it is having on him. Steadies himself, lifts a cup to get a drink of water. Fills it at the sink next to his workplace – Scottish tap water, the sweetest-tasting drink; that's what he always thinks; not today, however. But as he raises it in his still-trembling hand, the cup slips free. Strikes the edge of the sink surround and disgorges its contents, some over Barney, mostly over the floor. He mutters a curse to himself. The water runs over the smooth tiles of the floor, a mocking river of humiliation to accompany his disgrace. Mumbling a few other appropriate words which come to mind, he grabs a towel to dry himself off. Wullie looks over at him, starts to walk into the rear of the shop.

'Ah'll get a mop, Barney, and clear it up,' he says.

Like burning someone's house down and then offering to replace the welcome mat, thinks Barney.

'Don't bother, Ah'll dae it in a minute,' he growls at him, but Wullie feels the restlessness of the guilty; scurries off to retrieve the mop anyway. Barney shakes his head, begins to clear away the final few things lying around his work area. He lifts the pair of scissors again and studies them, his eyes drifting to Wullie, his back turned to him in the storeroom at the rear of the shop.

What damage I could do with these, he thinks, but he knows he never will. If he is to avenge this crime, it will have to be by some subtle act of treachery, not a brutal and bloody stabbing.

He still holds the scissors as Wullie emerges from the storeroom with the mop, and walks towards him. Barney purses his lips, tries not to appear too angry.

'Look, Wullie, it's awright. Ah said Ah'd get it, did Ah no'?'

'Ah'll just gie ye a hand, Barney, it's nae bother.'

Fine last words.

Wullie steps forward to start clearing up the water, not noticing it has run so much towards him. His first step is firmly placed into a pool of lying water on a smooth tile; his foot gives way. He attempts to regain his balance, and in doing so falls towards Barney. Barney raises his hands to catch him. Automatic reaction.

Wullie slumps heavily into him and his outstretched hands. Neatly, exactly, with medical precision, the scissors enter through Wullie's stomach and jag up under his ribcage. He rests in Barney's arms for a few seconds, then pulls back to look at him, an expression of stupefied surprise on his face.

He lurches back, blood pouring from the wound, the scissors embedded in his stomach. Falls back against the chair, which topples backwards, allowing him to slump down onto the floor. His back rests against the bottom of the chair, his eyes stare blankly one last time up at Barney, his head falls forward onto his chest.

Barney stares mutely down at the body on the floor, and the pool of blood spreading across the tiles. His face mouths silent words of horror, his voice a hushed croak of wind, and finally, when it finds some substance, it is the weak and desperate voice of the frightened.

'Fuck,' he says.

Chapter 9

Garbage Removal

Holdall stares blankly out of the window and wonders why it has stopped raining. It deserves to be raining. It has been a bloody awful day, the sort of day when it bloody well ought to rain, because any other type of weather is just completely inappropriate.

Annihilated by McMenemy early on, and given instructions to set about investigating every missing-persons case that has been reported in the past week, interview every family, and to follow up every new case that comes in, anywhere in Glasgow. So he has been sent out on the rounds, and worst of all, Robertson has been put in charge of the investigation in his place. Detective Chief Inspector Brian Robertson – the biggest bastard on the force. Think yourself lucky you're not suspended, McMenemy had said to him. Quite the reverse, he thought.

The day has been spent trailing round Glasgow, wet and dreich and unremittingly miserable, interviewing a succession of pointless boring women whose sons have unquestionably run off to London, and one man whose wife has, without any shadow of a doubt, fled the country with her boss. Her husband, however, still holds out some hope that she has been brutally murdered, and is anxiously checking the post every morning.

The day was indeed long, and then, having returned half an hour earlier, he had to face Robertson to be given the latest update on the case, and his instructions for the following day. Which bear a remarkable similarity to his instructions for the day he has just endured. Any more than a week of this and he'll be resigning.

I may resign anyway, he reflects as he stares out of the window, noticing with some satisfaction that the rain has just begun to fall again.

Quiet descends upon the shop. The body lies inert and slouched, propped against the toppled chair, the blood slowly spreading across the floor. Barney stands over it, staring dumbly at the bloody scene. His mind is numb, his feet anchored to the spot, even as the blood begins to spread towards them.

'Shit,' he says eventually. It hangs in the air, awaiting addition. 'Shit, shit, shit, shit, shit.'

The blood about to touch his shoes, he jumps away from it, starts pacing around the room. His heart thumps loudly, he begins to sweat, his face beaded with perspiration. He is flirting dangerously with panic. He has killed Wullie. Christ, he's killed Wullie. Wullie. He might have been a gutless bastard, but he hadn't meant to kill him.

Not yet, anyway. If he had been going to do it, it would have had to have been on his terms. Shit, shit, shit. Why hadn't Wullie just let him clear up the water himself? The bloody idiot. And why did he have to sack him? If he hadn't done that, this wouldn't have happened.

The memory of that – the sacking – nudges at him again, the feelings of annoyance return. Maybe it is Wullie's own fault. If he hadn't sacked him, it wouldn't have happened. Good logic, absolutely true.

He stands on the far side of the shop beside the door, stares at the corpse, the steady flow of blood now beginning to ease. Don't feel bad about it, part of him is trying to tell him, he got what he deserved. Think about it – it's true. If he hadn't been such a gutless little bastard, then he wouldn't be dead now. Perhaps the punishment doesn't quite fit the crime, but then what had he been about to do to your life, Barney? Something as bad. Maybe even worse. He was going to humiliate you.

He stands for some minutes arguing with himself over the rights and wrongs of Wullie lying in a pool of blood. Suddenly it hits him – he is going to have to tell someone about it. He will have to call the police, he will have to tell Wullie's wife, Moira. It's not just about him and Wullie. There are other people involved. The guilt begins to grow. He tastes the blood, feels it damp on his hands. Thinks: Macbeth.

What is he going to say to the police after all? Well, Officer, he'd just sacked me, and although Ah didnae mean this tae happen, Ah think ye can see that it's perfectly justified. Very well, Mr Thomson, the officer will say, we'll let ye off just this once. No' even a manslaughter charge. But dinnae be lettin' it happen again.

Of course not. Of course it won't be that easy. And once the police find out that Wullie had intended to sack him, as they surely will from Wullie's father, then they will be more than willing to believe that Barney had meant to kill him.

The phone rings.

His heart stops beating for some seconds, while it clatters up through his mouth, hits the ceiling and bounces off the floor a few times. He gets over the shock, gathers himself together; the phone is still ringing.

He stares blankly at it. 'Shit, whit dae Ah dae? If Ah answer it, it places me at the scene of the crime.'

Somewhere in Barney's head there is a calm, calculating half, trying to get him under control. It is that which had reminded him of Wullie's treachery. It is that which now tries to drag him back from the precipice of panic.

'Ye work here, ye idiot. That places ye at the scene o' the crime, does it no'?'

He stares at the phone, trapped in his indecision. He still has much to decide upon, and this is forcing him to make his mind up much more quickly than he wants to.

'If Ah don't get it, Ah can say Ah left the shop around five wi' Wullie still here.'

'Don't be a fool,' his other half replies. 'What if someone sees ye leave the shop now? Ye're caught for a liar. Ye're bound tae go down.'

'But why should Ah? Why should Ah go down? Ah didnae dae anythin'. Not intentional, like.'

'Come on, ye idiot. No one's gonnae believe that. If ye leave the shop and let the body lie, ye've had it. Answer the phone. If it's someone looking for Wullie, say he's already left.'

Barney hesitates. Shit, shit, shit. Why does the phone never ring when you want it to, always ring when you don't?

Slowly he walks over, lifts the receiver. His heart thumps dangerously in his chest.

'Hello, Henderson's?'

'Oh, hello, Barney, it's Moira. Is Wullie still there?'

His heart crashes frantically out through his ribs, cannons off the wall, and after bouncing several times around the room, eventually returns to rest, shaken and battered.

Wullie's wife. It's Wullie's wife. Shit, shit, shit. Stay calm, Barney, stay calm.

'Eh, no, Moira, he's no'. He, eh, just left a couple o' minutes ago. He, eh, shouldnae be too long, ye know.'

'Right, thanks, then, Barney. Goodn . . .'

A thought suddenly occurs, and in his fright he does not ignore it. Give yourself more time, Barney, give yourself more time.

'Oh aye, Moira, Ah forgot. He said he was gonnae dae a bit o' shoppin' or somethin' before he went home.' Not bad for off the cuff, he thinks.

'Shoppin'? Whit shoppin's he daein'? Wullie's never been intae a shop in his life!'

'Eh, Ah don't know, Moira, he didnae say.' Maybe it wasn't so brilliant after all.

'Oh God, Ah wonder whit he's up tae now. Ah'll kill that eejit when Ah see him, so Ah will.'

Appropriate, but you won't have to. The dark, clinical half of Barney, which is beginning to emerge almost as an independent being, interjects into his thoughts – get off the phone before ye say anythin' else stupid. Ye've got work tae dae, it says.

'Aye, right, well, Ah'm sure it's nothin', Moira,' says Barney.

'Aye, well, it better no' be, or Ah'll skelp his arse for him.'

'Aye, right. Goodnight, Moira.'

'Aye,' she says, and then she's gone.

He hangs up the phone, slumps down into his seat, relief washing over him in great tidal waves. He's handled it reasonably well, and he's managed to get himself a little more time.

Then the waves wash away, and once again he is high and dry. His eyes fall upon the corpse, lying in the pool of blood. Blood – how odd it looks. Much darker than he imagined it would be. Maybe it is just the low lighting in the shop. That low lighting for which he has been profoundly grateful in the past, when, after dark on winter days, atrocious late afternoon haircuts have gone unnoticed.

A thought occurs. Maybe now he will get to keep his job. A smile wanders aimlessly across his mouth, stopping as it goes, to linger on the spoils of victory. They'll need the new barber to cover for Wullie, so they won't have any reason to sack him. Smashing. At least that's something. Only, however, if he can avoid being arrested for murder.

Harsh truth: he is going to have to do something with the body that lies before him. Whatever he does, he will have to be analytical and cold. This is not Barney. He needs this new, unrealised dark half to think for him. He sits back, attempts to focus. No time to waste, and whatever is to be done, it has to be done quickly. Finally, after staring blankly, but without horror, at the body on the floor, his dark half arrives, on a gleaming white horse and followed by a large posse.

'Now, Barney, ye've got tae be clear about this.' Barney sits back to listen, not really sure who is doing the talking. 'If the body is discovered here in the shop, then ye've had it. Ye'll be charged with murder, and ye'll spend the next fifteen years in gaol wi' yer bum tae a wall trying to avoid people wearin' rubber underwear.' Barney winces. 'Ye're gonnae have tae dispose o' the body. Ye have tae clean up a' traces o' blood fi' the shop, and remove yer bloody clothes and get rid o' them 'n a'.' Barney looks at himself. Christ! He's hardly noticed – the huge patch of blood where Wullie fell against him. 'Once he's reported missin', the polis'll call, so there cannae be any traces o' murder.

And ye're gonnae have tae be quick about it, so get tae work.'

Barney stares at the corpse a little while longer, deciding what has to be done. Finally, his mind put straight on the matter, he sets to work with feverish determination, thinking all the time that the police are about to come bursting in through the door.

They keep some large black plastic bags in the back of the shop, for the general detritus of the day – hair clippings, rubbish, corpses – and in these he wraps up the body, binding it tightly with string. As is always the case with new murderers, he is surprised by the weight of the corpse and how difficult it is to manhandle, but still he is able to work efficiently and quickly – more quickly than ever he cut anyone's hair. He cleans the blood that has collected on the outside of the bags, then places the body beside the door awaiting removal. Then there are the traces of blood to be removed, the large pool of it, and all the other smudges and marks which have been spread around the floor and the furniture.

Forty minutes later he stands beside the door and surveys the shop. It looks good. It looks like it is supposed to look. Barber Clears away Dead Body in Record Time. All traces of the murder are gone, and he has cleaned up Wullie's workplace and removed his jacket to make it look as though he had departed as normal. Over a hundred and fifty pounds in his wallet, another small bonus to bring a smile to his face. All that remains to tell the tale is the bulky black package on the floor, and the blood on Barney's clothes. There is nothing he can do about that until he gets home, but he is able to cover up the worst of it with his jacket.

All looks well – only one immediate problem remains. How to get the body out to his car, unseen. It is just after six o'clock, a busy hour, but the street in which the shop stands is off the main road and usually quiet.

He turns off the lights, opens the door, pokes his head out into the street. There is one car driving past, and the main road seems busy, but there are no pedestrians in the immediate vicinity of the shop. All seems clear. He has little option, however. He has to risk it. If the body is still in the shop the following day, someone is bound to notice – corpses do so stand out.

He walks up the road to where his car is parked – gives a small prayer that it was returned that morning, wonders what he would have done if it hadn't been – reverses it back down the road so that it is directly outside the door. Opens the boot, takes another few furtive looks over his shoulder, goes back into the shop.

He looks around once again in the near-dark, the light filtering in from the street throwing strange shadows into the corners; a final check to make sure that everything is normal; turns his attention to the plastic bags. First of all he attempts to lift it onto his shoulder, a task which he fails to do by about as much as it is possible to fail to do something. Shrugs his shoulders, resigns himself to dragging it along the floor. Lifts the bags firmly at one end, making sure to grab the body through the plastic so as not to tear it, and starts walking backwards out of the shop – into the murk and the drizzle, pulling the dead weight.

'Oh, hello there, Barney, how are ye?'

For about the fifteenth time in an hour, Barney's heart pushes vigorously against the restraining tissue around it, and on this occasion he also comes close to losing any semblance of bowel control. Dangerously close.

He looks up. Charlie Johnstone, one of the shop's regulars. Shit, shit, shit. Why didn't he check the road again before he dragged the body out? Too bloody impetuous.

He lowers the body to the ground, stands to look at Charlie. Fully expects him to say at any second, 'Here, is that no' Wullie inside those bags there?'

'Oh, eh, hello, Charlie. How's it goin'?'

Potential crisis point. Charlie stops to chat.

'Ach, no' sae bad, no' sae bad. Mind you, these headaches Ah've been gettin' are an absolute bloody nightmare, so they are. They're killin' me. And Betty, Betty, well, ye don't want tae ask about her.' Shakes his head a few times, and then continues before Barney has the chance not to ask about Betty. 'Awfy trouble wi' yon trapped nerve in her shoulder, so she has. Awfy trouble. Aye, an' she had a bit o' bother wi' her eye, ye know, her cataract, but Ah suppose we've been lucky really, and Ah shouldnae complai . . .'

Barney feels compelled to interrupt, even if it means drawing attention to what he is dragging out of the shop. The longer he stands here, the more likely it will be for a police car to drive by – a police car with a corpse detector.

'Look, Ah'm sorry, Charlie, but Ah'm in a bit o' a hurry here.'

'Oh, aye, aye. Sorry aboot that.'

He looks down, sees for the first time what Barney is dragging out of the shop. A look of curiosity passes fleetingly across his face. Applies his hands to his sides, widens the stance of his feet.

'Here, that looks like a bloody big thing, so it does. Dae ye want a hand wi' that?'

Barney shakes his head. Groans inside. 'Eh, naw, naw, it's fine, Ah'm awright, thanks.'

He bends to lift the sack, making sure to grab hold of the body again, while Charlie watches. There is little concealing the act now, so he decides to get on with it and hope that an arm or some other appendage does not spring free. As he does so, he begins to think of another eventuality. What to do with Charlie if he realises what is going on. There are still plenty of pairs of scissors in the shop.

He pulls the sack to the edge of the pavement, lays it behind the car. Stares at it, wondering if he's going to be able to lift it up over the high edge of the boot. Charlie bustles over.

'Here, let me help ye wi' that. Looks bloody heavy, whitever it is.'

Barney shrugs, feels the tightness in his chest. He has to accept the offer, begins to make mental preparations for taking care of Charlie if the need should arise. For how can he fail to realise what it is that he is lifting into the boot? Maybe he should just go back into the shop now, return with a pair of scissors, embed them in some suitable part of Charlie's body and then bundle his body into the boot as well.

He closes his eyes, breathes deeply. Feels the tremble all over his body. Hands shake.

He looks into the boot. Never. There is never enough

73

room to put two bodies in there. The back seat, then. He casts an eye over his shoulder to see if there is anyone abroad who might see what is going on.

Charlie studies the black bags, takes a gentle kick at them. Used to play wing half for Queen's Park. Long time ago. Christ, thinks Barney. Christ. Surely he must realise that this is Wullie, or a body of some description. He must.

'Look, just a minute, Charlie,' says Barney, taking another look up and down the road, 'Ah've got tae get somethin' fi' the shop. Ah'll just be a second.'

He walks quickly back through the door, lifts the first pair of scissors which come to hand at his own workplace, then returns to the street. Half expects to find Charlie kneeling beside the bags, tearing them apart to reveal Wullie's dead face, contorted in perpetual wonder. Prepares to wield the scissors.

However, Charlie stands alone, staring up the street, idly whistling some aimless tune. Might be Verdi, might be Manic Street Preachers, might be Val Doonican. Barney slips the scissors into his pocket. No need to do anything stupid yet.

Charlie turns to him. Smiles. 'Wullie's no' in the shop, is he, lettin' us two do a' the work?'

Barney swallows, tries to smile, doesn't answer.

'Right, then. Ye ready, Charlie?'

'Aye, aye.'

The two men grab the ends of the bags, and with some effort manage to lift them up, shovelling them over the edge of the car and into the boot. The bags at Charlie's end start to tear, but the body slumps down into the boot before anything is revealed. It comes to rest with the feet at Barney's side still protruding over the edge, and he has to bend the legs to fit the whole thing in – the body already less pliable than he thought it would be.

They are both breathing hard as Barney quickly closes the boot to prevent Charlie looking at the bags any further.

'Bloody hell, Barney, whit wis that thing? Jings, it feels like a body or somethin'.'

Barney coughs loudly, attempting to cover up the involuntary splutter. Automatically his hand drifts into his pocket, his fingers fall on the cold steel of the scissors. Cold, cold steel.

'Oh, eh, it's, eh, it's just some rubbish, ye know, that we've collected, and Ah'm taking it tae the dump.'

Charlie smiles, nods. Simple Charlie. Used to play wing half for Queen's Park.

'Rubbish? Bloody heavy rubbish, Barney. Ah don't know whit kind o' rubbish yese collect in that shop.' Gives Barney a wink and a nudge. 'Sure ye havenae been havin' arguments wi' Wullie or Chris, eh, eh?'

Barney tightens his grip on the scissors. 'Don't be daft,' he says, attempting a smile. 'It's just, well, ye know, stuff.'

Charlie winks extravagantly again. 'Aye, right. Stuff. Yer secret's safe wi' me, son.'

Barney nods at him, grimaces slightly. Thinks: Christ, Barney, the guy's joking, he doesn't realise anything. But the hand in his pocket is ready to strike. He looks up and down the road – the coast is clear. The opportunity is there. Wait. Just wait to see if he says anything else.

'Thanks for yer help, Charlie. Ah've really got tae be goin' now.' Charlie has the collar of his jacket pulled high up over his neck, so that is one point of entry removed. The eye socket, that would be a sure-fire place to do it.

'Aye, aye, awright. Ah'll be seein' ye, Barney,' and with a wave he walks off towards the main street. Barney watches him go; his whole body aches with relief.

'Here, Barney,' says Charlie from the end of the street. 'Wullie's no' in the shop, is he? I was needin' tae speak tae him.'

Barney doesn't answer. He can't. Stands and stares, feels the rain on his face. Charlie waits a second for the reply. When he doesn't get it he waves and disappears around the corner.

Barney groans, but there is nothing he can do about it now. He couldn't have realised anything. There was no hint of suspicion about him. Nothing.

As he walks back into the shop to return the scissors, the phone starts ringing again. He gives a little jump, but he has become immune to these shocks. Whoever it is, he is in no mood to talk to them. He quickly leaves the shop and locks the door behind him. There is a lot of thinking to be done.

He drives home as calmly as he can. He is not relaxed, however – his steering wayward, his gear changes edgy, and his avoidance of old people crossing the road at best uncertain. His thoughts are consumed with what he is going to do with the body. And as he drives the short distance home, he resolves to tell Agnes. He will have to. He needs someone to talk to, and if he can trust anyone, surely it is her. And perhaps she might have body-disposal experience, he reasons to himself.

He arrives home, parks the car outside, leaves the bloody booty of his misfortune congealing in the back, tramps upstairs. When he walks into the sitting room, his dinner awaits patiently and cold on the table, while Agnes watches television.

He removes his jacket and stands in the centre of the room, his clothes soiled with blood, a look of grim desperation on his face. A chainsaw would not look out of place in his hands.

'There ye are. Where have ye been? Yer dinner's been ready for ages,' says Agnes, without looking round. Blane and Liberty are getting married, and everyone is waiting for Sobriety to object.

He stands for a second or two before answering, waiting to see if she will turn to look at him, something which under normal circumstances he would know she would never do.

It rises within him, a pressure cooker waiting to explode, until he can't keep it in any longer. 'Ah've killed Wullie,' he blurts out.

Agnes gasps. It isn't Sobriety who objects. It's Bleach.

'Yes, dear,' she says finally, after coming to terms with the fact that Bleach is pregnant by Blane, when everyone believed that she had been artificially inseminated with Rock's semen.

'Are ye no' listening tae me? Ah've killed Wullie!' His voice has become a desperate plea for help, more strained than he imagined it could be.

'Oh yes, dear? What did ye do that for?'

He takes a step nearer to her. She isn't looking at him, but maybe she's listening at last. 'Ah didnae mean tae. It was an accident. Ah swear tae God, Ah didnae mean tae.'

Agnes briefly turns and looks at him. 'Don't worry,

dear, Ah'm sure he'll have forgotten all about it in the morning.'

Barney drops to his knees, puts his hands to his face. Finally, the magnitude of what has happened is coming to him, and the idiocy of what he has done. He has killed a man. Maybe not intentionally, but he has killed him, and now he is plotting to dispose of the body. Whatever trouble he was in when he started has now increased a hundredfold.

Why had he not just phoned the police and explained what had happened? Nobody would have suspected him of murder. Why should they have? He's known as a reasonable man. Just because he's about to lose his job is no reason why he should kill anyone.

He starts sobbing, loud retches coming from deep within, his chest heaving and the tears driving down his face. He bends over, putting his forehead to the floor, starts banging his hands on the carpet. With no force, however, just a quiet, pathetic gesture of desperation. The first time he has cried since the death of his father.

'Shh!' Agnes waves a desultory hand as she turns the volume of the television up with the other. Lance and Billy Bob are arguing over which one of them has the first refusal on Flame.

Barney quietens down, but remains on the floor, sobbing softly, his head in his hands. And slowly, a small voice begins to come to him, a small instinctive voice nudging at his subconscious. The small voice which everyone hears whenever there is a problem which they cannot resolve. 'Go to your mum,' it is saying. 'Go to your mum.'

He thinks. Maybe that's right, maybe that is the thing to do. She was almost gung-ho about killing the two of them; perhaps she would know what to do now. It seems ridiculous, but he needs help, advice at the very least, and it isn't as if he has too many options. He will go to see his mother.

He struggles to his feet, looks sadly at the back of Agnes's head, trudges into the bedroom. Changes his clothes and puts the bloodstained ones into a plastic bag, which he secretes at the bottom of the wardrobe. Walks back into the sitting room, a sense of purpose having crept unawares back into his stride.

'Ah'm goin' tae my mother's.'

'Yes, dear.'

And as Barney walks out of the door, Charity and Monogamy are trying to pick a dress for Cerise to wear to the christening of Cream and Hamper's daughter Tupperware.

Chapter 10

Making Soup from Wullie

There is a time of definition in the life of every man, when the pieces fall together, or events take place to shape the future. It may happen suddenly, or it may be a gradual process, a build-up of things over weeks or months. Sometimes when it occurs he is unaware that it is doing so, until one day he looks back and realises that his life has altered completely, for better or for worse. It could be that he has fallen in love. It could be that some outside event changes his whole attitude to life, so that he views everything from a different perspective, and then indeed is life new. It could be that someone dies, creating a hole in his life that cannot be filled. It could be a new job, or a new car, or a new interest of any kind. Or it could be that he accidentally stabs his boss to death with a pair of scissors.

Barney's life is changing, he knows it's happening, and there's nothing he can do about it. He tries telling himself that this is what he wanted, that he was planning to kill Wullie anyway, but deep down he knows there is no way that he would have been able to do it, had not fate forced his hand. And now he prepares to turn to his mother. Forty-six years old and still the same solution to his problems as he had forty-five years previously when he messed the inside of his pants, or spilled tomato ketchup on his bib.

He is still contemplating the fickle hand he has been dealt when he walks into his mother's house. He calls out to announce his arrival, a shout which is, as usual, greeted by silence. He can hear the television playing in the sitting room; he imagines that she will be engrossed in some dreadful quiz show.

He opens the door, immediately starts coughing as the great wall of cigarette smoke sweeps into his lungs. It's always the same when she has been sitting watching television all day, and it is only very rarely that she ever opens a window – and that is only ever likely to happen between the end of June and the beginning of September.

He walks into the room, extravagantly waving his arms in front of him, still coughing loudly.

'For God's sake, Ah wish ye'd open a bloomin' window in this place, if ye're gonnae smoke sae much, Mother,' and he walks between her and the television to pull back the curtains, and let in some fresh air. Cemolina scowls at him, but she is more concerned with the television, and *Give Us Your Body Fluids.*

He stands by the window breathing deeply, as much for show as clean air, before moving back into the room, when he realises that she is paying him no attention. Slumps down into a seat, leans forward, resting his fore-arms on his knees, looks keenly at his mother. He stares at her for a while, hoping she will notice him, but her attention is undivided. This show is her favourite. Finally, he feels bound to speak.

'Mum, Ah've got tae talk tae ye. Ah'm in trouble.'

She doesn't answer for a while, then eventually lifts a dismissive hand, waves it in his direction.

'Shh! No' when they're tryin' tae guess whose fluids these are. Who dae ye think? This bloke says Alfred Hitchcock, but Ah thought they looked mair like Lennie Bennett's. Whit about you?' She turns, gives him a brief look.

Barney faces the realisation that all the women in his life are more interested in television than they are in him.

'Mum, Ah need tae talk tae ye. Ah'm in trouble. Real

trouble.' He hesitates, but he has her attention. 'Ah've killed Wullie.'

Her eyes widen, her jaw drops. The expression holds on her face for a few seconds, and he knows he has her complete attention when she lowers the volume of the television. If he isn't mistaken there is a glint in her eye, a smile forming upon her lips.

'Wullie! Ye've killed Wullie, did ye say?'

'Aye, aye Ah did. Christ, Mum, Ah'm in real trouble. Real trouble,' and he runs his hands through his hair and looks at her with desperation. Comfort me, his face says, I need it.

'Jings! Well done. Ah didnae think ye had it in ye.'

'What?' he says. Despite the night before, it is not the reaction he has been expecting.

'Well, ye wanted tae, didn't ye? Ye said ye wanted tae kill him. Ah'm proud o' ye.' She pauses, reflects a little. 'Although, dae ye no' think it would huv been better if ye had taken care o' the papist first? Can't stand they bastards, so Ah can't. Bastards the lot of them.'

He looks upon her with wonder. How can she take it so lightly?

'Well, then, how did ye do it? Whit wis the instrument o' his destruction? Dinnae tell me poison or Ah'll be right upset, so Ah will.'

When the scales fall from his eyes, they do so quickly and dramatically, cascading and tumbling away in a frantic rush. He looks upon his mother in a new light. She is mad. Of course she is. Completely mad. Perhaps it's senility, but if he thinks about it, he is sure he can recall examples of her madness throughout the years. She has always been insane, but since it has been with him all this time, he has come to take much of her behaviour as normal. But this isn't normal.

All the plans and schemes and silly ideas she has. He has liked to think of her as vaguely eccentric, perhaps even extravagantly eccentric, but it is more than that. Worse than that. And now, what about this reaction? How can she possibly be enthusiastic about him killing Wullie? Killing anybody? What mother could be so welcoming about her son committing such an act?

What is he doing here, and what advice can he possibly

81

get from her that will be of any use? Christ, he's been a fool. He was a fool to tell her what he had been thinking in the first place, and he is a fool to come here tonight with a bloody corpse in the boot of his car.

'Accidentally. Wi' a pair of scissors,' he mumbles, wondering why he is bothering to tell her.

She shakes her head, tuts loudly, displeased by the lack of drama in the description.

'Wis there a lot o' blood?'

'Aye,' he mumbles. 'A lot o' blood.'

He stares at the floor. He has no business here. There are no great answers to his problems to be found in the home of his insane mother. He is going to have to solve them himself.

'What have ye done wi' the corpse?' she asks, the glint returning to the eye. He doesn't notice, so much attention is he giving to the carpet. His heart has sunk. He is afraid.

'It's downstairs, in the boot of the car. Wrapped in several large plastic bin-liners.'

'Crike! Bring it up, then. Ah'll make soup!'

Barney looks up, aghast. 'Mother!'

She smiles, has the decency to look slightly embarrassed, but he knows it is feigned. They cast a quick glance at the television as the presenter produces a bag of thick, lumpy green liquid, but Cemolina is too intrigued by Barney's predicament to raise the sound. Barney turns away from the TV with a look of disgust. Cemolina comes with him, her finger momentarily twitching over the volume button.

'Well, whit are ye gonnae dae wi' it, then?'

He shakes his head, lets it hang low, enveloped, as he is, by dejection. 'Ah don't know, Mum, Ah really don't know.'

She stares at him. He stares at the ground, there being very little else for him to say. He is going to have to leave and get on with things, but when he gets outside there will be a body which he is going to have to dispose of, and he has no idea how he's going to do it.

Slowly he drags himself out of his seat, stands up.

'Look, Mum, Ah really ought tae be goin'. Ah shouldnae have come here and brought ye intae this. It's my problem tae solve . . .'

'Now, none o' yer nonsense,' she chides. 'You sit right back down and we'll talk this through, awright? Ah'm yer mother, and Ah'm here tae help ye.'

He pauses at her words, grudgingly lowers himself back into his seat, his reluctance to get help from his mother fighting his desperate need for help from anywhere.

'Now, tell me everythin' that happened, and we'll see whit we can dae.'

Barney stares at the floor for a while. What options does he have? He hardly has any friends with whom he can share the story. Wonders if he can go to the Samaritans about it; doesn't think they have a murder line. So, it might do him some good to tell his mother, even if there is nothing she can do to help him. And all the while, something at the back of his mind is hoping that she will advise him to go to the police and get it over with. It isn't a decision he can possibly make for himself, but he knows it's the right thing to do.

He lays the story out for her, trying not to miss anything out. For almost all of it she sits quietly taking it in, except for pitching in to suggest that he really ought to have killed Charlie Johnstone when he'd had the chance. When he is finished he is distraught, rests his head back against the seat, tries to stop the tears spilling over onto his face. His hands are shaking, and now that he has related it all and confronted the full awfulness of his situation, he is close to panic.

He opens his eyes to Cemolina bending over him and forcing a large whisky into his hands. He takes it and shakily lifts it to his mouth. Christ, it feels good. Talisker, he thinks, although he is no expert. Probably been there since his father died. Breathes deeply as it burns its way down his throat.

Cemolina settles back into her seat.

'What dae ye want me tae dae, Barnabas?'

He leans forward, rests his forearms on his knees. Head shaking.

'Ah don't know, Mum. Ah cannae ask ye tae dae anythin'. What am Ah gonnae dae, that's the question?'

'Why don't ye bring the body up here, son? Let me take care o' it.'

He stares at her, a wild look in his eye. It's ridiculous.

What can his mother possibly do with a human body? But no matter how ridiculous it seems to him, he loves the idea. If she takes the body, he is free of it. He can wash his hands. It would be wonderful.

'But what are ye gonnae dae wi' Wullie that Ah cannae?'

She bustles.

'Never you mind. Just comfort yersel wi' knowing that Ah can take care o' it. Ye can always rely on yer auld mother. Now you run downstairs and bring the body back up. And mind and try no' tae let anyone see ye this time.'

Half an hour later Barney is driving home, feeling moderately relieved. Feels like a weight has been lifted. Notices other cars on the road; remembers to use all the gears. He has no idea what his mother intends to do with the corpse, but whatever it is she has in mind, she had a reassuring look in her eye, and enough confidence in her voice to put him at ease. It isn't over yet, but the immediate worry of the corpse is gone. Gives him plenty of time to worry about all the other problems which will arise.

Something makes him drive past the shop. Just a hunch, a vague feeling of unease. He doesn't know what he expects to see. Wullie's ghost, perhaps, his face pressed against the window, his features contorted in eternal agony. However, the shopfront stares darkly and mundanely back at him. Quiet, deserted. Deathly quiet.

He walks into his flat at just after ten o'clock. Surprised to be confronted by the sounds of silence, rather than some abysmal Australian or American Deep South soap opera. Stops and listens before he walks into the sitting room, but there is nothing. Maybe Agnes has gone to bed already, but something tells him it isn't going to be that. The hairs on the back of his neck stand to attention, his skin crawls. Panic.

Tentatively, he opens the door to the sitting room, with expectations of a massive police presence behind the door. The television is on, but with the sound turned down. Agnes sits, cup of tea in hand, a concerned look on her face; next to her on the settee is Moira, Wullie's wife, tear in her eye, cup of tea untouched on the table. They look at Barney as he walks in the door, and such is their relief at seeing him that neither of them notice that he completely shits his pants.

They don't say anything; watch closely as he removes his jacket, letting it fumble out of his hands and fall to the floor. He comes into the room and sits down in a seat opposite them, not wanting to say anything. Doesn't want to betray his secret. Feels like he has blood all over him; the word 'murderer' carved into his forehead.

Agnes finally speaks. The silence cannot be allowed to extend for the entire evening. Quick look at her watch. Twenty minutes until *Rectal Emergency Ward 6*.

'Moira's here,' she says.

Barney nods. Aye, Ah can see that, he thinks.

'She's pure dead worried, so she is.'

Barney nods again, tries to look interested but not too concerned. Telling himself to behave as if he doesn't know why Moira's here. Act natural. He's nervous; feels like the slightest hint might give him away. Has to ensure that there is nothing in his demeanour that will strike a discordant note. Act natural, Barney, act natural. Thinks of the Beatles. They're gonna put me in the movies. Wasn't the Beatles who wrote it. Who did it first?

'Barney?' says Moira.

'Ah didnae dae it!' he blurts out, fingers gripping the seat.

'What?' say Moira and Agnes in unison.

He closes his eyes, tries to take hold of himself. Don't be such a bloody idiot, Barney. They don't suspect you of anything. Why should they? Just be calm, ye dunderheid, and don't put your foot in it. Opens his eyes. Determines to play the part; the grand conspirator.

'Oh, sorry, nothin'. Ah thought, well, Ah don't know. Ah was thinkin' about somethin' else. In a daydream, ye know.' He pauses, tries to regain his composure. 'Whit's the problem, Moira?' he asks finally, his voice just about steady enough for them not to notice the difference.

'It's Wullie, Barney, he didnae come home the night. Are ye sure he didnae say anythin' else when he left the shop? Just that he wis goin' shoppin', is that a'?'

Barney thinks. Looks like he's giving the question serious thought – trying to compose himself, however.

85

Never felt so uncomfortable in his life. Fighting the urge to blurt out the truth, but knows he's already gone too far for that.

'Aye, that was a',' he says eventually. 'He left about quarter past five, and said somethin' about goin' tae the shops. That was it, ye know.'

Moira waits for something else, but Barney is finished. How can he give her more hope than that? She's lost her husband, although she doesn't know it yet. Her head drops into her hands and she starts crying in gentle sobs. Agnes moves closer, puts an arm around her shoulder.

'Whit kind o' mood wis he in, Barney? Did he seem tae be awright, ye know? Think aboot it, 'cause Moira's pure upset, so she is.'

Barney stares into space for a while, casually lifts and drops his shoulders. Hopes it's casual. 'Aye, well, ye know Wullie. He just looked like he normally does, ye know.'

'Ye don't think he's been nabbed by yon serial killer, dae ye? That's whit me and Moira have been talkin' aboot.'

Barney scoffs, nearly chokes on it. At least he can deny that one.

'Naw, naw, dinnae be daft. He husnae fallen intae the hands o' any serial killer. Don't worry aboot that.'

Decides it is time to look unconcerned, make them think they're overreacting. Which is exactly what he would have thought, if he hadn't just stabbed Wullie in the stomach. He stands up, stretches, yawns.

'Look, Moira, Ah wouldnae worry about it. He's probably just gone doon the boozer and had a few too many tae drink. Ye know what he's like, eh? Ye know Wullie.'

She shakes her head slowly, mumbling through the tears. 'No, no, it's no' like him. No' Wullie, so it's no'. A Friday night, aye, but never durin' the week. No' ma Wullie.'

Barney waves this away, casual, dismissive, but the next question hits him harder. Full in the face at about a hundred miles an hour.

'Dae ye no' think we should phone fer the polis?' says Agnes.

The polis! Shit. He hasn't really thought of that yet. He knows it will come to it, but not yet. It is too early for the polis to be involved. Christ, Wullie could be sitting down the pub for all anyone else knows.

'Eh, naw, naw, no' yet. Ah think that might be a bit hasty, ye know. Wait and see whit happens. Maybe if he hasnae shown up by mornin', gie them a call. Ah'm sure he will but, so Ah wouldnae worry about it.'

'Dae ye really think he's awright, Barney?' Moira says to him through her tears. Desperately seeking reassurance.

Barney looks into the damp eyes, finally is overwhelmed by guilt, to the point of not being able to reply. Mumbles some attempted words of comfort to her, squeezes her hand, mutters that he is tired and has to go to bed.

He walks to the bedroom, an air of unconcern about him; the great lie. And when he gets into the room, he collapses on the bed and weeps.

Chapter 11

Not the Maltese Falcon

Holdall stares disconsolately at the list of names. Another six people have been reported missing this morning. Another six groups of worried relatives he has to trawl round, and whose minds he will have to try to put at ease. Christ, he hates Robertson. The man is a total bastard, and if ever he has the chance to get his own back, then he'll bloody well take it. And if it involves several blunt instruments and a lot of blood, well, all the better.

He looks at the names and the ages, trying to decide by looking at them what might have happened. As usual, four of the six are teenagers. The options are numerous for this lot, and dying at the hands of a serial killer is not one of them. They could be lying in a gutter somewhere, creamed out of their faces from the night before; they could be on the bus to London with £50 in their pockets and a collection of ridiculous dreams in their heads; they could be lying in some bed somewhere enjoying again all the things they have enjoyed the night before (lucky gits); or, and at this he brightens up a little, they might be lying dead in a ditch somewhere, by their own hands. There will probably be at least two of them already reappeared by the time he gets to their houses. At least there is that consolation.

He studies the other two on the list. A thirty-eight-year-old woman with seven children, aged between eighteen and two, all of whom still live at home. There appears to be no particular father figure. Big mystery, he thinks, and mentally crosses that one off. She will be back in a day or two, feeling guilty, and pissed off that her children have phoned the police.

One remains. A man in his late twenties. Runs a barber's shop, lives with his wife, no children. This one isn't so easy to dismiss, he decides. Might have gone out and got drunk, ended up in some woman's bed somewhere, but he would usually have turned up by now.

Maybe this is it. For all he scoffs at this ridiculous goose chase, there is a fair chance that he will come across victims of the killer at some stage. They will, of course, already be dead by the time he begins to investigate their disappearance – a small flaw in the great plan – but perhaps he might stumble across some clue. The exercise itself isn't a waste of time, but he resents Robertson having given it to him.

He looks out of the window, at the rain ricocheting steadily off the glass. Of course it is, he thinks, this is Glasgow in March. It always bloody rains.

The door to his office opens. Detective Sergeant MacPherson comes in, his face the usual mask of taciturnity. The two men nod at one another; MacPherson places some papers on Holdall's desk.

'When'll ye want tae start out this mornin', sir?' he says, having withdrawn to a respectful few feet.

Holdall sighs heavily, stares at nothing. The horror of going out. He doesn't even want to think about that yet. Wet and cold – concerned mothers and children. Jesus. He thinks some more, his mind on a variety of things, and just as MacPherson is beginning to shuffle his feet and glance at his watch, Holdall looks up, makes up his mind.

'Let's give it about half an hour, eh, Sergeant? I think I need a good deal of coffee and something to eat before I can face the rigours of the day. If rigours they are to be, eh?'

MacPherson nods, issues a short 'very good, sir', and marches out of the door, a hundred things to do in the next half-hour.

Holdall sits back, laces his fingers behind his head, stares at the ceiling. How long can he do this before he'll tell them to stuff their job? So, it'll be a blindingly stupid thing to do, and Jean will be unbelievably pissed off at him, but he's buggered if he can put up with much more of this. He can find something else to do, it can't be that difficult.

Maybe he could set up his own private detective agency. That might not be a bad idea. Sure, he'll have to start with small-time stuff. Divorce cases, and missing children. He winces at the thought. But it won't be long, surely, before he's getting into adventures, mixed up with glamorous women, being sent on the hunt for golden falcons and the like. God, that'll be the life. Maybe, he reflects, maybe Jean won't be able to handle it. She might even leave him, but hey, he thinks, what the heck. There'll be plenty more babes out there given what he's going to be doing. He's watched enough private-dick shows on the TV to know that it would be one stunning chick after another in that job. Heaven.

His eyes fall on the list in front of him, the pile of papers MacPherson has placed on his desk. With a weary sigh, and wondering if MacPherson will have taken the hint and instigated a cup of coffee on his behalf, he turns off his dreams and looks at the pile of reports by his right hand.

'And when did ye last see Stuart, Mrs Hutchinson?'

The woman stares over her cup of tea at the wall, tries to remember. 'Tuesday,' she says eventually. 'Tuesday about eight o'clock. Aye, that'd be about right, naw?'

MacPherson nods, looks at his notepad. Holdall is sitting beside him, quietly sipping a cup of tea, doing his best not to listen to any of what is going on. The chief inspectors' trick – let the sergeant ask all the questions while pretending to be coolly paying attention at his side.

'And ye expected him back about when?'

'Oh, well, Ah don't know. He says he wis just goin' doon the boozer, ye know, so Ah thought he'd be back about eleven or something like that, ye know.'

MacPherson nods, looks concerned. 'So, if ye expected him tae return at about eleven o'clock on Tuesday, why did ye wait 'til this mornin' tae report him missin'? Did ye no' think aboot doin' it yesterday?'

She takes a loud slurp from her cup, places it on the table.

'Well, ye know, Officer, Ah jist assumed he'd scored wi' some bit o' skirt, an' buggered aff back tae her place, ye know. It widnae be the first time that's happened, ye know.' She smiles weakly at MacPherson; he nods back. 'Ah wis a wee bit worried by yesterday afternoon, but Ah don't know, Ah just didnae like tae bother anyone, ye know. Ah mean, Ah remember once when Missus Thingwy fi' doon the road reportit her boy missin', and if it wisnae just the thing, but he turns up . . .'

Holdall interjects. Strained patience; teeth grinding together.

'All right, Mrs Hutchinson, can we just stick to the story?'

'Oh aye, aye, nae bother,' she says.

MacPherson scribbles something else in his notebook.

'Look, Mrs Hutchinson, ye've done the right thing by reportin' yer son missing now, and ye're no' puttin' anyone tae any trouble.'

Like hell she's not, thinks Holdall, as his thoughts drift on their way out of the conversation.

'Now, can ye tell us who he usually met down the pub, and if ye've been in contact wi . . .'

There is a noise at the front door, followed by the sound of footsteps marching into the house. Holdall rolls his eyes extravagantly, stands up. The prodigal bloody son, he thinks. No point in delaying; might as well get out of the damn house before she kills him.

MacPherson joins him as the door to the sitting room opens, and a young man of around nineteen walks into the room. He stops, stares at the two strangers, looks at his mother. His mouth opens, but he doesn't get as far as formulating a sentence.

'Where the bloody hell have you been, eh? Ah've been worried sick, so Ah huv, but no, you widnae gie a shit about that, wid ye? You're too bloody busy thinkin' aboot yersel', an' tae hell wi' everybody else, no'? An' look whit ye've made me dae, ya stupit bastard. Ah've called the polis, so Ah huv. Ah'll probably be in trouble now, but you'll nae gie a shite aboot that, will ye? Naw, ye bloody won't. Ye're just too busy thinkin' aboot yersel'. Bloody hell, tae think that Ah raised you fi' nappies. An' whit thanks dae Ah get?'

She pauses for breath, starts talking again before anyone else has time to speak.

'Look, Ah'm really sorry aboot this, Officers, wastin' yer time an a' that. Can Ah no' offer ye another biscuit?'

Holdall and MacPherson hold up their hands in unison to refuse, inch slowly towards the door. Following the biscuit refusal, the mother turns once more upon her son.

'Well, don't stand there like a bloody great puddin'. Where huv ye been?'

He shrugs, stares at the floor. 'Ah just met this girl, Mum, ye know. She wis really nice. Anyway, Ah spent the night wi' her. Nothin' happened! An' then we went away for the day yesterday. Millport.' Ah, Millport, thinks Holdall. Land of Fantasy. Or is he confusing it with California? 'Ah tried phonin' but, honest Ah did, Mum, but ye wernae in. Then Ah ended up spendin' the night last night 'n a'.' He stares at his mum, then turns to Holdall. 'Am Ah in trouble?' he says.

Holdall shakes his head, lays his hand on the lad's shoulder. 'No, son, you're not in trouble.' He smiles, begins to walk past him. Stops, looks the boy in the eye. 'Was she a babe?'

Stuart Hutchinson – Hutch to his friends – looks surprised, then the smile breaks onto his face.

'She wis a wee stoatir,' he says.

Holdall grins, turns to the mother. 'We'll see ourselves out, thank you, Mrs Hutchinson.'

He walks from the sitting room with MacPherson at his heels, and as they open the front door they can hear the woman begin to berate her son in earnest now that they have gone. They stand out in the light rain for a second, looking at the dank and depressing street before them. Lost in thought.

'This is a lousy job, Sergeant,' says Holdall, beginning to trudge towards the car.

'Bloody right it is,' says MacPherson, following on, his stride nevertheless the more purposeful.

They get into the car and MacPherson studies the list he is carrying with him.

'Just one more tae go, sir. A Mr William Henderson. The barber.'

Holdall winces at the thought that this one might prove to be more serious than the others, starts the engine and drives off into the gloom.

Chapter 12

Interview with a Barber

Big Billy McGoldrick is in danger of getting his ear cut off, so animated is he becoming in the discussion; trying to turn his head to look at Chris every time he says something with which he doesn't agree.

'But, Chris,' he says, 'why is it that our fitba' teams cannae beat anyone in Europe? Christ, we lose tae them a' these days. Teams we'd have pumped the pants aff o' twenty years ago. A' they wee pish teams. Now we're the wee pish teams.'

Chris studies the back of McGoldrick's head, executes a couple of smooth moves – the scissors sizzling in his fingers – then straightens up, catches his eye in the mirror.

''Cause, and this is whit Ah keep trying tae tell ye, they play cultured fitba', no' like oor kick an' rush game. Wi' us it's a' heids doon and last one in the penalty area's a big poof.'

McGoldrick shakes his head, narrowly avoiding a scissor in the ear. 'Aye, a' very well, but why can't we play cultured fitba', if they can dae it? It's places like Turkey an' Latvia, for Christ's sake, we're talking aboot here, no' Brazil.'

'Because the fans widnae stand for it. Naebody in Scotland wants tae see cultured fitba', do they?'

'Are you saying that Ah don't like cultured fitba'?' McGoldrick says, straightening his shoulders and slightly raising his head, changing for ever the course of the growth of his hair.

'Who does in Scotland?' says Chris, already beginning to make the necessary adjustments. 'Ah mean, look. Dae any of us really want tae see our team come out an' fanny aboot in the midfield and kick the ba' about like a big bunch o' poofs? It's no' the Scottish mentality. If the Thistle huvnae scored after about ten minutes, we're all baying like dogs for them tae blooter the ba' up the park as hard as possible. That's whit Scottish fitba's a' about. None o' this fart-arsin' about in midfield. It's a load o' shite, so it is.'

McGoldrick looks doubtful. Chris is flowing, the barber in his element.

'It's typical o' the generally aggressive nature o' Scottish behavioural patterns. It's like if two blokes get intae a fight in a pub. Whit dae they dae? Dae they glass each other, or dae they pass the ba' about in midfield? And ye know Ah don't need tae tell ye the answer tae that one.'

McGoldrick holds up his hand and makes to reply, but Barney switches off, tries not to listen to the rest. He is in the middle of a haircut, and has already committed two or three too many stinkers this day – doesn't want to do any more.

He is attempting to indulge in denial, but it's not easy. He's never had to deny anything before. Combined with worry about what Cemolina will do with the corpse, and worry about what he will say to the police when they finally show up – he expects the inevitable – his head is a mess. Much the same as most of the customers he has dealt with this black day.

Moira phoned the shop that morning to say there was still no sign of Wullie, asked Chris if he knew of anywhere he might have gone. If Chris is worried about his disappearance, he doesn't show it, thinking to himself that Wullie has probably just gone off somewhere, got drunk and fallen in with some woman. He will stagger home some time today, an apologetic look on his face, and a stream of spectacular excuses pushing each other out of the way in order to be first to get to his mouth.

Barney surveys the task in which he is currently embroiled – wonders about how hideously wrong it has already gone. The man has asked for a Charlton Heston '86, always a tricky proposition, but especially so since Barney's hands are shaking – involuntary spasms, sporadic bursts. He has been tempted to suggest that his customers take out ear insurance before they sit down. Thinks, however, that if he had nothing to do but sit and brood he would feel even worse.

Of the customers that have come in looking for Wullie, some immediately departed on finding him not there, and the rest mostly have gone to Chris. There are a couple who reluctantly agreed to be prey to Barney's fickle hand, being rewarded with hair which gets a fright every time it looks in a mirror.

The morning is dragging on, long and slow, when finally the door opens. Two men walk into the shop, their coats buttoned up against the rain. They look miserable and unhappy, but it isn't the usual misery of men coming to get their hair cut. They stand for a few seconds looking at the barbers, and then one of the men walks forward, his hands fishing around in his pockets. Finally he produces his card, holds it up between Chris and Barney.

'Chief Inspector Holdall, Maryhill. I wonder if I could have a word with you two gentlemen?'

'Is it aboot Wullie?' asks Chris. The police – instant worry. Same for Barney, but for different reasons.

'Yes, it's about Mr Henderson.' Holdall waves a hand at the two men, moves to sit down. 'The two of you finish what you're doing, and we'll speak to you then. It shouldn't take too long.'

They sit down at the end of the queue. The two customers ahead of them look nervous at the closeness of the law, and shuffle as much as they can towards the other end of the long bench. Finally the strain becomes too much for one of them, and he stiffly rises, walks quickly from the shop. MacPherson looks suspiciously after him – he's arrested people for less – but Holdall quells his enthusiasm with a wave of the hand. Whatever reason the man has to remove himself from the presence of the police, it isn't their problem. If they chased every idiot who looked suspicious . . . he lets the thought run away.

Barney, meanwhile, is considering doing the same thing, but manages to persuade himself not to. Instead, he attempts to concentrate on the haircut he is committing, but it isn't easy. Fortunately, in a Charlton Heston '86, there is more blow-drying and brushing to be done than scissor work, and after he lays the scissors down – the very instruments of death from the previous evening – he finds that his hands stop shaking, the work with the hair-dryer altogether more straightforward. So much so that, to his dismay, he finishes his job off before Chris. Thinks: Bugger. He's first to interview, but there's nothing he can do about it.

The customer seems reasonably content with his thatch – he knows a girl in his local who goes mad for men with Charlton Heston '86 haircuts – and after thrusting an extra couple of pounds into Barney's hand, he walks sus-piciously past the police and out of the shop. Barney swallows hard, tries to compose himself the best he can, turns to face his tormentors. Can't open his mouth – doesn't yet trust his vocal cords – but stands in front of them looking like a stuffed fish.

Holdall and MacPherson walk towards him.

'Is there somewhere we can talk?' says Holdall, doing his best to keep the disinterest from his voice.

Barney waves his hand towards the door at the back of the shop – in off the alcove, behind the fifth seat; a place of mystery for the customers who never get to see what goes on within – leads them into the room. It is not large – used mostly as a storeroom, although there are a couple of chairs so the barbers can nip out and take a break, should the work allow. There is a large window in the back of the room, with bars across it, looking out onto a grim and tiny courtyard, where the rain falls on dirty and cracked stones. Barney looks through the bars, considers that this could be his fate – turns to the policemen after they have closed the door.

MacPherson produces his notebook, prepares to start. Holdall pulls out one of the seats, prepares to look bored. The shop and this back room depress him, and he is beginning to think that he can't blame one of the barbers for wanting to run away from it.

'Mr Thomson or Mr Porter?' asks MacPherson.

'Thomson,' mutters Barney, still not entirely trusting himself to open his mouth.

'Why don't ye take a seat, Mr Thomson?'

'Ah prefer to stand, thanks.' Barbers are used to standing.

'Very well.'

MacPherson stares at his notes. Barney tries to prepare himself to do his best not to give away his guilt. This is just routine, he says within, routine. They have to speak to him, he's the last person who will say he saw Wullie. It doesn't mean they suspect anything.

'Now, Mr Thomson, this is just a routine missin'-persons inquiry. Moira Henderson's reported her husband missin' since late yesterday afternoon. Now, she told us that you were the last person she knows tae have spoken tae him. Is that correct?'

Barney considers his answer, as he will after every question; all the better to avoid self-incrimination.

'Aye, aye, that's right. He, eh, left here about quarter past five, as far as Ah can remember.'

'And did he say where he was goin'?'

Another pause. 'Naw, naw, he didnae. He just says somethin' about goin' tae the shops, but he didnae say which shops, ye know. He asked me tae lock up, then he left. That's a' really, Ah think.'

MacPherson makes a couple of scribbles in his notebook, lifts his head to look at Barney.

'He didnae mention goin' anywhere else, or goin' away or anythin'?'

'Naw, naw, nothin' like that.'

'And was it normal for Mr Henderson tae go tae the shops after work?'

Barney shrugs – almost too hastily; holds it back, looks non-committal. 'Ah don't know. Ah didnae really know what he did outside the shop, ye know, we werenae really friends.'

MacPherson raises his eyebrow, looks at Barney in such a way as to make him feel extremely uncomfortable. Barney tries to think of what he has just said, and how it might have been incriminating.

'You *were* no' really friends, Mr Thomson?' MacPherson's voice is low and hard; Holdall looks up

98

with some interest. What is he doing, he wonders. 'Surely ye mean, ye *are* no' friends? Or d'ye suspect somethin' might have happened tae Mr Henderson which you're no' tellin' us about?'

Barney lets a laugh erupt from some unknown region of his throat, an attempted dismissive, apologetic laugh, which unfortunately sounds as if he has just murdered someone and been caught with the scissors in his hands.

'Aye, aye, o' course. We are no' friends. That's what Ah meant. Slip o' the tongue. Ye know how it is, eh?'

MacPherson slowly lifts an eyebrow. Mr Spock never looked so cool. 'How what is, Mr Thomson?'

Holdall watches his sergeant with some fascination. MacPherson is taking the piss out of the barber, trying to make him as uncomfortable as possible. He shrugs. Why not? It's one of the few pleasures left to the police – to put people to as much discomfort and unease as they can. And, he has to admit, there is no better exponent of the art than MacPherson.

'Oh, ye know, nothin', nothin'. You, eh, know how it is when ye get interviewed by the polis. Ye always get worried, even when ye havenae accidently stabbed someone wi' a pair o' scissors' – what are you saying!!! – 'which o' course Ah havnae, and, well, ye know, and ye, eh, know how it is.' He finally shuts up, stands with a stupid grin on his face.

Holdall watches with wonder, finds himself almost bursting out laughing. MacPherson is a genius. Here is some poor sap who has nothing whatsoever to do with the guy disappearing, and the sergeant has him acting like he's in the dock on a multiple murder charge.

MacPherson stares thoughtfully at him; taps his pen on the notebook. Brilliant, thinks Holdall, brilliant.

'And where was your colleague, eh, Mr Porter, when Mr Henderson left the shop?'

Barney relaxes. An easy one, thank God. 'He'd gone home early, at about three o'clock, because we were so quiet. Wullie sent him home.'

'And did that happen often?'

Another easy one. Holdall smiles. Another calm before the storm, if he isn't much mistaken. Relax them, then grab them by the balls. Terrific fun.

'Naw, naw,' says Barney easily. 'Ah don't know what happened yesterday. Just a quiet day, Ah suppose.'

'So, how many customers were there in the shop?'

Jings, this is a dawdle, thinks Barney, an absolute dawdle. 'Oh, Ah don't know. Maybe fifteen a' day. No' many.'

MacPherson nods, scratches behind his ear with the pen. Time to crank it up again. Holdall knows what's coming, enjoys the show.

'And dae you and Mr Henderson get along awright, seeing as ye're no' really friends?'

Shit, what does he say now? He can hardly lie, because they can easily find him out from Chris. The truth it will have to be, however incriminating.

'Naw, Ah don't suppose we did get . . . do . . . do get along very well.'

'Why is that, Mr Thomson? Everyone else we've spoken tae seems tae think he's a nice enough chap. What's so different about you?'

Everybody else they've spoken to? Who the hell could that be? Holdall almost bursts out laughing. This is wonderful. The *Godfather Part II* of police interviews. Hard, powerful, but cracking entertainment. Wait till the lads down the station hear about it. MacPherson's a genius.

'Eh, Ah, eh, don't really know. Just a personality clash, Ah suppose. Different generations, interested in different things, ye know. Something like that.'

MacPherson nods, looks doubtful.

'Ah don't like football,' mutters Barney in his defence. Quite the wrong thing to say to MacPherson, who looks at Barney as if he suspects him of being a master criminal.

Barney hears his heart beating faster and faster, hopes they will be done with him soon. What else can they have to ask him, after all?

'We understand that Mr Henderson was about tae ask ye tae leave the shop. Had he done that yet, Mr Thomson?'

Barney's mouth opens slightly – return of the stuffed-fish look, hook in upper lip.

Christ! What dae Ah say tae that? They must have spoken tae Wullie's father. Bloody hell, if they know that, maybe they'll suspect me of anythin'. Maybe they've already spoken tae Charlie Johnstone. Maybe they're about tae arrest me . . .

A thought strikes him, uncomfortable, unpleasant. Why are two detectives doing a routine missing-persons inquiry? Surely it should be a couple of uniforms. They must already suspect something. Shit, shit, shit. What is he going to say? Only one thing to do. Deny everything!

'Jings, Ah'm sorry tae look shocked, ye know, but Ah hadnae heard that, naw. They were gonnae sack me? Who told ye that?'

He looks hopefully at the sergeant, wondering if his acting has been of sufficient merit. MacPherson studies his notebook, raises his eyes.

'We understand fi' Mr Henderson's father, a Mr James Henderson, that he intended tae tell ye yesterday.'

Barney shakes his head, mumbles a denial, stares at the floor – a child with crumbs around his lips denying having broken into the biscuit tin.

MacPherson raises the eyebrow once more, then scribbles something else in the notebook. Decides to put Barney out of his misery. Certainly he's acting a little suspiciously, but then so will anyone if you treat them the right way. They're looking for a serial killer, not some boring old barber who wets his pants the minute the police hove into view.

'Ah don't think there's anything else for the moment, Mr Thomson. We may want tae speak tae ye again, however. Ye're no' thinkin' of goin' anywhere, are ye?'

Barney stares at him, eyes wide. No, he hasn't been thinking of going anywhere, but now that he's mentioned it . . . It's obvious. That'd be the easiest way out. Run away! Disappear up to the Highlands, or down to England. Or France even. Just get out of Glasgow.

'Naw, naw, Ah'm no' goin' anywhere.'

'Right then, Mr Thomson. When ye go out, will ye ask your colleague tae come in here, please?'

Barney nods, tries not to show the smile of relief which itches to burst free from his face. Nods at Holdall, walks back into the shop.

'Brilliant, Sergeant,' says Holdall, smiling, when the door is closed. 'You took the piss out of that guy something rotten.'

MacPherson looks quizzically at him. 'What dae you mean, sir?'

Holdall doesn't answer, shakes his head, stares disconsolately at the floor.

Barney walks back into the shop, relief smothering him. For all their questions, the police obviously don't suspect him of anything. And why should they? He is also comforted by the thought of running away from it all; imagines a variety of exotic locations. America would be a good one – he doesn't think they play football there.

Chris is halfway through a regulation short back and sides, and has almost finished a half-hearted discussion on how Partick Thistle can best go about winning the League. He looks at Barney as he comes through the door.

'They'd like a word wi' you now, Chris,' he says.

'Aye, OK.'

'D'ye want me tae finish that off?'

The customer's strangled cry of 'no' is cut off by Chris's acceptance, and Barney – with new lightness in his heart, new vigour – goes about his business with a whistle on his lips and a nimbleness in his fingers. Suddenly he is a man transformed, in his relief almost able to forget his troubles. He polishes off the haircut to general satisfaction, and has started on another before Chris emerges back into the shop, a worried look on his face, the police close behind.

They nod at Barney as they walk past, then they are gone, out into the morning rain. Chris and Barney look at each other. Barney doesn't know what the look says; no words are exchanged.

An hour and a half later they find themselves alone in the shop, having worked their way through half a dozen customers. Barney is feeling rather pleased with himself as he grabs a look at his paper. In quick succession he has executed a 'long at the back, short at the sides', a 'not too much off the top, tapered at the sides and back', and a 'Bobby Ewing '83'. They have each, in their own way, been immaculate haircuts, barbery out of the top drawer – smooth, elegant and polished. A trio of satisfied customers. The money from the healthy tips still jangles in Barney's pocket. Had this been America there would have been loud whoops and cheers, and cries of 'Good hair!', and he and Chris would have exchanged high fives and banged heads. Barney imagines the word will already be going around Partick – 'Want good hair? Barney Thomson's your man'.

The door opens and a young lad comes in. He nods at the two barbers. 'Wullie not in today?'

'Eh, no, he's got the day aff,' says Chris. 'Ah'll dae yer hair if ye want tae sit down.'

The lad hesitates, looks a bit embarrassed. 'Naw, it's all right, I'll go to this other bloke, if that's OK?'

Chris shrugs his shoulders. 'Aye, sure, nae problem, mate.' He doesn't care.

Barney does, however. He lowers the paper and looks at the boy as he walks over. He's delighted. This is the kind of thing he's always wanted, and it hasn't taken long. Should have killed Wullie ages ago.

He stands up, offers him the chair.

'Hello, young fellow, how's it goin'?' Tries to keep the enormous grin from his face. Doesn't entirely succeed.

'All right, mate,' says Allan Duckworth. 'How about you?'

'Aye, aye, cannae complain, cannae complain.' He swirls the cape around dramatically, drapes it over the customer, reaches for the towel to put at his neck. 'So, what will it be the day, my friend?'

'Oh, you know, just a haircut,' he says.

Just a haircut. Music to the barber's ears. *Carte blanche* to do as you please. What could be easier? The smile on Barney's face increases by another inch or two on either side, and he picks up the electric razor.

'What dae ye make o' those Rangers, eh?' he says after a minute or two. 'Lost four games in a row now, eh? Really strugglin'.'

'Aye, but they're still six points clear at the top of the League.'

'Five.'

'Five, is it?'

'Aye. But ye know, they're only that far aheid because everybody else is sae crap.'

'Aye, you're right about that.'

And so the conversation goes on, and so the day goes on. Barney cuts more hair than he has had to do in a single day for many a year, and he loves every minute of it. Quite forgets about Wullie, other than to be glad he isn't there to take business from him. And customer after customer leaves the shop with hair from the gods – hair for which movie stars would pay hundreds of dollars, for only four pounds plus tip. People will recall this day for years, and how they were privileged to have had their hair cut by a man at the zenith of barbetorial invention.

They have seen the final customers off by ten past five. Chris has grown more and more uneasy during the day as no word has come from Wullie; his initial lack of concern giving way to extravagant worry. He imagines all kinds of disasters – but never the truth.

He exchanges few words with Barney, and after everyone has gone tells him to leave, and that he will lock up. Barney accepts, and after clearing away the fallen hair around his chair – unusually equally distributed on either side – puts on his jacket, walks from the shop. It has been a grand day for him, the best that he can remember since he first lifted a pair of scissors. And any day which he doesn't finish by stabbing someone will be viewed as a success from now on.

But as he steps out into the bleak rain of an early March evening, he is forced to return to the real world. He is going to have to face the consequences of his actions of the previous day. He has to go and see Cemolina, discover the gruesome truth of how she has disposed of the body. He hasn't worried about it all day, because he hasn't thought about it. Now, however, the time is at hand.

And however bad he imagines it is going to be when he gets to her house, it is nowhere near as bad as it actually is.

Chapter 13

A Freezer Full of Neatly Packaged Meat

Barney stands on the threshold of his mother's door, gives himself pause. Tries to come to terms with the ill feeling he has about what lies within. Jodie Foster in *Silence of the Lambs*. It is not just his mother's 'soup' remark which still rings in his ears; something else – a sense of grave foreboding.

He opens the door, walks into the flat, calling out her name. There is no reply, but that is not unusual. However, there is an ominous feel to the house. Silence. No television plays in the sitting room, there is no other sound. He senses death; smells it. Perhaps she is out on her grotesque errand, he thinks. Somehow he knows it is not that.

He walks quickly along the hall and into the sitting room. At first he sees nothing, because he isn't expecting to see what he does. Then he realises that his mother is lying sprawled on the floor, her head resting at an awkward angle. A cup lies spilled at her side, its contents splashed across the carpet; a murky brown stain, all that is left of a milky coffee, three sugars.

He stares at her, rooted to the spot. Shock. Then through the gloom, he sees her eyelids flicker, dashes to her side, kneels down.

'Mum! Mum! Are ye awright?'

Cemolina flickers her eyelids. Bloody stupid question, she thinks, of course I'm not all right. But she has not the strength to say it. Her life is fading quickly, the strain on her heart almost intolerable. Had he come but two minutes later, Barney would have found her dead.

She tries to lift her head off the carpet. She has something to tell him. She must before she goes.

'Ah'll call an ambulance,' he says quickly, begins to get up, but he is stopped by the slight movement of her head.

'Naw,' she croaks, 'too late for that.'

He can barely hear her, but he knows what she is trying to say. Puts his mouth up close to her ear, gently squeezes her hand.

'It's no' too late, Mum, ye've still got a chance. Ah'll get an ambulance.'

He starts to get up again, but she touches his hand as she makes an effort to grab it before he moves away. He looks at her; she says something to him which he cannot make out. Torn between fetching help and letting her talk to him. Doesn't know what to do. Knows deep down that it's already too late. Bends down, puts his ear close to her mouth. Fights back the fear – his mother is dying.

'The fre . . .' she whispers, her voice on the point of expiration.

'Sorry, Mum, Ah didnae hear ye. Did ye say "frisbee"?'

It hits him; he is listening to the last words of his mother. Her dying words. He puts his head nearer, as the tears start to form at the sides of his eyes.

'Free . . .' she croaks, her voice barely audible.

He screams within his head. These are his mother's dying words, he has to hear them. She's making the grand effort, so must he. This could be what stands for ever on her headstone. He has to understand.

'Frisbee, Mum? What about a frisbee?'

She summons up the juices of life for one last great effort. Holds her hand out, grabs the sleeve of his jacket to pull him closer, although no closer can he get. She pauses to conjure up new energies, then speaks slowly and powerfully into his ear.

'Not frisbee, ye dunderheid. Freezer! It's in the freezer!'

The words 'What's in the freezer, Mum?' – pointless

words, for he knows well what she means – hang suspended on his lips, half uttered and then forgotten, as his mother folds from her last great effort. Having said what she must, the will is gone, and her body settles lifelessly onto the floor. Her fingers remain fastened on his jacket. Death grip. He grabs her head, presses his cheek against it and weeps, his other troubles forgotten.

He stays like that for a long time, unable to let go, as if by hanging onto her body he is in some way hanging onto her life. Finally, he pulls himself away, and after having trouble detaching her gripping fingers, he sits wearily down beside the telephone and starts making calls.

Two hours later, Barney and his elder brother Allan sit and blankly stare at the carpet. They don't see each other much, have never got on particularly well. Here they sit, sharing something for the first time in over twenty years.

Allan lives a moderately opulent existence on the periphery of Perth, in a house which Barney envies, with a wife that Barney yearns for. Three children and a dog complete the picture-perfect life, and Barney need never know that Allan is even more miserable than he is himself.

'Well, my brother, I'd better be getting back. Barbara will be wondering what's happened to me. I didn't leave much of a note.'

Barney's grief is marginally pushed aside for a second; easily done. He hates it when Allan calls him 'my brother', which he always does, and the mention of Barbara – attractive, intelligent Barbara, who has never watched a soap opera in her life – brings pangs of jealousy thumping loudly at the doors of his grief, demanding entry.

'I'll be back early tomorrow morning to get on with the arrangements.'

'Ye can stay the night wi' Agnes and me, why don't ye?' says Barney. Something within wants Allan to say yes, some basic fraternal thing making him want to hang on to his brother, even though he knows that there is no way he will accept. And would he not be ashamed to take his brother back to his flat in any case?

'No, that's all right, Barney, thanks. I'd better be getting back. Thanks all the same.' He stands up, starts to put his jacket on. 'Will you be going to your work tomorrow?

107

You know, it's all right if you do, because I can take care of everything.'

Like the unwanted belch of curry back into your mouth, four days after you've eaten a vindaloo, reality kicks Barney stoutly in the balls.

His work. The shop. Wullie. The corpse. The freezer.

Shit.

He shakes his head to clear the image away, looks at Allan. Maybe he should tell him everything. Allan, the older brother. The sensible older brother. He'd know what to do.

Phone the polis and get him locked up, probably.

'Aye, aye, Ah've got tae go tae work,' he says. He isn't telling Allan anything. 'There's one o' the other lads aff at the moment, so there's only the two o' us the now, ye know. Ah'd really better go in.'

Allan nods. 'No problem. Don't you worry, I'll see to everything.'

They say their farewells, Barney sees his brother to the door. Returns to the sitting room, stands thinking. He has to go and look in the freezer, but he desperately doesn't want to. Tries to persuade himself that he can postpone it until morning, but he knows he might as well get it over with.

His mother has a huge freezer, he knows that. Plenty of space for a body. He and his brother have always asked her why she bothers; now it has been of use. Has she known all this time that she might one day have need of concealing a corpse? Of course not, Barney, don't be so bloody stupid.

He walks with some trepidation into the kitchen. The big freezer dominates the room, taking up one whole wall to the left as he walks in. He stops and stares at it. Not just big enough to hold one body, he thinks. Big enough to hold several.

He puts his fingers on the handle and leaves them there. Whatever he is about to see, he knows it isn't going to be pleasant. Wullie's body, hideously curled up, his face distorted in agony and shock – is that what awaits him?

He swallows, slowly lifts the lid of the freezer. A plume of vapour drifts out to meet him, and he stares into it, waiting for it to disperse. Suddenly it's all there in front of him. Meat. The freezer is packed with meat. And then it strikes him and he feels his stomach push at the back of his throat.

This eclectic array of packets, frosted-over reds and browns. This is Wullie. Neatly packaged, easy to handle, ready to use – Wullie.

He prods something. It is frozen solid. She must have worked fast, he thinks, because it has all been in here a long time. The freezer is tightly packed, every inch taken up with bones and various chunks of meat and flesh. He pokes at a couple of things, his face a mask of horror and wonder, then wriggles something free from the frozen mass.

It is a foot, sweetly severed below the ankle. On the side of the package, neatly printed on a white label, are the words 'W. Henderson / 11 Mar / Left foot'. He drops it back into the crowd, lifts out another one. An indeterminate lump of flesh and organ. 'W. Henderson / 11 Mar / Part of viscera (not sure which)', it reads. Quickly he puts it back, lowers the lid. Doesn't want to see any more.

He rests his hands on the edge of the freezer and stares blankly at the top of it for a while. Swallows hard, tries to examine his emotions to discover what he really thinks about this.

'What were ye doin', Mum? Ye labelled Wullie. Did ye have tae go so far as tae label him? Was this thing no' grotesque enough for ye?'

He shakes his head, lowers it still further. And as he stands hunched over the freezer, the thought which has been nagging away since he first looked inside finally breaks out into the open. It has been a distant nag, something he couldn't place, but then suddenly it is there; stark naked in front of him, screaming. The thought of it chills his heart; hairs rise slowly on the back of his neck.

The freezer is full, absolutely full to the brim. There is no way that the whole of this huge compartment is taken up with Wullie.

He opens the lid again, looks inside. Starts picking up bits of Wullie, dumping them on the floor out of the way. A femur. The heart. An arm. The head. Christ! The head, the eyes removed. Packages of flesh, all expertly wrapped and labelled. He quickly lifts them all, and then dumps

109

them noisily on the floor. There seem to be hundreds of them. Untidily arranged in ill-fitting row after ill-fitting row. God! he thinks, these can't all be Wullie. It can't possibly be as he fears, but his blood thumps through his body, his breath catches in his throat. What else can it be?

Finally he dares to look at another of the packages. His heart freezes, his mouth drops in horror. The writing is neat, and in his mother's own hand. 'Louise MacDonald / 5 Mar / Respiratory system.'

Louise MacDonald. The name had been in the newspapers that morning. The latest victim of the deranged killer.

He lets the package fall out of his hand, back into the freezer. It lands with a metallic thud. Christ almighty! His mother. His own bloody mother! What has she left him with? More than just Wullie. A lot more than just Wullie.

He closes the lid, slumps down onto the floor, resting his back against the freezer. Sits amongst Wullie, the frozen packets strewn about the floor. The closest they've been in a long time.

Barney Thomson, barber, runs his hands through his hair and closes his eyes. His breath comes in spasms. His heart thumps. The doorbell rings.

He jerks his head back and smashes it into the freezer. Bites his tongue.

'Christ!'

He stands up in a panic. The door! It can't be the polis already. He stares out of the kitchen into the living room as if expecting Special Branch to come charging into the flat. Feels hot and cold; frightened.

The doorbell rings again. Quiet, urgent, wanting. Come and get me.

He swallows. Might just be Allan having forgotten something. He looks at the mass of frozen food on the floor, decides to leave it where it is. Kicks it into the centre of the kitchen then closes the door behind him as he walks into the living room. Down the hall, round the corner, looks at the door. Can see the outline of a man behind the frosted glass panel.

A man alone, although it is not Allan.

Barney hesitates, stares at the grey figure. Imagines

Death standing there, come to collect his dues. But it is he himself who is Death. He shivers, doesn't want to answer the door, but now the man on the other side might be aware of Barney's presence. The light behind him.

The doorbell is rung again. Get it over with, Barney.

He steps forward, pulls open the door. Stares at his tormentor. A young, nervous-looking man stares back. Late twenties perhaps. Checked jacket; Kay's catalogue. Debenham's tie; small blue and red bicycles on a yellow background. Mole beneath his lower lip, skin like feta cheese. Big hair; a Marc Bolan. Faint smell of cheap after-shave. Apples.

'Aye?' says Barney, as the younger man does not appear to be about to start the conversation. Feels the commotion of his heart begin to dampen.

Young man coughs, continues to look embarrassed. Nervous curiosity. Eventually he speaks.

' "Mature woman, looking for love"?' he says in a small voice.

Chapter 14

Fish for Dinner

Barney sits quietly munching his dinner, Agnes opposite him at the table, a mug of coffee in her hands. He is glad that she's cooked him fish, because he doesn't think he'd be able to face meat. Nor will he for a long time, he reflects, as he stuffs a huge chip into his mouth.

The thought of the freezer turns his stomach; he tries to force it out of his mind, concentrate on his dinner. He is hungry, but knows he won't be able to eat anything if all he can think about is Wullie, and all those others.

Agnes is looking at him, attempting consolation, the memory of her own mother's death stirring within her feelings of sympathy for her husband which she hasn't felt for some years. The television is playing in the background, but for once she is paying more attention to Barney. She does have one ear, however, listening out for what is going to happen when Chenise and Manhattan discover that Blade has been doing nights at a working men's club.

Finally Barney gives up the ghost, pushes the plate away from him. The memory of Wullie's face, twisted and distorted under a clear plastic bag, is too much for him. And how many more distorted faces are in that freezer?

he keeps asking himself. What are the newspapers saying now? Five or six? Is the freezer really that big?

'Ye no' feel like eatin', Barney?' she says.

He shakes his head, stares blankly at his chips. Should he come clean? It's on his mind. He wants to own up to the whole sordid mess. But then, how can he? Not now. Before, perhaps, when it was his mess. But now? How can he reveal to the world that his own mother was the mad Glasgow serial killer? And who is going to believe him, anyway? Wouldn't they all just think it's him who's been doing it?

No, he has to finish what he's started. He is going to have to get rid of those bodies somehow. They are safe enough where they are at the moment, but some time he will have to get on with it. Corpse disposal; or what is left of the corpses. Death or glory, he tells himself. But he knows there is no real way out. However this thing finishes, his life is never going to be the same again. Unless he can make the acquaintance of denial.

'Ah don't blame ye,' she says, and they sit in silence for another few minutes. Every now and again she is tempted to look over her shoulder at the television, but at times like these, soap opera is almost incidental. Almost.

'Oh aye,' she says. 'Bill phoned ye earlier. Sounded quite anxious tae talk tae ye, but Ah told him about yer mum, so he says he'll get ye in the next day or two, ye know. Passes on his condolences, 'n that, ye know.'

Barney looks at his watch. 'It's only quarter past ten. Ah'll maybe gie him a wee call the now.'

'Aye, why don't ye dae that?' says Agnes, relieved that she will be able to watch the television again. Things look as if they are picking up; she submits to her addiction.

Barney raises himself from the table, slumps down into another seat beside the phone, dials the number. It does not ring long.

'Hello?' says Bill. There would seem to those who know him a slightly anxious quality to his voice. The effects of his knowledge of Barney's murderous intent of two nights before, preying on his mind; uneasy rest.

'Hello, Bill, it's me.'

'Barney,' he says. Sounds relieved. 'Ah'm glad ye called.'

He pauses, knows that delicacy is required; is as

incapable of it as every other man in Scotland. You do not lightly accuse a man of murder at the best of times, and certainly not when he is racked with grief.

'Did Agnes tell ye about my mum?' says Barney.

'Aye, aye, she did. Ah'm really sorry, Barney, that must have been a great shock. She wis always so lively for her age, ye know. Whit happened?'

'Well, ye know, Bill, it wis just her heart. She wis an old wummin.'

'Aye, aye, ye're right. Still, it's aye a shock.'

'Aye, aye, ye're right.'

'Ah know it's a bit early, 'n a' that, but huv ye any idea when the funeral will be?'

'Ach, well, Ah'm no' sae sure about that. Probably no' until Monday now, ye know. Maybe even Tuesday. We'll find out the morra. Allan's gonnae take care o' most o' the arrangements. Elder brother 'n a' that.'

'Aye, aye.'

There is a pause. Barney doesn't know what else to say. Bill wonders how long to leave it before he can bring up the subject of the missing Wullie. And just exactly how is he going to put it?

Barney interrupts the flow of his thoughts.

'Did ye phone for somethin' else earlier, Bill?'

Bill pauses briefly, tentatively sticks his finger into the honeypot. 'Aye, well, actually there was somethin', Barney.'

Another brief lapse in the conversation, while Barney waits to hear what it is. Bill tries to decide how best to delicately probe the accused. He's read plenty of Henry Kissinger; tries to think of hints on diplomacy.

'Em, Barney . . .?'

'Aye, Bill, Ah'm still here.'

'Ah, eh, understand, eh, that Wullie's missin'. His, eh, faither wis on the phone tae me earlier the night,' he says, finally taking his clothes off and diving into the honeypot, bollock naked.

Barney puts his hand to his head. Of course that's why he's phoned. He's bound to have heard about it by now. Shit, shit, shit.

Be assertive, Barney, it's the only way.

'Ah didnae kill him, Bill, if that's what ye're gonnae

ask,' he says, not quite sounding as hard as he wants to. It works, however. Bill springs onto the defensive; like Italy in the '94 World Cup final.

'Naw, naw, Ah wisnae gonnae say that.' He stops, reflects. They're old friends. He might as well tell the truth. 'Well, aye, aye, Ah wis gonnae say it. But whit can Ah think, Barney, eh? A couple o' days ago ye were talkin' about killin' him, and now he's missin'.'

Barney shakes his head, tries to play the part. 'Ah know whit ye must think, Bill, but wherever he's gone, it's nothin' tae dae wi' me. Ah wis just haverin' the other night. Ye know me, full o' shite sometimes, sae Ah am.'

Bill tries not to feel guilty. Not entirely convinced by Barney's protestations of innocence. Years of reading philosophy have made him wary of coincidence.

'Have ye any idea whit's happened tae him, then?'

Barney is starting to get annoyed, knows it's because his friend's questions aren't misdirected. But still, he didn't murder Wullie – as such. It wasn't his fault.

'Ah don't know, Bill, Ah told ye that. Look, ma mother's just died, for God's sake. Gie us a break, will ye no'?'

'Aye, aye, awright, Barney. Ah'm sorry. Ah'd better go.'

'Aye, right. Look, Ah'm sorry Ah lost my temper, Bill. It's been a long night.'

'Aye, aye, Barney, dinnae worry about it. Ah'm sorry for suggesting whit Ah did.'

'Aye, right enough. Ah'll speak tae ye the morra, eh?'

'Aye, aye.'

Bill hangs up, wonders if he should call the police. Maybe you shouldn't do that to your friends, but then you shouldn't commit murder either. Wullie's father is his friend also, and he's known young Wullie since he was a bairn. He makes his decision. Prevaricate; sleep on it.

Barney hangs up, wonders if Bill will go to the police. Maybe it isn't the sort of thing you should do to a friend, but then Bill is also friendly with Wullie's father. And besides, he's always thought Bill was a slimy, underhand sneak anyway – the sort of bloke who would report his own grandmother for taping a song off the radio. He's never trusted him when they were playing dominoes. Kicks himself for telling Bill his thoughts in the first place. Sees conspiracy everywhere.

He lies in bed that night wondering how he can shut Bill Taylor and Charlie Johnstone up, stop them from talking to the police. So consumed is he by these matters that he hardly thinks of his mother's freezer, and of his mother herself. An advert in the paper; young men enticed to her flat. The great Glasgow serial killer.

Chapter 15

Step Up to the Big Chair

Holdall sits at his desk, considers the new list of missing persons that has arrived with the dawning of Friday morning. Another five, with the usual specifications. There will be nothing for them here. And of the eight they ended up looking into the previous day, only two remain unaccounted for. The barber, and a young seventeen-year-old lad from Milngavie. Only the missing barber troubles him, and he realises that there is more work to be done on that. He expects MacPherson will be eager to get back to the shop, have another go at Henderson's colleagues. They will chase up another couple of things about him today, then return to speak to them again in a day or two if need be. They aren't going anywhere.

Today, however, will also involve the usual round of concerned parents. Bloody marvellous, he thinks, as he pulls hard on his first coffee of the day; absolutely bloody marvellous. Another day wallowing in the sewer of disenchantment.

The door opens. MacPherson walks into the room, the usual blank expression stamped on his face. Holdall looks up; the two men nod at each other.

'Good news, Sergeant?' says Holdall, not quite sure what MacPherson can tell him that will qualify.

'Ah have some news, sir, though Ah don't know whether ye'd call it good or no'.'

Holdall sighs, rests his chin in the palm of his hand. 'Let's hear it, then, Sergeant,' he says; resignation.

'It's about Jamie Lawson, sir.'

Holdall stares blankly at him, narrowly avoids asking who the hell Jamie Lawson is.

'One o' the two unaccounted fors fi' yesterday, sir,' says MacPherson, reading his mind. Holdall nods, tries to look like he knew that all along.

'Dead in a ditch, is he?' he asks, no sympathy and almost a little hope in the voice.

MacPherson coughs. 'As a matter o' fact, aye, he is. Stepped in front o' a train, sir. On the west coast line, near Dalry. Killed instantly, o' course.'

Holdall shrugs. He doesn't really care. If these bloody stupid teenagers want to do that to themselves it isn't their problem. Wastes everybody's time.

'Why on earth would anyone go to Dalry to kill themselves, Sergeant?'

'Ah really couldnae say, sir.'

Holdall grunts, thinks about the half-hour they wasted yesterday talking to the boy's mother.

'Don't suppose he left a note confessing to a host of murders in and around the Glasgow area, did he?'

'Not as far as Ah'm aware, sir.'

'No, I didn't really think that he would.'

He takes another gulp from his cup of coffee, considers the awfulness of the day ahead. It lies before him like a rotting cow on the pavement.

Friday is a long day in the shop. Many customers come in, as is always the case at the end of the week, and the barbers are kept busy. Wullie's father, James Henderson, even returns to work for the first time in five years, to help out for a couple of hours in the afternoon. Some old-time regulars are glad to see him, but they are nevertheless wary of submitting to the whim of his scissors – most of them having been burned by an out-of-practice barber at some time in their lives.

His first two haircuts are indeed dangerously close to being suitable cases for litigious action. However, he is a

118

past master of the water-disguise treatment, so his initial embarrassments are well covered up. After half an hour he is back in form, cutting hair with the light-fingered panache of old. Like a spy called out of retirement, who takes one last covert dip behind enemy lines, he takes to his task with a smile on his lips and a glint in his eye. The old magic is still there.

He is telling himself that his son has probably just gone on an incredible two-day drinking binge; feels quite proud of him, having done it himself a few times in his younger days. Knows, however, that he will not be able to keep the worry at bay for much longer.

Every now and again Barney casts an eye over the work going on next to him, and is suitably unimpressed. He has always thought that James is a lousy barber, and as he studies the work he is now doing he concludes that five years' abstinence have done him few favours.

And this, his blighted mind keeps telling him, is the man who would sack him. However much guilt Barney feels about what he has done to Wullie, he still feels hurt and betrayed that they were intending to let him go. And if Wullie was the agent of the dismissal, it was James's finger on the trigger.

He finds he can't work and think about what is to be done at the same time; does his best to push to the back of his mind the horror of what lies in front of him. Having to dispose of five or six frozen bodies. You just don't get training for that in life. Should have done Pathology 'O' level. Cannot even begin to think of what is to be done with them, so he concentrates on his work instead. If the whim takes him, he attempts some inane conversation. Anything to push away the thought of the contents of the freezer.

James leaves the shop at around four o'clock, saying that he will return in the morning if Wullie has not yet shown up. His parting words to Barney – 'Come in early so that I can have a word with you' – have Barney almost cutting the ear off the customer beneath his trembling hand.

It is late in the afternoon, with the day seemingly drifting to a quiet conclusion, when disaster strikes. The rush of customers to the shop has ended, the skies outside are grim and dark with foreboding, the March rains returning with a vengeance, having given the city a few hours' respite. Barney and Chris are cutting the hair of one last customer each when the door opens and a figure dashes into the shop out of the rain.

Flat cap pulled low over his eyes, the collar of his coat high up the back of his head. He shakes himself off, removes his cap and looks at Chris.

Charlie Johnstone.

'Ah know it's late, Chris, but ye wouldnae be able tae squeeze me in, would ye?'

Chris glances at the clock, but is not really concerned with it. 'Aye, nae bother there, mate, Ah'm nearly done here. That auld carpet o' yours shouldnae take too long, eh?'

Charlie laughs, and removes his coat to sit down, nods at Barney as he does so. Barney nods back; wishes the floor would open up and swallow him, or that a lightning bolt would strike. He returns to cutting hair, but he can't ignore the feeling of dread. Will he mention what he helped Barney do two nights before?

Barney's stomach churns, great armies of nerves and fear stampede through his body. The hairs on the back of his head begin to prickle and stand to attention. He has to do something.

He glances at Chris to see where he is with his haircut. If he can get his finished first, then maybe he will be able to cut Charlie's hair; it'll be easier to control the conversation, stop Charlie mentioning the other night. It is his only chance.

Too late. As he looks over, Chris removes the towel from the back of his customer's head and shakes the fall-out from the haircut to the ground. Barney is still minutes away from a conclusion. Curses quietly to himself, concentrates on what he is doing. Perhaps if he avoids Charlie's eye he won't speak to him.

His penultimate customer sent packing, Chris invites Charlie up to the big chair and prepares for the final haircut of the day.

'Thanks for this, Chris,' says Charlie, upon his ascent.

'Ach, nae bother, Charlie, nae bother at a'. Mind ye,

it's been a right long day in a', what wi' Wullie no' bein' here.'

Charlie glances around him, observing for the first time that Wullie isn't present; notices Barney trying to disappear inside his pullover.

'Oh, right. So where is Wullie, then? Away on holiday or somethin'?'

Chris shrugs. A concerned shrug. 'Tell ye, we don't know, Charlie, ye know. Don't know whit's happened tae him. He left the shop on Wednesday. Barney saw him go. Said it wis about quarter past five, that no' right, Barney?'

'Aye,' says Barney, the presence of his heart lodged firmly in his mouth making it difficult for him to talk. If Charlie says something now, Barney is in trouble.

'And no one's seen him since. He's just disappeared aff the face o' the earth. Even Moira hasnae heard anythin'.'

Charlie slowly shakes his head. 'Aye, aye, that's right strange, so it is. Right strange. Ach, he's probably sittin' on a park bench somewhere drunk out o' his face. Ye know whit Wullie's like.' And he laughs, but there is no humour or comfort in it.

'Aye, we know Wullie.'

Barney's hands tremble, the sweat beads on his forehead. This is going badly, he thinks. Badly. Then, out of the corner of his eye, he sees Charlie turn his head towards him. Knows what is coming. At least, presumes he knows what is coming.

'Here, Barney, that wisnae him in . . .'

'What dae ye make o' those Rangers, eh, Charlie?' asks Barney. Smooth, cool, natural. Desperate.

Charlie looks quizzically at him. 'Whit are ye talkin' about, man? Ye ken Ah'm nae interested in the Rangers. Ah wis gonnae say . . .'

'Aye, aye, Ah know that, it's just, ye know, it's gettin' taewards the end o' the season, and Ah thought ye might be goin' tae the odd game or two.'

Charlie shakes his head the best he can, given that Chris is now at work in and around the area of his left ear. 'Ah huvnae been tae see a game o' fitba' since ma playin' days huv been over, Barney, ye know that, for God's sake.'

Chris looks up from the waves of hair. 'What's a' this great interest in fitba' ye've been takin' all of a sudden,

Barney? Ye're talkin' about the Rangers tae just about everyone that comes in here.'

Barney shrugs, attempts a smile. 'Ye know, Ah just like tae take an interest in what's goin' on. Fitba', that kind o' thing. Ye know me.'

Aye, Ah do know you, thinks Chris, that's what's so strange about it.

Barney stares at them for a second or two to see if they are about to add to the conversation, but neither of them looks likely to talk immediately. He breathes a sigh of relief. The danger might have been averted.

'As Ah wis tryin' tae say, Barney . . .' Charlie starts up again.

'So, how's Betty and a' that, Charlie? Ye were sayin' somethin' aboot her the other night.'

Shit! Barney, you stupid idiot. Don't mention the other night. Don't remind him, and don't give him the opportunity to ask about it.

'Aye, well she's no' sae bad. But ye know, it wis the other night Ah wis gonnae mention. Was Wullie no' still in the shop when Ah saw ye? Ah thought he wis and Ah couldnae get a straight answer fi' ye. Heid in the clouds, Ah thought, ye know.'

'Naw, naw, Charlie,' says Barney. Big relief – thought he had been about to mention the plastic bags. If he doesn't say anything else, Chris needn't suspect anything. He might yet get away with it. 'He'd already gone a while earlier.'

There is near-silence. The mellow clink of scissors. Barney feels the beating of his heart. He is getting to the end of the job he is doing, and surprisingly, it doesn't appear to be going too badly. Don't mention the plastic bags, Charlie, he thinks, please don't mention the plastic bags. Or I'll be forced to kill you.

Charlie nods suddenly, grunts. 'Aye, aye, o' course. That wis aboot six o'clock, was it no'? He'd huv been long gone by then, so he would.'

Shit! The time. He'd forgotten about the time. Starts cutting frantically with nervous fingers to cover up the panic. His customer semi-dozes beneath him, unawares.

Chris looks over at him. 'Six o'clock, Barney? What

were ye still daein' here at that time? Couldnae have been that busy, surely? And no' if Wullie had gone.'

Barney stares intently at the back of the head in front of him, as if trying to sort out some intricate piece of hair sculpture. Tries desperately to think of what to say. He believes himself to be a wonder when it comes to cutting hair, but he's crap in a crisis, and he knows it.

'Oh, aye, well, ye know, it was stupid, but Ah just sat down at the end o' the day, after Wullie had gone, and fell asleep. Who'd huv thought it, eh? Woke up about six o'clock, feelin' like a right eejit, so Ah did.'

He glances over at Chris, sees the doubtful look in his eye. Chris looks away, returns to Charlie's hair. Barney can still get away with it if only Charlie keeps his fat gob shut. Should have done it when he had the chance. What difference would one more corpse make now?

The shop lulls into silence again, as they think their private thoughts about Wullie. Barney relaxes; the conversation might be at an end. If he can just finish this haircut and get out of the shop . . . There has been nothing said to arouse the suspicions of Chris too much.

With a final couple of snips, and an unsteady sweep of the comb, Barney is done with the chap under his knife. Lifts the towel, draws off the cape, and the bloke is free. A final glance in the mirror, the customer is happy that the cut isn't as awful as he first suspected it might be, then, with a brief exchange of cash, he is gone. Barney busies himself with clearing up, hopes he can make it out before anything else is said.

'Ye were sleepin', Barney?' says Charlie suddenly, as if he's just been plugged in at the mains. 'Ah thought ye were gettin' together a' that . . .'

'What dae ye make o' yon serial killer, eh? That no' terrible,' says Barney, but the words stick in his throat. He knows he is beyond stalling tactics.

'Whit, whit? Naw, naw, Ah wisnae talkin' aboot that. Yon pile o' garbage ye were takin' oot on Wednesday night, that Ah helped ye wi'. Ah thought that that wis whit ye had worked late tae dae, that wis a'.'

Chris looks up. Curious. Pile of garbage? Penny does not yet drop. 'Oh, aye? And whit pile o' garbage wis this, Barney?'

Barney swallows, desperately tries to think of what he can say. There isn't much for it, though – there's nothing he can say. He's going to have disappear.

Looks up from where he has been busy arranging his scissors neatly on the counter, starts to walk backwards. Trapped cat – without the claws.

'Whit? Oh, aye, well, Ah've got tae be gettin' tae the toilet, if yese'll jist excuse me a second.' And with that he vanishes through the door at the back of the shop, hoping that by the time he emerges the conversation will have been dropped.

Charlie is busy shaking his head as best he can, under the steely click of the scissors.

'Bloody heavy, so it wis. Ah had tae gie the lad a lift wi' it tae get it intae the back o' his motor, so Ah had. Jings, but it wis heavy. And big too. Long.'

'Is that right?' says Chris. The idea has come to him; comprehension slowly dawns. But it can't be. Barney? Mild-mannered, boring-as-you-can-get Barney?

'Aye, it is right. Whit kind o' garbage dae you lot produce in here, anyway?'

Chris shrugs, avoids the question. This is to be between Barney and him. 'Well, ye've got tae work in a barber's shop before ye know the kind o' things that we have tae put in the rubbish.'

Charlie nods gravely. 'Aye, aye, Ah suppose ye're right. The ways o' many men are indeed mysterious.'

The conversation lulls, and Chris is swift coming to the conclusion of his business. Barney skulks in the back room for a couple of minutes and then, to his horror, as he emerges to make a quick exit, is just in time to see Charlie put on his coat and head for the door.

'Oh, there ye are, Barney,' he says. 'Ah'll be seein' ye.'

Barney has no words, returns the farewell with a lame nod.

'Right, Chris, thanks a lot for squeezin' me in,' says Charlie. 'Ah hope Wullie turns up in the next day or two.'

'Aye, aye, Ah'm sure he will.'

And with that Charlie is gone. After he has stepped out into the street, Chris slowly closes the door behind him, locks it, slips the key into his pocket. He turns round and faces Barney. Barney stands with his back up against the rear wall; frightened eyes, muscles tensed.

It is time.

Chapter 16

Jolene Stabs Billy Ray Bob Billy Bob

The two men stand face to face across the shop, the tension of unstated convictions thick in the air, Chris's finger twitching at the trigger of his suspicion. He stands in the centre of the shop, hands steady, eyes narrow, stance broad. Gary Cooper.

Barney presses against the rear wall, where his hand falls on the broom which he has just been using to clear up the detritus of the day. Grabs it tightly, holds it to his side, knuckles white. Beads of sweat appear on his forehead, his face is pale. Knees weak; his heart thumps, hands tremble. Gollum; he wilts under the persistence of Chris's gaze.

Neither man yet feels confident enough to speak. Chris doesn't know what to say, still incredulous that Barney could have had anything to do with Wullie's disappearance. Barney waits only to react to whatever Chris might say, for he knows some accusations will soon fly. He should be desperately trying to think of excuses or stories to tell, but his mind is thick with fear. Clogged up. Needs a chimney-sweep. His tongue flicks out to remove the moustache of sweat which has appeared above his top lip; a lizard surreptitiously reeling in a small insect.

Chris finds his tongue. He can't stand there all night,

and although he doesn't have a clue what to say, or how this might progress, he knows he must say something.

'And whit heavy bag o' rubbish might this have been that ye were takin' oot tae yer motor on Wednesday night? Eh, Barney?' he says. Spits out the name.

Barney cowers before the question, his eyes ever more fearful. His tongue darts out in quick jabs, his fingers take a feverish grip on the broom, a staff for fighting. Now he's Robin Hood. A frightened Robin Hood.

'Well?' Chris sneers at him, accusing finger pointing. 'Ye cut a lot o' heavy hair on Wednesday, did ye, Barney, is that whit ye're gonnae tell me?'

Barney speaks. 'It wis just some o' ma own stuff.'

'Whit!' he shoots back. 'Whit own stuff? You don't have any o' yer own stuff. Whit stuff o' yours were ye puttin' intae rubbish bags?'

With the words comes the doubt. What if it was something of his own that he had been taking out? Why should he tell Chris about it? It isn't as if they are friends. He might do a lot of things that Chris doesn't know about. Shit, maybe he's making a complete idiot of himself. What is he doing anyway? Nothing less than being on the point of accusing Barney of Wullie's murder. Bloody hell. That's a bugger of a thing to be doing. It's not a throw-away line, a casual, easily ignored remark. Working late and carrying a heavy bundle to his car does not necessarily add up to Barney being a murderer. It is strange, and he is acting suspiciously, but it doesn't make him a criminal. This is mild-mannered Barney. Mild-mannered, Barry-Manilow-with-scissors Barney. Not some bug-eyed psycho.

'Look, it wis just stuff, awright? None o' yer business.'

Chris has been walking towards him; now he hesitates, stops. He is at an impasse. He can't force Barney to tell him what was in the bags, and it is still a giant stretch of the imagination to assume that it was the body of Wullie Henderson.

Still, there he stands before him, clutching desperately onto the broom handle. Would he be acting so suspiciously if he had nothing to hide? Why be so defensive if his actions are innocent? And the consistent interruption of Charlie when he had been trying to speak to him.

Obviously he hadn't wanted him to mention what he had been doing on Wednesday evening. Didn't want Chris to know about it.

He gets there eventually; arrives at a conclusion. Barney is hiding something. Definitely. Perhaps it's nothing to do with Wullie, but then perhaps it is. It isn't going to cost him anything to accuse him – not his friendship, that's for sure. And Barney is due for the chop, he knows that. Not a friend, not a colleague.

His mind is made up.

'Did ye kill Wullie?' he says.

Barney reels, squeezes the broom handle ever tighter. 'Naw!'

'Well, whit wis in they bags, then, Barney, whit wis in they bags? Eh? Eh? Ye think Ah'm some heid-the-ba', or somethin'?'

Chris walks slowly towards him again, finger jabbing out, the aggression on his face far greater than any confidence he feels that Barney stands rightly accused. But the closer he comes, the more he sees the fright in Barney's eyes. Knows he is right; Barney's the man.

'Ye did kill Wullie, didn't ye? Didn't ye? Ye knew he wis gonnae sack ye, didn't ye, ya miserable bastard!' he shouts, his voice consuming the small shop.

Barney bends his knees, almost squatting. On his way to cowering on the floor. 'Naw!' he squeals, a scream of pathetic denial. 'Ah didnae mean tae. It wis an accident!'

The words fall dead in the air.

Silence envelops the shop. Barney is down on the floor, pressed against the wall as much as he can be. Chris stands three or four feet away, amazement on his face. So Barney had killed Wullie! He had been right.

Now that the information is out there, neither of them knows what to do next. Chris stands over him, astonishment and anger growing on his face; Barney cowers beneath him, awaiting his fate.

Several things are flying around Chris's head. He wants to kill Barney. He knows he shouldn't. Call the police, make sure Barney doesn't get out – that's what he should do. But what then? What if he tries to keep Barney in here until they arrive? Barney is a killer, he's just admitted to it. What if he goes for him as well? God, he looks pathetic enough, but he killed Wullie somehow. Christ, maybe he's *the* killer. Perhaps he should just get out while he can, go straight to the police. Shit. And what might this bastard have done to Wullie's body? Chopped it up? Christ almighty. A piece of Wullie could be sitting in the post waiting for delivery to Moira's house the following morning.

His wrath rises once more within him, the fire blazes in his eyes. Barney sees it, knows what is coming. Holds the broom handle tightly in his grasp, prepares to defend himself.

Finally, Chris's temper snaps. He leaps forward, hands outstretched, searching for the killer's throat. Barney is ready for him, however, does what he can in his pathetic, overtly defensive position. Thrusts the broom hard at Chris as he dives towards him, hitting him square in the chest with the thick brush. The broom is old, but the handle holds, and such is the force of Chris's onslaught that the full weight of the broom on his chest unbalances him; sends him toppling backward. He grabs at air to try to balance himself, but there is nothing to grab hold of. His feet slip from under him, he falls back.

His head cracks off the sharp edge of the counter with a strange thud. Almost hollow, thinks Barney, as he watches in horror. In a flurry of arms and legs, Chris collapses to the floor, his head thumping down onto the ground; and there he lies. Motionless.

After the brief commotion, silence descends. Barney, still cowering against the wall, the broom clutched in his trembling hands, stares at Chris. Chris is silent and unmoving on the ground. And then slowly, from where his head lies on the floor, a pool of thick blood begins to spread out, stealthily creeping across the tiles. On his face can still be seen an expression of surprise, but the features of his face will not move again.

Slowly Barney rises, crawls over beside him. He gingerly places his ear on Chris's chest, holds his breath as he listens. Nothing.

He sits back on the floor, stares at Chris. Can't believe it.

'Christ, not again,' he says.

Barney eats his dinner. Once again he is practising a good deal of denial in order to be able to eat, as it is the last thing that he feels like doing. But he is temporarily trying to forget the previous three days, to relax before he has to face the awfulness of what is to come.

He read somewhere once that the best way to rest the mind is to think of some idyllic and peaceful setting, to concentrate on it, imagine that you are there, smelling the aromas, hearing the sounds. So, as he sits at the dinner table, Agnes's tinned beef stroganoff – beef! – flitting quietly between plate, fork and mouth, he imagines himself to be at the foot of Ben Ime, where the forest track comes to an end beside the small dam with the beautiful clear pool of water behind it.

The sun is shining, there is a crispness in the air, the snow still covers the top half of the hills. He is sitting back after a hard day's walking, a cup of tea in one hand, a roast beef sandwich in the other. All of a sudden, a small grey rabbit, its nose snuffling, overcomes its fear and emerges from its hiding place in a nearby bush. It stands on its hind legs and sniffs the air, attempting to fathom what it is that Barney is eating. 'Ahh, roast beef sandwich,' it says to itself. 'Like a bit of cow, so I do.'

Barney looks away from the rabbit and back up the hill which he has just descended. The last section was steep and tricky in the snow, but hardly treacherous. He can still see the footprints he has left, stretching back up the mountain. He sighs a contented sigh, and looks again at the rabbit. 'Would you like some sandwich, Mr Rabbit?' he says, and the rabbit nods his head, his nose twitching in anticipation. Barney tosses the remains of his sandwich towards the rabbit, a few inches above his head. Mr Rabbit leaps majestically up to grab the bread, and seems to pause in midair while he plucks the flying sandwich out of the sky. He cannot keep his balance, however, and falls backward, landing flush on his back, impaling himself on a broken beer bottle.

Barney has killed Mr Rabbit.

He snaps out of his idyll, jolted and unhappy, and stares once again into the abyss of real life. He has accidentally killed his two work colleagues, and his mother has died

130

leaving him a freezer full of butchered corpses. Maybe he'll be able to keep his job now, of course, but only if he can keep out of prison.

Chris's body lies dumped in the boot of his car, where he left it half an hour previously. Barney has no idea what to do with it. Or Wullie's body for that matter. Or any of the others. Maybe he can just mail them all to the relatives, bit by bit. Bloody expensive, though.

The one small piece of breathing space he has is that Chris lives alone. It might be a while before anyone reports him missing. Perhaps it will even have to be Barney himself, when Chris doesn't turn up for work the following morning.

He thrusts a contemplative lump of potato into his mouth. If he is lucky, he thinks with a smile, the police might assume that Chris has killed Wullie and done a runner. Not much chance of that, though. More like they'll have him for both.

He glumly stares ahead as he spears the final potato, pops it into his mouth, contemplates his fate. He does not even notice Agnes squealing with delight, as Jolene accidentally stabs Billy Ray Bob Billy Bob in the throat with a pencil.

Chapter 17

The State of Russian Toilets

Saturday mornings are always busy in the shop. They close at lunch-time – there being football matches to attend – and usually have a rush of people to deal with before twelve thirty. They are especially busy this morning because Chris doesn't show up for work. Old Man Henderson is there, and in Wullie's continued absence he has also called for their occasional Saturday girl, Samantha, which clearly goes down well with all the men who come into the shop – Samantha dresses for the occasion. Some consolation for not having either of their preferred barbers there. Few are those, however, with enough neck to sit it out and wait for her in particular, most preferring instead to leave it to chance, scowling disconsolately when they are called by Barney or James.

James is somewhat disgruntled when Chris doesn't show up, and makes a few phone calls to his apartment. Decides he won't bother Chris's parents with it, but he might see them later that afternoon if he hasn't been able to get in touch with him. With Wullie having seemingly vanished, it is giving him an uneasy feeling. No believer in coincidence either is Old James Henderson.

He is now exceptionally worried about his son, although at least the post arriving that morning did not bear any of his body parts. Still, the family are convinced that something must have happened to him. Whatever is the case, he is upset enough that morning that he doesn't feel like telling Barney he isn't wanted any more; decides to leave it until the following week. He is still trying not to contemplate the 'what if' of Wullie not returning.

Barney is cutting hair with robotic repetition. Trying not to think about the freezer, he finds he has to think about nothing at all. Cut hair as if in a dream. Consequently, he gives some strange haircuts that morning, but such is the peculiar glint in his eye that few complain.

However, this is not to say that some of those strange haircuts are not dream tickets. Indeed one chap, as a direct result of the haircut he receives from Barney, pulls a sensational woman that night. A babe, if ever there was one in Glasgow. And it just so happens that two weeks later she murders him in cold blood. So it could be said that Barney is responsible for another murder, but that might be unfair.

All morning, however, something niggles at his mind. Something he had thought about the night before. Whatever it is, it is a good thought. He can't remember it, but he's aware that it's helpful; but every time it's almost there, something snaps and it's gone.

The morning drags on, haircut after haircut, a busy and endless stream, and fortunately a long line of people who are not interested in conversation. He has to briefly concentrate when one chap asks him for a 'Brad Pitt Vampire', but that doesn't prove as difficult as he thinks it might. After that, things are pretty much plain sailing. There is one customer who is used to seeing Wullie, and who wants to talk about football. He asks Barney what he thinks about Rangers' game against St Mirren in the Cup, but Barney has only looked at the Premier League table; never even heard of St Mirren. The bloke realises quickly that he isn't getting anywhere; falls into silence.

Finally the long morning begins to draw to an end. The 'Closed' sign has been posted on the door, and each of the barbers is left working on the final head of the day. As the hour has approached, Barney's stomach has begun to churn. He realises that something is going to have to be done with this great weight of dead bodies that is in

133

his possession. He can no longer afford simply not to think about it.

Unfortunately, for his last job, he gets what all barbers hate to get when it's not looked for. A talker. A man with no particular favourite amongst the barbers, and whose hair Barney regularly cuts. Something in computers, as far as he is aware. At least with this chap he hardly has to say anything; an occasional nod will suffice. His concentration drifts in and out of what the man is saying, catches the odd word or sentence. He starts off on football, which Barney completely ignores, and then moves on to the weather, and as Barney delicately negotiates the ears, he goes on to the subject of toilets.

'And Russian toilets! Let me tell ye about Russian toilets.' He stops, catches Barney's eye in the mirror. 'Ye ever been tae Russia, Barney?'

The question sinks in only a second or two behind schedule. Barney shakes his head, mumbles a negative.

'Ye wouldnae believe it. These people are incredible. Now, me and Wendy went there last year, and ye couldnae credit it, so you couldn't. Ye think the toilets in Buchanan Street are bad, they're nothin' compared tae these. The smell hits ye fi' about twenty yards, and then ye go down the stairs tae them and there's just shite everywhere. Shite! Everywhere! The floors are covered wi' it. Then there's these stalls wi' just a small swing door on them, wi' a hole in the ground tae use. There's pish and shite everywhere, and there's nae bog paper. And there's always some huge fat Slavic-lookin' bird, who looks like she cracks walnuts in her thighs, sittin' there, and you've got tae pay her for the privilege of wading through gallons o' shite.' He pauses for breath. Barney nods at what he presumes is an appropriate moment. 'And bloody hell, the toilets on the trains. Unbelievable. There's nae bog paper, o' course, there's water or pish or something everywhere, they smell terrible, and ye get pubic hair in the soap because these people have never seen soap before, so they take the opportunity tae wash themselves a' over. Of course they dae, Ah mean, whit dae ye expect, ye know. Bloody awful country. And Ah'll tell ye another thing,' he says, finger wagging with the flow, 'it's the same wherever ye go. The minute ye cross the Channel, ye're lucky if ye'll ever see a decent toilet again. These people just have nae conception. The French, the Belgians. They're a' the same. The Belgians pish in the street, for God's sake. And then the Italians. Christ, try sitting doon for a crap in that country. Maybe the Germans are awright, but they've got plenty o' other deficiencies to make up for it. And the further south ye go, the worse they get . . .'

Barney switches off completely, leaves him to it. The annoying nag at the back of his mind is right there, on the cusp of his memory, waiting to be plucked out of the air; then it is gone, and he's lost it again. The more he thinks about it, the further away it gets.

He vaguely turns his attention back to the inane ramblings of his last victim of the day.

' . . . and then he downloaded the whole bloody lot. So ye know whit he did then?'

Downloaded? He's not still talking about toilets, is he? Barney shakes his head, feigns interest, as he applies the finishing snips to the back of his hair.

'Well, Ah must admit, he was pretty cunnin', 'cause Ah wouldnae have thought of this masel'. Ye see, this guy Johnson left last week. No' sure where he went, but basically, nobody's ever gonnae see him again. So Ernie works out whit the guy's password wis, don't ask me how . . .'

'Probably just his birthday, or someone else's birthday or somethin' like that. Saw that in a film once.'

'Oh, aye, *Clear and Present Danger*, was it no'? Anyway, whatever. He works out the password, gets intae his computer and fixes it so it looks like it was Johnson that made the initial balls-up in the first place. Brilliant! So when the Big Man finds out about it, which he did yesterday afternoon, he doesnae suspect a thing. Just assumes that it was Johnson all along. Ernie gets aff scot-free, and Johnson's name is mud. But he doesnae care 'cause he's buggered aff and is living in Switzerland, or some shite like that. Amazin',' he says, laughing quietly to himself. Then he lifts a finger as he thinks of something else. 'Switzerland! Now there's a place where ye'll get a decent toilet, if Ah'm nae mistaken. Mind ye, ye cannae flush them after about five o'clock in the evening. Think about that.'

Barney nods, then with a swish of the comb and a pat

or two on the top of the head with his hand to ease the hair into its final, respectable shape, he is done.

He has only been half listening to his customer, but there is something in what he has said that brings the irritating nag back to his mind. What is it, for Christ's sake?

He removes the towel, then the cape, steps back. The man rises, brushes his hands over the shoulders of his jumper – an act Barney usually hates to see customers performing, but today he couldn't care less – then he searches his pockets for the cash. The money and tip safely thrust into Barney's hand, he puts on his jacket and heads out into the Saturday afternoon rain, cheerful goodbyes all round.

Barney slumps down into his seat. Thinks: God, what is it? It has to be so simple.

And then, like a pebble falling from someone's hand and splashing easily into the water, it comes to him. Simple indeed, so very, very, simple. Taking candy off a wean; sticking the ball into an open net, thinks Barney the football fan.

He shoots up out of his chair, quickly clears up the remains of the day. Easily done, and soon he is on the verge of leaving the shop. Turns to James just as he is going. He has to know how much time he has.

'What are ye gonnae dae aboot Chris, James? You want me tae go round an' see if he's in?'

James looks at him, slowly shakes his head. It has been a long morning for him. His hands are tired, he dearly feels the strain of Wullie's disappearance. 'Naw, naw, it's awright, son, leave it tae me. Ah'll gie his parents a call when Ah get in, and see if they've heard anythin'. We're probably worryin' over nothin'. We'll gie the polis a call later, maybe. See what his folks think. Jings, but Ah've got a bad feelin' aboot this.'

'Aye, well, Ah'm sure he's awright, ye know,' says Barney. James has no answer.

Barney nods, says his farewells, walks out into the cold of early afternoon. He isn't going to have too long, so he has to get on with it.

Quick pace, steady hand, glint in his eye. Gary Cooper.

Chapter 18

Chicken, Chips, Ice Cream and Three Fish Fingers

The phone rings. Holdall snaps out of a deep sleep. His eyes open and he's looking at horse-racing on the television. Can't immediately tell how long he's been asleep. There had been a horse race on when he drifted off in the first place, but there's probably been another ten in between. Bloody horse-racing, he thinks – the bane of Saturday afternoon sports programming.

He looks at the clock as he struggles out of his seat. Half past three. Stoatir. There will be football commentary coming on the radio shortly – he won't have to suffer this damned horseshit any more. He can fall asleep in front of the radio instead.

'All right, all right, I'm coming,' he grumbles to the insistent ring of the phone. This had bloody well better not be work, he thinks. Lifts the receiver, knows as he does so that it's bound to be work.

'Hello?'

'Hello, sir, MacPherson here, sir.'

Buggerty-shit-farts. Bloody Scottish Cup on the radio this afternoon as well. This had better be bloody good.

'Sergeant, hello.'

'Good afternoon, sir.'

'Now, what could be so important that it requires you

137

to rouse me from an afternoon of quiet slumber in front of the TV? Is it important?'

His voice is level, but he is daring MacPherson to make it interesting. Too often, he has always believed, some idiot thinks that every time there is a crime committed the obvious thing to do is to call a policeman who is off duty, as if, by definition, being on duty renders you totally ineffective.

'Ah thought ye might like tae know, sir. We've had another report o' a missin' person.'

Bloody hell, he thinks. Bloody hell. Another fag-arsed teenager runs away from his parents because he thinks it'll be cool to hang out around the streets of London and sleep in a bin-liner. Jesus Christ, and they disturb his Saturday afternoon for this.

'Bloody hell, MacPherson, it's the Scottish Cup this afternoon. What the hell are you thinking of? Did you suppose that I was going to think it more important that some pain-in-the-arse fourteen-year-old believes that his parents don't understand him than whether the Rangers get into the semi finals of the Cup. Come on, MacPherson, you've got to do better than that. Tell me something I might be interested in.'

MacPherson is well used to his chief inspector's outbursts. Quite enjoys them sometimes. Has been known to incite him.

'Well, ye might like tae know that the Rangers are gettin' beat one-nuthin', sir, but the main thing . . .'

'What! By bloody St Mirren?'

'But the main thing, sir, is the person who's disappeared.'

Holdall slumps further down into his seat. Christ almighty. He doesn't like the sound of this. Getting beaten by St Mirren. What next? It was bad enough losing to Mickey Mouse sides in Europe every year, they didn't need to be losing to Mickey Mouse sides in the Cup as well.

'All right, MacPherson. Who is it? The Rangers forward line, by any chance? They certainly appear to be missing.'

'Naw, sir, Ah think they're a' present and correct.'

'Present, at any rate.'

'Aye, well, you know they're a load o' pish, so Ah don't know why ye should be surprised.'

'Sergeant . . .'

'It's another of they barbers. Ye know the ones we talked tae on Thursday about their colleague. The younger one, Chris Porter. He's gone missing now as well. His parents called up tae report it half an hour ago, and the local boys passed it on tae us. Thought we might be interested.'

Holdall has been roused. 'We certainly bloody are, Sergeant. Hold the fort, and I'll be there shortly.'

With a few more bloody hells muttered under his breath, he readies himself to go out.

Holdall and MacPherson sit in their car in the midst of a splendid traffic jam in the centre of town. They have visited Old Man Henderson, and now are on their way to see Barney Thomson. The radio plays quietly as they sit, while MacPherson continually annoys Holdall by attempting to discuss the case. Not until he has heard that Rangers have moved into the lead is he able to relax and give him any kind of attention.

'Ah, that's better. Three-one,' he says, pointing at the radio. 'Still can't believe they don't have commentary of the game, though. Who the hell is interested in Aber-bloody-deen. Even people in Aberdeen don't give a shit about them. Average crowd, two and a half.' He drums his fingers on the steering wheel, looks irritatedly up the line of traffic. 'So, what was that you were saying, Sergeant?'

MacPherson has been looking at some notes in his book. There is nothing he can't remember, but he likes to be sure. A good policeman knows his facts.

'Well, there's an obvious link here. On baith days, at the end o' the day, the two missin' men were alone wi' this Barney Thomson. That two barbers should find themselves alone the gether at the end o' the day appears tae be a rare thing. And yet, after these two occasions, the men go missin'.'

Holdall looks at the couple in the BMW in front of them. Angry words are being exchanged; he is delighted he can't hear them.

'You think Barney Thomson is a killer, Sergeant? Did he strike you as such?'

'He was nervous, certainly.'

'The way you talked to him, I was nervous.'

'Ah just questioned him like that because Ah sensed somethin'. He wisnae sure about what he wis sayin'. Ah think he might've been lyin'.'

Holdall nods, shifts into first gear so that he can crawl forward another few yards. The rate they're going, if Barney Thomson is going to try to run from them, he could be in the Bahamas by the time they get to his house. The woman in the car in front raises a fist to her husband; a child in the rear seat raises his ugly head.

'A bit stupid, though, surely, if you want to kill your two work colleagues, to do them both inside three days.'

MacPherson shrugs. 'Ah don't know, sir. Maybe he kills the first one out o' malice, and then this Chris Porter finds out, and he kills him tae keep him quiet. Who knows?'

Holdall shakes his head. 'No, no, I don't think so, somehow. Not this man. He just looked like a quiet, boring, middle-aged fart to me. The sort of guy who picks spiders up and puts them out the door, instead of squashing them to buggery like the rest of us. No, I don't think Barney Thomson's a killer. And certainly not our killer, this bastard that's been taking the piss. No way.'

MacPherson rubs his chin. Not convinced, but beginning to see another possibility. Even more far-fetched, perhaps, but you have to cover the bases in this job.

'What if we're completely on the wrong track, and someone is after all three barbers in the shop. It could be that, rather than this man being our killer, he's the next victim.'

'Ye mean a sort of mass revenge from someone who's had a real stinker of a haircut, or something like that?' Holdall laughs at the thought. 'Lovely. I like the sound of that. Still, I think we're getting a bit ahead of ourselves, Sergeant. We're not even sure that these men are dead yet, never mind that they've been murdered. Their disappearances could be entirely coincidental, and entirely innocent. Although, I have to admit, I don't think Henderson'll be coming back. Not now.'

Suddenly a gap opens up ahead, a clear lane of traffic

appears. It is lined with plastic cones, but whatever road-works are due to take place over the next three years, they have not yet started. Seeing his opportunity, Holdall goes for the space and the free lane; passes by the attempted murder of the man in the BMW by his wife; hands at his throat, while the child screams.

Holdall is in a plain car, and he considers putting his light on top to let the people past whom he is driving know that he's on police business. Then thinks: Bugger it. If they don't like it, they can clear off. And if it incites a whole bunch of others to do the same, well, it'll be someone else's problem.

'So, how dae we treat Thomson when we talk tae him, sir?' says MacPherson. Knows how he would like to treat him.

'Oh, I don't know, Sergeant. I think maybe you should treat him much the same way you did the last time. Let's see how he handles it. You never know. You might be right.'

'Very good, sir.'

MacPherson smiles, wonders if he'll be able to get away with using a truncheon.

Barney stands in the middle of the kitchen in Chris's flat, wondering what he's going to do next. It's a good plan. Deposit all the bodies around Chris's place, except the body of Chris himself. Make it look as if he's the killer and has fled the city. It should work well. All great plans have their logistical problems, however.

Plastic bags containing the bodies of seven people lie in his car out on the street. Individually wrapped, a mass of limbs, organs and general viscera sit waiting to be disposed of. Fortunately it is cold and damp, the winter chill still lingering in the air. They are not about to begin to defrost. Nevertheless, he has to get rid of them quickly, and as he surveys Chris's freezer, he realises he's in trouble. It currently contains two packets of boil-in-the-bag chicken supreme, half a bag of chips, an insubstantial carton of ice cream, and three fish fingers. And it's full. Whatever else he can do with the frozen meat, he isn't going to be able to put it into this freezer. Part one of his plan is down the toilet.

141

Shit. What had he been expecting? He rubs his forehead; tries to get his brain to function properly. Of course Chris doesn't have as big a freezer as his mother. Who the hell has, for God's sake? Nobody has freezers that big. Nobody. Not even frozen-food shops.

Frozen-food shops! He could casually walk around them, depositing bits of meat into their freezers as he goes.

Bugger it, don't be an arse, Barney. That will hardly incriminate Chris. And anyway, it'll take bloody ages. No, he's going to have to do something here. He can't just leave them all in the bags, because it'll be obvious they've been sitting in a freezer somewhere else. It must be two months since that first one died; murdered by Barney's own mother. If he hadn't been in a freezer all that time, he would be fairly pungent by now. Are corpses still 'he', or are they 'it'? he wonders.

He can cook them. That's a thought. Maybe if they're cooked they won't smell so bad.

He pulls a chair out from under the kitchen table, slumps down into it. Bugger it, that isn't going to work. Even if they have been cooked, these people are still going to be off after this long. And there's no way that he has the time to cook God knows how many pieces of meat. The police will be called shortly, if they haven't been already, and then they will very probably come around here.

And then there is still going to be Chris's body to take care of. God, that's bad enough, never mind all this extra baggage that's been dumped on him by his mother.

He buries his head in his hands, tries to think of a way out of the hole. Knows he just doesn't have the imagination for it. Barney Thomson, barber, he is; not Barney Thomson, screenwriter.

Agnes Thomson opens the door, a look of annoyance on her face. Coralie and Cordelia are about to be sucked into a lesbian lovefest by Cassandra, who is only doing it to wreak revenge upon Cosmo and Clovis. It is the steamiest thing to happen on *Aardvark Road* for years, and she has known for months that it was coming on. The videotape is running, but she's annoyed all the same.

The expression on her face changes when she sees the two men, heavily coated and serious. There is one in his forties, the other maybe ten years younger, and whatever they're doing, they don't look happy about it.

'Mrs Thomson?'

She nods slowly, not sure what the actions of her tongue might be if she attempts to speak.

The younger man holds out his identification card. 'Detective Sergeant MacPherson, ma'm, and this is Detective Chief Inspector Holdall. Is yer husband at home, Mrs Thomson?'

The look on her face changes again. She folds her arms across her chest. 'Naw, he's no'. Whit's he been up tae now, eh?'

'As far as we're aware, he's no' been up tae anythin', Mrs Thomson. We'd just like a word wi' him. May we come in?'

Her expression tells the story – why should they? – but she holds the door open, beckons them inside. There will be no cups of tea offered, however.

They follow her into the sitting room, sit down. She only partially turns down the sound on the television, notices that they appear to be interested in what is going on – it seems that Candice and Clarabel are being drawn into the whole sordid business by Coralie, who has never really loved Clint – and switches it off. She can watch it later in peace.

'Could ye tell us where your husband might be, Mrs Thomson?' asks MacPherson. Suppresses his disappointment, hopes Mrs MacPherson is taping the same programme.

'Aye, Ah could tell ye where he is. What's a' this aboot, anyway?'

'Oh, it's nothing tae worry about, Mrs Thomson. Just a routine inquiry. It appears that a Mr Chris Porter, who works wi' your husband, has gone missing.'

'Naw, naw, naw, ye dunderheidit eejit.' Already on the point of reaching for the TV control, if this is all it amounts to. 'It's no' Chris that's missin'. It's Wullie, the other yin. An' Barney spoke tae a couple o' your lot two days ago. Says they were a right couple o' old farts,

143

whoever they were. So, get away wi' yersels and don't bother me on a Saturday efternoon.'

MacPherson shakes his head, decides not to indulge in police brutality. 'No, no, Mrs Thomson, ye don't understand . . .'

'Dinnae tell me Ah don't understand, ye great lummox.'

'Mr Porter has now gone missing as well. They're both missing.'

Her high dudgeon vanishes; she stares at them a little more warily. What are they after, then? Better watch what she's saying.

'We'd just like tae speak tae yer husband about when he last saw Mr Porter, that's a'.'

'Why? Dae ye think he's got somethin' tae dae wi' it, or somethin'?'

'No, no, nothin' like that. We'd just like tae talk tae him, that's a'. You said you could tell us where he is?'

She thinks about it. Barney called earlier and said that he wouldn't be home because he was going to watch a game of football. It didn't strike her as odd, because she didn't bother thinking about it. But now? Barney hates football, so what the hell is he doing? Unless, of course, he's lying. In which case, what the hell is he trying to cover up? Oh God, she thinks, what's the stupid bastard been up to?

'Aye, he's away tae the fitba'.'

'Oh, aye?' says Holdall, speaking up for the first time. 'What team does he support?'

She thinks about this for a second, trying to remember if she knows the names of any football teams, but none in particular come to mind. Shakes her head, mumbles something incoherent. Holdall shrugs, stares at the floor, his interest once again extinguished.

'So you can't tell us when he'll be returning to the house?' says MacPherson.

She shakes her head, and bites on her fingernails. 'Naw, he didnae say. But Ah'll be makin' his dinner for him, so he better come home or Ah'll skelp his arse for him, so Ah will.' A thought comes to her; an infrequent occurrence. 'Ye don't think that if somethin's happened tae the other two, that it might happen tae him 'n a', dae ye?' Is he insured?

144

MacPherson stands up to go, and Holdall, who is no longer paying any attention, absent-mindedly follows him.

'Ah think it's a bit too early for that kind of assumption, Mrs Thomson. We'd just like tae speak tae him at the moment. So, if ye could get him tae gie us a call as soon as he gets back, thanks very much. Ah'll gie you a note o' the number.'

'Aye, fine. Whitever.'

MacPherson hands over a piece of paper, then he and Holdall make their way to the door. Before it is even closed behind them, they can hear Cruella and Candida arguing about Crevice's relationship with Collage.

They walk down the stairs to the car, Holdall with ill-concealed lethargy on his face. He's fed up trailing round all these sad people. Perhaps there's some sordid story to be revealed in this awful barber's shop; maybe there are foul deeds going on between these men; but it isn't what they're supposed to be investigating. They have a serial killer to find, and that's all he's interested in. Finding this bloody murderer, sticking him in Robertson's face, and then telling the sodding police what they can do with their sodding job.

'What now, sir?' says MacPherson as they reach the car. Looks around at the bleak row of tenements, damp and dreich in the rain.

'I suppose, Sergeant, that we should go and see if we can take a look at the flat of this Porter fellow. All might be revealed. You never bloody know, do you?'

'You didnae have any plans wi' Mrs Holdall this afternoon, then, sir?' MacPherson asks, as they slump into the car to escape the cold and deepening gloom.

'Knowing my interest in football, Sergeant, Mrs Holdall moves house every Saturday and takes up residence in Marks and bloody Spencer for six hours. I expect I'll see her around seven o'clock this evening, heavily laden with goods, but light of cheque book.'

'Ah. Just like Mrs MacPherson.'

Chapter 19

Boil-in-the-Bag Hand

Barney stares at his handiwork, considers all that he's done in the past couple of hours. The freezer compartment in the fridge is tightly packed with one small body part, suitably labelled, from each of the deceased. It isn't much, but it's all he can squeeze in, and it links Chris with every one of the murder victims.

To add some grotesque effect, he has left some of Wullie stewing in a pot, to make it look as if Chris has been in the habit of cooking his victims, and has fled the city even as the last one boils. After partially cooking the body parts, he has replaced the boiling water with cold to ensure that no one will come across still-hot water in the kitchen. It had been mildly disgusting when he removed the hand and the mélange of viscera from their plastic bags, but a couple of hours of transferring body parts from the freezer to his car has toughened his stomach beyond reason.

Still he is left with seven bodies of which he must dispose, and quickly too, before they begin to stink his car out; before Agnes notices that the rear seat is piled high with black plastic bags. He will have to sneak out tonight on this gruesome errand, but first he has work to finish in Chris's flat, making it look as if he has made a hasty exit. Clothes lying around, a bag half packed but left behind, another bag and some clothes gone. Someone might know that they are missing. He thinks of leaving a meal half eaten on the table, but that would be unnecessarily dramatic. And time-consuming. Perhaps he has another couple of hours to spare; perhaps he doesn't.

On his way to the flat, he had gone into Central Station and purchased a one-way ticket to London using Chris's credit card. He was not sure how quickly the police could check up on that kind of thing, but it might be quite effective if they did. Rather pleased with himself for having thought of it.

He walks around the house, does what he thinks is necessary to make it appear that Chris is in flight. Finds a set of three travel bags of different sizes, perfect for his requirements. Removes the middle one, hopes that it's noticed, while he half packs untidily, with a random selection of clothes, the bigger one. The bed has been made, so he ruffles the sheets, lies down in it for a while to give it the correct appearance.

After twenty minutes of stalking around the flat, deciding what else he can do to precipitate the belief that Chris is a killer in flight, he is done. Gathers up the bag with whatever articles from the flat he decides should be removed, prepares to leave.

A good afternoon's work is complete.

Holdall parks his car outside the tenement block where Chris has his flat. In front is a car with black plastic bags piled high in the back seat. He stares at it for a second or two, shaking his head.

'Look at that, Sergeant. How the hell can that idiot see out of the back? If I could be bothered, I'd find him and book him. I don't suppose we've got something we could use as a parking ticket to stick on the guy's window?'

'Don't think so, sir,' says MacPherson. Ponders letting the air out of the tyres for annoyance's sake.

They get out of the car, stand on the pavement in the lightly falling drizzle, look up at the third floor. It is a typical West End block; huge rooms, large bay windows looking out onto the street; not far from the university. The lights are out in the flat, as Barney has toiled on in the ever-deepening gloom, frightened to illuminate the windows.

'Nice block,' says Holdall. 'How the hell can a sodding barber afford to live here? Tell me that, Sergeant.'

'Lucrative business, barbery, Ah suppose. There's always people wantin' tae get their hair cut. Big tippers in this area too, Ah expect.'

'While we toil away doing the Queen's bidding, working with the scum and filth of the world, and we get paid a bloody pittance. Bastards.'

'The Queen's biddin'?'

'You know what I mean, Sergeant. I was being poetic. Now, have you got those keys?'

'Yes, sir. Should dae the trick.'

The door into the close is locked, and MacPherson produces a huge bundle of keys from his pocket, starts working his way through them. No point in letting any caretaker know the police are here, if they don't have to. There will be time enough for all these obstructive bastards to get in their way. He's really hoping that they won't be able to get into the flat itself, because that'll give them an excuse to kick the door down. Hasn't had to kick down a door for a couple of years now. One of the staples of a policeman's diet.

At the fourth attempt the door clicks open, and the two men trudge into the dreary close, the door slamming shut behind them.

Upstairs, Barney hears the faint rumour of the door closing; jumps. Thinks about it for a second, realises he has no reason to worry. There are plenty more people in these flats to be using the door, there's no reason why anyone should be coming here. Very likely the police haven't even been called yet. And it isn't as if Chris is going to be coming back.

He quickly looks around the dark of the room, the lights from outside sending strange shadows shuttling into the corners. A shiver drifts lazily up and down his back at the thought. He has seen enough horror films in his time not to even need to use his imagination.

He dismisses the thought, pulls himself together. It isn't going to be Chris coming up the stairs, or anyone else coming here, for that matter. Still, better get a move on.

Everything is done that he can think to do; the bag waits ready at the door. He just has to hope that he's done enough to incriminate Chris, without making it look like the set-up job it is. All that remains is to dispose of seven bodies. Piece of cake. He wonders if they ever had to do that on any of his mother's game shows. *Lose That Corpse!*

He presumes he'll have to face the police another few times. If his nerve holds, and the police are as stupid as everyone thinks they are, he might get away with it.

The doorbell rings.

Barney loses momentary control of his bowel and bladder functions, only manages to get them together after the initial damage has been done. His heart starts thumping extravagantly – will it ever stop? – his head spins into a frantic muddle.

Christ, there's someone at the door. Who the hell is it going to be? A friend of Chris's? Chris's ghost? His parents? The police? A host of seven dead bodies reassembled to take their revenge?

Pull yourself together, for God's sake, Barney! Ghosts don't ring the doorbell. The police? Would the police ring the doorbell? Probably not. Those bloody thugs would just barge the door down. It must be friends of his, someone like that.

A key! They might have a key! You can't just stand here like a lettuce, Barney. Hide!

He quickly dashes through the flat, tries not to make any noise with his footfalls, anxiously looks in every doorway to see if there is any cupboard space. Finds it behind a door in the hall, next to the bedroom. There are shelves inside, with sheets and blankets, but there's enough space at the bottom to crouch down and pull the door shut.

He holds his breath and waits, trying to think if he has left anything of his own lying around.

His heart jumps again as the doorbell rings once more, and then keys are pushed into the lock. Whoever it is seems to be having some trouble, because they can't open the door immediately. Funny if it's someone trying to break in, he thinks. Even funnier if they then trip over

149

the bag he's left just behind the door. Too bad he can't see it.

Shit! The bag. The bloody bag. He's left it lying in the hall. Christ, he has to get it.

He closes his eyes and tries to think. Dare he go out? Every few seconds a key is inserted in the lock, and then withdrawn. Whoever it is, they don't have the actual door key; must be trying a bunch of skeleton keys. What does that mean? Christ, think, man!

The police! The police maybe. Bugger, if that's who it is, then he has to get the sodding bag. He has to risk it.

He waits until the latest key has been tried and failed, gently opens the door, pokes his head round. The bag sits in the middle of the darkened hallway, about six or seven yards away. One more attempt with the key, he thinks, and hope they don't get in.

The key fumbles in the lock and then is withdrawn. In the silence he hears some curse at the door. Can't wait any longer. He stands up out of the cupboard, quickly runs the few yards to the bag. As his hand falls on the handle, another key is inserted in the lock. There is a deafening, damning click, and if his pants haven't quite been laid waste from the previous occasion, they are now. The door is pushed open, he hears a 'Thank God for that'; dashes back to the cupboard. The brief second that it takes for the key to be removed from the door gives him just enough time to get back into hiding.

He gently closes the door of the cupboard, just as the first man pokes his face around the door.

MacPherson flicks the light switch, and they look around. It is a large entrance hall, several doors leading off. The walls are hung with various pictures of exotica, and Holdall grunts as he looks upon a flat which is clearly going to be a lot nicer than his own house.

He wanders off to the front, where he presumes he will find the sitting room and possibly the main bedroom. Walks through the door, flicks the switch. He is indeed in the sitting room. Curses under his breath at the decoration and furniture. The three-piece suite looks just the kind he will never be able to afford. Wishing to make himself feel worse about it, he slumps down into one of the seats to see how comfortable they are.

Unbelievably bloody comfortable, he reflects as he looks around him. There is a huge television, two video recorders (if the bastard ever turns up, he thinks, we can probably get him for pirating), a music system the size of a small African republic, and a computer which has clearly been rescued from a spaceship. He curses, rolls his eyes. What a bastard, he thinks. What an absolute bastard.

'This guy has got to be up to something more than cutting other bastards' hair.'

He stands up, walks out of the room and through the one next door. The bedroom is equally huge, similarly extravagantly furnished, dominated by an enormous bed, the sheets ruffled and unmade. Above the bed, clinging to the ceiling, is a mirror the size of the bed. Holdall lets out a low whistle; despite himself feels some admiration for Chris Porter. The guy has no class, but at least he has no class with style.

He steps out of the bedroom, looks at the door next to it. Probably a cupboard which is going to be bigger than his house, he thinks, as he puts his fingers on the handle.

Inside Barney is tensed, waiting for the moment. Feels as much as hears the hand touch the door above; prepares to dash out. Guesses that if he hits the man in the face with the bag just as he opens the door, he might be able to get past him and out of the front door before he can do anything about it. Has no idea what he will do when he gets downstairs, because he can't afford to let them see him driving off in his car. He can worry about that when he gets down there, however.

The door starts to swing open. He tenses his legs, holds the bag up, ready to pounce. Cold palms, head thumping, nerves raw and bloodied. Last-second decision; don't wait for the door to be fully opened – crash out, hitting the bastard with it. He starts his leap . . .

'Sir!' MacPherson calls from the kitchen. 'Ah think ye should take a look at this.'

Holdall holds the door half open; Barney manages to stop himself hitting it by less than a centimetre. Rests back on his haunches, chest heaving. The door is closed. Not closed shut, however. It is left marginally open, so that he can hear the conversation that goes on a short way down the hall.

Holdall trudges resignedly to the kitchen. He really doesn't want to see it, because he presumes it is going to be one of those huge white things that people have in adverts for floor cleaner, but that no one has in real life.

He is pleasantly surprised. It's tiny. Smaller than his kitchen by a long way. Small enough, indeed, to win small-kitchen competitions. The thought might have struck him that a single bloke would probably be more interested in pulling women that in having a huge kitchen – if it hadn't been for something else which grabs his attention.

MacPherson is standing in the middle of the room holding up someone's left hand with an exceptionally large pair of tweezers.

Chapter 20

Run Away

Barney holds his breath. They're not supposed to have found anything this quickly, whoever they are. His mind and body are disintegrating into a tangled mass of frayed nerves and gelatinous visceral substructure. This is awful; bloody awful. He wishes he had turned himself in right at the beginning, as he listens to the voices from without.

'Well, bugger me with a pitchfork. Who do you suppose that belongs to, Sergeant?'

'Nae idea, sir. It's male, certainly, but further than that Ah'd only be guessin'.'

'Anything else in that pot?'

'Meat o' some kind, sir. Who knows? Half cooked, too, but Ah wouldnae like tae guess which part o' a body it might be. Could be a bit o' beef for all we know. Ah'm nae pathologist.'

'Me neither. Looks like we've got a few phone calls to make.'

The voices continue. Barney stops listening. He's recognised them; the same policemen who were in the shop two days ago. And they've found the hand a hell of a lot quicker than he wanted them to. The place will be crawling with police within minutes, turning it upside down. He has to get out.

He slowly pushes the door further out, so that he can glance down the hall. The voices are clearer, but his view of the action is obscured by a corner wall in the hall, between the kitchen and the front door.

He is just going to have to make a dash for it, hope for the best. Tentatively, he puts his foot out of the door, and then, crouching, the rest of his body. Clammy hands, trembling with fear. If he is to escape it has to be in the next few seconds, or not at all.

He is into the hall and moving noiselessly and quickly to the door. He is at his most vulnerable, caught between hiding place and exit, should one of the police walk back out into the hall. And as he puts his hand on the door handle, begins its silent downward sweep, the conversation in the kitchen stops. He hears footsteps coming towards him.

He freezes. Still like ice. Something screams at him to run, but he knows it is too late. They will see the door closing as they come into the hall, there will be a brief chase, and then he will be caught. That's all there is going to be.

And so, silently, finally, the flight and fear die within him and he stands waiting upon his fate; waiting upon his executioner.

The legs and then the body of Holdall appear at the corner. Barney releases his breath, lets all hope fall from him. And then, as Holdall turns the corner and stands not three yards away from him, MacPherson calls out again – he has discovered the freezer – and Holdall turns his head away from the hall and Barney, before he has set his eyes upon him.

So bereft of hope has he been that Barney does not immediately dive out of the door. Still frozen, before finally the impulse to move comes to him, and slowly he opens the door, steps out, closes it quietly behind him. His body disintegrates even further with relief. Stays calm, because he is empty of all emotion and anxiety.

He does not rush thereafter. The police are hardly likely to be turning up in droves in the next half a minute; he does not think that he will be followed down the stairs. So, with strange assuredness, he walks quietly down, bag in hand, and out onto the street to his car.

As he starts the engine he thinks perhaps someone is looking out of a window at him, but he doesn't glance back. Never look back. That is the way he will live his life from now on. And so he drives off down the road and disappears into the gloom and dark of late afternoon.

The drive home is short, and it isn't until he is about to park his car that he thinks to turn on the radio to get some football scores. He is going to have to tell anyone who asks that he has been at a game, and it will be a good idea to know the score.

He has to listen for ten minutes before finally they give a score from a match which he recognises as being in Glasgow. Partick Thistle versus Aberdeen. He isn't sure exactly where Partick Thistle's ground is, but it seems a fair bet that it's in Partick somewhere. Lived in Partick all his life, never seen it; how big can a football ground be?

There is parking attached to the flats in which he lives, but he has a lock-up for the car about two minutes' walk away. Is glad of it now, as he can get the heaps of plastic bags out of sight. A short walk back to the flat; he is reminded that he needs to change his underwear. Too exhausted to be embarrassed.

He heads straight for the bedroom before announcing himself to Agnes. It is hardly likely that she will be interested in his arrival anyway. A quick wash and a clean pair of trousers later, he walks into the sitting room. Finds her watching the television; the table set, awaiting dinner.

'It's in the oven,' she says to him, without bothering with a 'hello', or to look over her shoulder. Flange and Fleurelise are trying to fit Gossamer's body into the back of a Mini, after he has been stabbed by Luge for having an affair with Peppermint. He grunts, realises with some surprise, as he goes into the kitchen, that he is very hungry. All that handling chopped meat, he reflects.

The usual unappetising fare greets him, but twenty-five years of it have quite lain waste to his taste buds. He is happy to eat anything. As always, he forgets to put on oven gloves, burns his fingers on the plate. Eventually he proves equal to the challenge, retrieves his dinner.

He consumes himself in thought as he plunges into his meal. What is he going to do with the eight hundred pounds or so of dead meat? Maybe he should just have left it in his mother's freezer, and then brought it home bit by bit for Agnes to cook. By the time she'd finished with it, it would have been quite unrecognisable. Still, don't be daft, Barney. You were never able to stomach Wullie alive. He smiles grimly. And it doesn't strike him, how easily the grotesque becomes acceptable.

And then somewhere between a chip and a mouthful of savoury pancake, he realises that while he has to take care over what he does with Chris's body, he can dispose of the others as he pleases. Christ, Ah should have thought of that earlier, he thinks; stabs another chip with a little more venom. So what if they find the other bodies? It makes no difference. It is only Chris's body which will have to remain concealed for all time.

Agnes's sweet voice drags him from his deliberations.

'Here, you! Ah hud the polis lookin' for ye this afternoon.'

Bloody hell.

'The polis?'

'Aye, the polis. They said that Chris wis missin'. Did ye know that?'

He stares at her, wonders if the visit would have been anything more than routine.

'What did they say? What did they want wi' me?'

'Well, Ah don't know, dae Ah? They probably just want to ask ye the same kind o' thing they asked ye the other day. Right strange, though, is it no', Wullie disappearin', and now Chris? Ye don't think somethin's gonnae happen tae you, dae ye?'

Slowly he shakes his head, stares into space. So, the police had already been round, even before they visited Chris's flat. He thinks he'd better remember that football score. Two–one to Aberdeen. Don't forget it.

'They left a number that they said ye had tae call when ye got in. Ah left it by the ph . . . Here, whit's goin' on?'

She turns her head back to the television. Dexter has just stabbed Deuteronomy, because it appears that it's Pleasure who's drowned Patience and not Leviticus as everyone has thought.

Barney looks at the phone with dread, but something lightens his heart. It is unlikely that those two will come flying round to him, having just found what they've found. There will be no immediate reason to suspect him, after discovering the cooking pot in Chris's kitchen, and they might leave him alone for a while. They'll be back, but he should have given himself some breathing space.

Whatever else he does, he will have to report in, or else arouse suspicion. He happily spears three chips, pops them into his mouth. He isn't home and dry yet, but things could definitely be worse. Much worse.

Chapter 21

Waste Disposal

The sweat pours down Barney's face, mixes with the light drizzle which had begun to fall the instant he stepped out of the car. His clothes and his skin are soaking. Barber Drowns in Own Body Fluids. He hasn't had this much physical exercise since he was about twelve, and his body isn't coping too well. He is having to stop every half-minute or so, and it is taking him a long time to get where he wants to go – the mirror of life. He takes another look at his watch – already nearly four o'clock. He must get a move on.

He straightens his back once again, puts his shoulders into the task, sinking the oars deep into the water and dragging the boat forward as fast as he can. The weight at the back of the small rowing boat, however, is dragging it down, and it would take a much fitter man than Barney to manoeuvre it with any speed out into the centre of the loch. He curses himself for not bringing gloves, as his hands are numb with cold, and he begins to feel the first tingle of pain, heralding the arrival of blisters on his fingers.

Once again he has to stop after no more than a few strokes. He looks over his shoulder and is surprised to see that he is nearer to the opposite shore than he thought he was. He's as near to the middle of the loch as he is able to get. Almost immediately the pain in his hands and shoulders eases, and he draws the oars into the boat.

There is another awkward moment coming up, and not the first of the night. He has to tip the bundle at the back of the boat into the water, without capsizing or without taking himself over the edge with it.

He pauses to get his strength back, looks around him. The hills are etched black against the night; the shores of the loch are visible, dim and dark through the drizzle, on each side. He can remember when his father used to bring him here for picnics when he was a very young child. Loch Lubnaig, a mile or two past Callander. Distant memories. Hot summers, smiling father. Someone to look up to. It isn't as remote as he would have liked, but he doesn't have time to go driving up into the Highlands.

He waited late into the evening to see if the police would turn up at his house, and when by midnight they hadn't, he decided to make his move. With the final soap opera of the day finished, and Smoke and Dandelion safely locked up for the murder of Blanchette – a story in which even Barney had found himself interested – Agnes had trundled off to bed, and Barney knew that within minutes she would be blissfully snoring and unaware of his movements.

He had headed off on the Stirling road, not entirely sure where he was going. On a whim, however, he had driven through Glasgow rather than go straight onto the motorway, and just before he had come to Glasgow Zoo – which had given him an idea or two – he had come across what he had been looking for. A dump. A bloody huge dump. And there he had deposited the remainder of the bodies of the victims of his mother, and of Wullie. They will be discovered at some point, but that isn't really important. It is the body of Chris Porter which needs to remain concealed for a long time.

And now he sits in the middle of a loch, about to dump it over the side. Once he had pulled off the road beside the water, into what he hoped was an area of solitude, he had got to work with heavy stones and rope and enough plastic bags to wrap up a very large horse. He wasn't sure if it would all be sufficient to keep the corpse at the

159

bottom of the loch, but it was all that he could think of at the time, and he had to hope that it would be. It seemed the only thing he had left to chance was finding a rowing boat lying conveniently at the side of the water, waiting for him – and there it had been, almost as if he'd had an accomplice. Divine assistance. A bona fide miracle. God was on his side.

As the day has worn on, the horror of manhandling corpses has slowly faded, and by now he is almost treating them like any other pile of garbage. That initial fear that any second a finger was going to move, or that Chris's entire body would suddenly sit up, has passed, and now he might as well be about to throw away a consignment of rotting chicken.

He braces his feet against the side of the boat, with the bundle between his legs. Stretches forward and slowly tries to lift it onto the edge of the boat, which he manages without too much difficulty. Now he has to transfer the weight of the package until it topples over, while at the same time keeping his weight far enough back to stop it dragging the small boat underwater. And with almost consummate professionalism, he fails to do it. Half a minute later, Barney slides slowly into the water, arms and legs flapping. The package immediately begins to descend to the depths, sucking Barney with it at first, but he soon struggles to the surface, coughing and spluttering, arms flailing; desperately hopes that whichever hand of fate had left him the rowing boat will now throw him a life-jacket.

The boat, however, stays upright, despite taking in large quantities of water. He manages to grab hold of the sides, slowly pulls himself together. It is only then, when he has time to think about it, that it hits him.

The temperature of the water. Anyone who has ever dared to stick the merest end of their big toe into a Scottish loch in mid-afternoon in high summer will know. This is March, in the middle of the night.

Barney will later reflect that there are no adjectives in the English language of sufficient adequacy to describe the coldness of the water. But without undue care and attention, he has to get out of it as quickly as possible, and in doing so almost topples the boat over. The fates are with him, however – even if they had briefly taken the piss by dumping him in the water – and he manages to avoid further excitement as he returns to the boat. After that, the row back to the shore is a long and slow and hard one. And cold; very, very cold.

Half an hour after getting back to the shore, he is driving home, bollock naked, the heating up full, his clothes squeezed dry of water as much as possible and drying on the rear seat. He hopes desperately that he won't pass a police car along the way.

He has decided to take the roundabout way back to Glasgow through the Trossachs, thinking that the roads will be even more deserted, and that he will be more likely to find somewhere to put his clothes back on before he returns to the city.

It works out well, a smooth drive home – with the exception of passing another middle-aged man alone in his car, who also appears to be bollock naked. The things you come across, thinks Barney.

And so, by just after seven o'clock on Sunday morning, he is back in bed, pyjamas safely on. Falls into an immediate and deep sleep, free of dreams and nightmares. Minutes later Agnes awakes, mooches into the kitchen for the first soap of the day.

Chapter 22

Grandmother from Hell

Monday morning. The room is thick with cigarette smoke, the air heavy with the rancour of aggressive argument. It seems as if the five policemen each have differing views on the crime, although that's not quite the case. The two detective sergeants have taken a back seat – such is their lot – and let their superiors get on with the argument. Still, they have managed to express their opinions without getting dragged into the open war which is developing.

McMenemy sits at the head of the table, watching over proceedings, asking pertinent and tough questions – so he believes. Gives his men free rein to indulge their tempers. Another dictum: a station divided is a station easily controlled.

It all seems clear cut to Chief Inspector Brian Robertson – a fellow of infinite lack of imagination. Chris Porter is the mad Glasgow serial killer, and he has fled the town after committing a crime which was a little too close to home. In fact, it is out of their hands now. They know that he purchased the ticket to London, and now that they have issued the countrywide alert, what else is there that they can do? Chris Porter is their man, and it's just a matter of sitting and waiting for him to show his hand. And if he never does, well, it isn't their problem.

As long as he never returns to Glasgow. 'QED,' he says at the end of one of the explanations, although he doesn't know what it means. Hopes he hasn't made an idiot of himself.

Chief Inspector Robert Holdall is not so easily led by the glaring evidence. The whole thing reeks of a set-up, although he is not convinced of it, and is unsure of how to play his hand. Robertson is in the ascendancy in the case and he has to be careful what he is doing. Still, there are things which have to be said.

He is airing his views, enjoying the disdain with which they are being treated.

'We spoke to Barney Thomson again yesterday. All right, so I've no idea what he's got to do with it, if anything, but he creams his pants every time we walk into the room. The man is nervous.'

'Aw, come on,' says Robertson. Waves an extravagantly dismissive hand in the air. 'This Barney whatshisname of yours. You really think this bumbling moron is a mad serial killer? I don't care what you say about serial killers, but there has to be some spark about them, surely. Something different, something to set them apart from the rest. This guy is about as interesting as a two-hour Nescafé Gold Blend advert. Get a life, Holdall.'

'Bullshit, Robertson. What are you gibbering about? What's this difference you look for in your serial killers, eh? That they carry around a chainsaw, perhaps? That all their clothes are made out of women's skin? Come off it. How the hell are you supposed to be able to tell that someone's a serial killer just by looking at them? Bloody hell, you can't work like that.'

'So what are you saying, then, Holmes? That Barney bloody Thomson is our killer? That this poor sad bastard, with no friends and a pathetic wife, is the type of guy to chop people up into little pieces and go scuttling down to the post office? The guy is just a dork, and that's it. He couldn't kill Jack shit.'

Holdall laughs. He hates Robertson. Christ, I want to punch him in the balls, he thinks.

'Jack shit? Been watching *NYPD Blue* again, Robertson?'

McMenemy finally holds up his hand to stop the men,

although he is loath to do so. Loves it when his detectives get into an argument – allows him to appear even more statesmanlike and superior.

'Calm down now, gentlemen, please. Now then, let's consider all the facts. Three oh one, if you could just run down all the relevant details for us, please – and no asides, gentlemen, if you would be so kind.'

MacPherson looks quickly at his notebook, while Detective Sergeant Jobson frowns, wonders why he hasn't been asked to go over the facts of the case. Thinks MacPherson is an all-right copper, but can't stand him all the same. Guilty by association.

MacPherson starts reading in a subdued monotone. 'Chris Porter last seen on Friday night by Barney Thomson when he departed his barber's shop in Partick. Reported missin' by his parents early Saturday afternoon. On entering his flat later on that afternoon Chief Inspector Holdall and I discovered a small freezer full o' body parts, a bit fi' each o' the victims o' our serial killer. There wis also a hand, and some viscera lying cooked in a pot on the cooker. This, as yet, remains tae be identified. Checks made wi' travel firms and companies yesterday show that Mr Porter had purchased a one-way ticket to London on the train early on Saturday afternoon. We have yet to identify who might have sold this ticket, but we should be able to do that today.'

'Yes,' interjects McMenemy, 'that might tell us something.'

'There are a lot more details, sir,' says MacPherson, looking up, 'but those are the most pertinent.'

'Exactly,' says Robertson, laying his hands in an expansive gesture on the table. 'It's bloody obvious. This Porter fellow is clearly our killer, he's buggered off to London, and within a week or two people in Wimbledon and Balham will be having pieces of their children turn up on their doorstep, while they're getting tucked into their cornflakes.'

McMenemy grunts, hunches his shoulders even further. It just so happens that he agrees with Robertson, but there is no way that he is going to give him any encouragement. He is about to say something challenging and spymaster-ish, which he hasn't thought of as yet, when there is a knock at the door. He grunts loudly, bellows a command.

The door opens, and a rather dishevelled middle-aged man trudges in. His clothes are old-fashioned – designer stains on the shirt collar – the watch chain dangling from the tweed waistcoat setting the whole off beautifully. He is fiddling with his horn-rimmed spectacles and looks rather embarrassed, as he always does when confronted with a room full of more than two people.

The pathologist, Jenkins, has arrived.

'Jenkins!' booms McMenemy. 'What have you got to tell us, man? Make it quick. Don't just stand there looking like a piece of pumpkin pie, for God's sake.'

Jenkins stares at the floor, fiddles with his glasses some more, puts them on and looks at his audience. Coughs quietly, removes his spectacles again before he speaks.

'Hm, I'm not sure how you're all going to take this, gentlemen.' Pauses again, puts his glasses back on.

'Get on with it, man!'

Takes off his glasses, lets a look of worry career with abandon across his face. 'Well, what I have to tell you all seems rather strange, and I know you won't want to accept it.'

'Good God, man! You're not giving us the chance. Bloody well get on with it, and tell us what it is!'

Independently, Holdall and Robertson smile to themselves. It is always the same. Jenkins would bumble and fudge, McMenemy would bluster and shout, and eventually they would get somewhere.

'Mm, well, it seems, gentlemen, that it wasn't your Mr Porter that chopped and packaged these bodies so beautifully. And can I just say that whoever it was made a lovely job of it.'

Holdall can't stop himself clapping his hands together. Encourages a raised eyebrow from McMenemy, a scowl from Robertson.

'Hah! I knew it! I knew it wasn't that Porter bastard.'

'It was an old woman.'

The words fall softly into the room and lie there, no one particularly keen to pick them up. The five men stare at Jenkins, who wilts under the glare, tries not to be too embarrassed. Wonders if he still has some of his breakfast on his chin. Finally, McMenemy explodes.

'What on earth are you talking about, for God's sake! An old woman? How the bloody hell can you tell that from a few packets of meat?'

'Dead skin cells,' says Jenkins, voice even more of a mumble than normal. 'There are skin cells left on the outside of some of the packages. We found some that belonged to a man, but mostly they're off an old woman. A very old woman.'

The rest of them are looking at him in amazement. 'You're joking, right, Jenkins?' says Holdall. Aghast, angry, his moment of triumph rudely snatched away. 'How can you people tell that stuff? Why couldn't you tell it before from the packages that came through the post?'

'She wore gloves, presumably, when sending the packages in the post. It's not normal, of course, to find skin cells attached to everything that people touch, but in this case it was the vigour of the chopping activity that must have gone on. We're not sure about this man's involvement, but certainly almost all the work appears to have been done by the woman.'

McMenemy has temporarily lost the look of the head of the Secret Service. Covers his face with his hands, mutters about the press.

'And when you say old?' asks Robertson. Not smiling, because that would be out of place; still very relieved that he isn't the only one around the table looking stupid.

'Eighty. Eighty-five. Difficult to say exactly at this stage. Might know a bit more when we've done some more tests.'

McMenemy lets out a loud groan, chin slumping into the palm of his hand.

'What the hell are we going to tell the press?' he says, a question directed at thin air. 'They'll love this, won't they? The great granny from hell. Christ almighty, we're in trouble. We've been farting around for the last two months looking like a complete load of bloody oafs, and all the time there's some antediluvian witch charging about with a two-foot butcher's knife. Jesus Christ.'

'But whoever's granny she was, how did all the stuff

end up in Chris Porter's fridge? Was it his granny, perhaps?' says MacPherson.

McMenemy straightens his shoulders, attempts to regain his appearance of authority. Looks around the room. The command is back in his eyes. M has returned.

'Gentlemen, we need to find out who this damn woman is, and we need to find out quickly.' Has the tone of a washing-powder advert. 'Check out his grandmothers, and find out if he knows any other elderly women as well.'

'And Thomson,' says Holdall, 'what about him? There's got to be something there. I just know it.'

McMenemy shrugs. 'Very well, one two seven, do as you will. Just remember that three nineteen's in charge of this one.'

Holdall nods, can't keep the scowl from his face. The men rise and leave the room. Robertson is out first, waits for Holdall to follow him. Delighted that his authority in the case has once more been asserted.

'Right, Holdall, you heard the man. I'm in charge, so you'll bloody well do what I say. As far as I can see this Thomson git of yours has as much to do with this case as a gold watch, so we'll just leave him out of it at the moment. If anything, he was only likely to be another victim of this Porter and his vicious female accomplice, and if I find you harassing this man, you'll be in trouble. You're a stupid, wasted old fart, Holdall, and it's about time you got put in your place.'

Holdall stares at Robertson, fights the urge to head-butt him. He has never head-butted anyone before, but a football thug he arrested once gave him instructions on exactly how to do it – he still has the scar – so he is pretty sure he could carry it off. Forehead to the bridge of the nose. Straightforward enough. And the bastard is asking for it.

'So,' says Robertson, with some relish, 'I'd like you and MacPherson to go to all the old people's homes in the area. Find out if any of them recognise our Mr Porter. Think you can handle that, or are you not sure you can cope with the strain?'

The foosty moustache which crawls along the Robertson top lip curls slightly, and then he is gone – seconds before Holdall can choose to make the career-ending decision of acquainting Robertson's nose with the inside of his head.

Holdall and MacPherson stand and watch him go, biting their lips and their tongues. They stay like that for several seconds, as they each consider what other lines of work it would be possible for them to enter.

'Ye know, sir,' says MacPherson finally.

'What, Sergeant?'

'If Ah'd been you, Ah'd have head-butted that cunt.'

Chapter 23

A Prayer for Cemolina Thomson

A Davie Provan. A Gene Wilder. A Jack Nance (*Eraserhead*). He grimaces. An electrocution special. A John Lennon (pre-Yoko). A regulation US Marine.

Barney reels off the haircuts of the men as they walk past him, shaking his hand. He gives not a thought to the hair of the women. He knows nothing of hairdressing, except that you can charge a lot more money for doing the same amount of work.

'She was a good woman, Barney,' says a mourner, clasping Barney's hands. Barney nods, stares at his Sigourney Weaver (*Alien*). Odd haircut for a bloke.

A good woman? What might the definition of that be? A woman who lured men back to her flat and then murdered them. Chopped up their bodies. He doesn't like to think about the fact that maybe she ate some of them, but the thought keeps intruding.

Another man walks by and shakes his hand, another friend of Allan's whom he doesn't recognise. He is surprised by the turnout at the funeral, but he hardly knows any of these people. They're all associates of his brother, all here for Allan, not Cemolina, and certainly not Barney. An endless line of them pouring out of the crematorium, shaking the hands of the bereaved brothers.

169

It might have been a good service, but Barney wasn't listening. A few words from a minister who had never met her, a couple of hymns which Allan had chosen and which Barney didn't know – what hymns did he know? – then a lengthy eulogy from the elder son, talking about his mother's good nature and her remarkable and amusing eccentricity. Nearly made Barney weep, so he switched off.

A man with a completely inappropriate Michael Jackson '75 walks past Barney without even acknowledging him.

Eccentric? Is that what his mother was? A lovable eccentric?

His immediate job is done. The bodies disposed of, and the police fended off as best as he could manage. The interview on Sunday morning with Holdall and MacPherson had been uncomfortable, but he didn't think they were any closer to him. A few words about Partick Thistle and Aberdeen, eased by having had time to read a report in the morning paper, and they had seemed satisfied. It had all been, as far as he could tell, routine. Little or no suspicion on their part. Holdall had seemed more interested in his description of the first goal, in fact.

And so now, with those unpleasantries out of the way, he has had plenty of time to reflect on all that has happened. To think about the deeds his mother committed.

An advert in the newspaper. No artifice about it. Mature woman, mid-eighties. And there were young men who replied to it. He cannot begin to believe that, but it must have happened. He himself had had to dispose of the evidence. And the woman that was his mother's final victim, what about her? How did she come to be sucked into it? Had she answered the ad in the paper?

A kid with a Soapy Souter shakes Barney's hand and trudges off, looking miserable in his Sunday best.

And what would have happened once they had arrived at his mother's flat? He can see the extensive range of butcher's tools and the five cut-throat razors he had found in the kitchen. Had that been it? A cup of tea, perhaps something stronger, then what had these men been expecting? Not their little old lady suddenly appearing beside them, her hand poised with a razor – then slice!

170

the throat open and bleeding. Or had she waited until they were in bed?

Almost a more distasteful thought: his mother in bed practising her Eastern lovemaking. Barney shivers, accepts the weak hand of a man with a Bruce Forsyth '74.

The line is drawing to an end. Bill Taylor stops in front of Barney, holds out his hand. Their eyes meet. Lock. The full horror of the police findings at the flat of Chris Porter are only at this moment being made public, so Bill knows nothing.

'Terrible business,' he says. Edge to the voice.

'Aye,' says Barney.

Bill's suspicions of Barney are running rampant. He sees himself as some kind of defender of truth and justice. Superman! But he has no proof, and has not yet done anything. Not told anyone, made no effort to discover what has happened to Wullie and Chris. Frightened perhaps. Not Superman at all. Vacillationman.

He nods. Barney nods. Bill walks on and wonders. Barney remains distracted.

A final couple pass by, the woman with the hair of Queens, the man with an indeterminate eighties cut which Barney can't quite place. Then the line is over and the minister is with them, shaking them both by the hand.

'Thanks a lot, Michael,' says Allan. Allan wears an expensive dark grey suit. Bought especially for funerals.

The minister smiles.

'It was an honour. She was a most singular woman.' Extends his hand to Barney, who takes it.

'I'm sorry I never got to meet your mother, Barney. Quite the eccentric, by all accounts.'

Barney smiles weakly. Christ! He wants to scream. If he hears that word one more time. Eccentric? She was mad! A killer! A freezer full of them now, and how many more throughout her life?

He has spent the past couple of days wondering about it. Could there have been earlier signs that he ignored? Madness and murder. And another horrible thought lurking at the back of his mind. The death of his own father; had she been responsible for that? A heart attack, she said, but the boys had been on holiday at the time with their grandmother. It could have been anything.

All those strange jams and wines and pies she's made all her life; what had been in those? Barney stares blankly back at the minister. He is getting carried away. Cannot stop himself thinking of his mother handing over a fruit loaf for sale at a coffee morning, wondering exactly what the ingredients were. Everything he can ever remember her doing – and he has over forty years of a dominated life to look back upon – is now shrouded in suspicion; every act potentially barbaric.

Maybe he is doing her an injustice, or at least the memory of the woman she once was. Perhaps the eccentricity gave way to madness only in the last few months.

He realises he is still holding the minster's hand, shaking slowly. Lets go, and the Rev. Michael Flood smiles awkwardly and is led away by Allan Thomson, who eyes his brother with suspicion.

Barney is left alone with the macabre landscape of his imagination. Endless debate on endless questions he knows he will never have the answers to. He will one day rationalise it all, persuade himself that his mother's mental affliction had been with her for only these last few months. Might one day even see the funny side of it. An old woman luring young men back to her flat, then giving them so much more than they expected. But for now he is left to wonder what he is the son of, what evil begot him.

A soft hand on his.

'Are you all right, Barney?'

He awakes from the grotesque stupor, eyes wide open. Barbara Thomson stands in front of him, dressed in black. Auburn hair touching her shoulders. Autumn lips. Concern in her eyes, eyes pools of entrapment and impossible allure.

'Oh, Barbara, Ah didnae see ye there. Aye, aye, Ah'm fine.'

She smiles and he wants to leap into her mouth and lose himself inside her.

'I was watching you during the service. You never heard a word,' she says.

He shakes his head.

'Distracted, ye know,' he replies.

They stare at each other, nothing to say. Concern in the

172

one matched by longing in the other. Barney has forgotten about his mother. Wishes he could think of something to say. What smooth words had Allan first used to attract this prize of a woman?

'You were a lot closer to her than Allan was. It must be difficult for you.'

'Aye, well, ye know.' God! Barney, think of better than that. He stares intently at her. Suddenly has an idea. He could tell Barbara everything.

Of course, that was it! What has he been waiting for? Cool, sensible Barbara. She'd understand, she'd listen. She wouldn't immediately denounce him; turn him over to the police. Not Barbara. He could tell her now, where they stand. At least make the first noises about needing to talk to her. Get it all off his chest, the whole bloody thing. She might not approve of what he'd done, but at least she'd listen. Sympathise.

He imagines her advising him to run away, head for the hills. Confessing to him that she's fed up with Allan so she'll come with him. They could disappear together to some remote corner of the world where Barney could set up his own barber's shop. Barney's Hair Emporium. Barney's Place. Barney's Cut 'n' Go – Haircutting While U Wait: No Children. Has another thought. Maybe he could do what they did in olden times; become a barber surgeon. Haircutting one minute, surgical operations the next. That might be for him. Barney's Cut 'n' Slice. Sees a sign above the door; a pair of scissors dripping with blood. Just him and Barbara, together alone. No more Agnes, no more terrible soap operas.

'You look upset, Barney,' says Barbara. 'Maybe I should leave you to your thoughts.'

He stares at her, mouth open slightly. She answers his stare, wonders if he has indigestion. He can think of no words. His voice stalls. His brain automatically shuts down. She smiles and turns away. Barney watches her go, his dreams along with her. He had his chance. Barbara alone. He should have said something, and if he couldn't do it then, when would he ever be able to do it?

Never. That was the only answer to all the questions of his dreams.

Barbara disappears into the crowd. The image of his

mother, cut-throat razor slicing into soft throaty flesh, returns.

He stares at the hard, cold ground, does not even fight the vision. A vision which should be incredible, but is so very easy to see. He never could believe his mother's strength sometimes. She had always seemed so frail, and yet . . .

'Barney, ye better come on.' He looks up. Agnes in front of him. Attempting compassion. 'There's another crowd here for the next funeral.'

Move 'em up, get 'em in, shove 'em out. The cattle market of the crematorium. Barney nods.

'Ye awright tae go tae the hotel?' she says. Tea; cheese-and-cucumber sandwiches; funeral cake; polite chatter, sombre mood.

'Aye,' says Barney with resignation. 'Got tae dae it, eh?'

She smiles sympathetically and nods. Takes his arm as he walks away. Turning his back on his mother.

Agnes hopes she has set the video correctly. Today's the day when Codpiece and Strawberry will attempt to sabotage Zephaniah's hernia operation.

Chapter 24

The Anthony Hopkins

The steady click of scissors and the gentle flop of hair to the floor are the only sounds in the shop. The three barbers go about their business, solemnly and quietly, each lost in their own thoughts and leaving their victims to theirs. The row of customers sit along the wall, a couple reading newspapers, silently resigned to their fate.

It is Wednesday afternoon. Word has got out from the police about the gruesome findings in Chris Porter's apartment, and of the great supply of body parts which was discovered on a dump on Monday morning. These included the butchered corpse of Wullie Henderson.

There are some in the town who cannot understand why James Henderson has not closed the shop – at the very least temporarily – but they are those with no conception of the Calvinist work ethic, which Henderson imagines himself to possess. If there are to be members of the public needing their hair cut, then the shop has to be open.

Had it been a women's hairdresser's, the customers would have fled, and the shop would already have gone out of business. But men are lazy about hair, creatures of habit, and the previous two days have been as busy as normal. And besides, the word is getting out – there is a barber there at the top of his game. If Jim Baxter had cut hair at Wembley in '63, they are saying, this is how he would have done it.

The chair at the back of the shop is now empty. At the chair next to that James Henderson is working. He knows he shouldn't be. It is ridiculous almost, and his wife is furious, but he tells himself that this is what Wullie would have wanted. What is more important to him is that it gets him out of the house, takes his mind off what has happened. That is something he cannot yet think about.

The next chair along is worked by James's friend Arnie Braithwaite, who has agreed to start a couple of weeks early. His is a steady, if unspectacular, style, a sort of Robert Vaughn of the barber business. He won't give you an Oscar-winning haircut, but then neither will he let you down.

And then finally, working the prized window chair, is Barney Thomson. He moved into it with almost indecent haste, the day before. Perhaps if he had been thinking straight, then James would have considered it odd, but everything is a blur to him at the moment.

Barney cannot believe his luck. He hasn't heard from the police since his interview with Holdall and MacPherson on Sunday, and while he has still expected them to come marching back at any time and arrest him, it is now three days later and nothing has happened. And the interview that appeared in the paper that morning with some policeman, Robertson, seemed to indicate that they were after Chris; not pursuing any other line of inquiry. It has all worked like a dream. On top of that, the window seat has fallen into his lap, almost before he'd started to think about it.

Suddenly he is cutting hair with an extraordinary panache, now that he is free of his bitter rivals. If Arnie is the Robert Vaughn of the business, Barney is the Anthony Hopkins. Always good, and frequently magnificent. He is cutting with verve and style, each hair pruned to perfection. He can taper the back of a head with ease and the flick of the razor. Ears present few problems, so quickly has he become as one with their intricate curves. Layering, perms, short back and sides, Kevin Keegan '78s, they are all easy for him now. In a matter of three days he has become quick, efficient and composed, and now, when he feels like it, he will happily chat away to the customers on any subject they choose.

So, Rangers have been drawn against Celtic in the semi-final of the Cup? No surprise there. Bill Clinton – dirty big shagger if you ask me. Break-up of the Antarctic icepack – the cause of Chernobyl, he will opine to anyone who listens. *Blackadder*? The second series is definitely the best, but if you push him he might say the fourth. If someone wants to chat, Barney is there for them.

The afternoon is drawing to a pleasant conclusion, the customers beginning to dwindle away, when the door opens and one last customer, his collar pulled up against the driving rain, comes rushing into the shop. It is Bill, Barney's dominoes partner; Barney's nemesis.

He catches sight of him in the mirror as he walks through the door. They haven't spoken since the funeral, and with all that has happened, Barney has quite forgotten about worrying whether or not Bill will go to the police. From the fact that they haven't turned up on his doorstep, jangling handcuffs and waving a search warrant, he presumes that he has never made the call.

However, this is quite a bit out of his way, so he surely hasn't just come for a haircut. He must want to talk.

They look at each other in the mirror. Bill nods at Barney, Barney nods at Bill. Bill sits down and waits his turn, steely determination in his eye. Bill the Cat.

Barney returns to his haircut, mildly perturbed, yet strangely confident. It is a simple and requested US Marine job, for a chap who says he is going hillwalking in Africa; wants to reduce the chances of getting huge bugs in his hair. Barney has been knocking it off quite quickly, but now, as he hopes Bill will go to one of the others, he slows down. No other customer awaits – Bill is next in line.

'So, where abouts are ye goin' walkin' in Africa, young man?' he asks, neatly executing an ear bypass manoeuvre.

'I'm going to climb Kiliminjaro,' says Malcolm Harrison. Does his best to sound cool.

'Oh, aye, aye, that's near Cape Town, is it no'?' says Barney, using his new-found confidence and knowledge to their fullest.

177

Harrison pauses briefly before answering, unsure exactly whether to tell a man from the Barber Death Shop from Hell with a pair of scissors in his hands that he is talking rubbish.

'Well, it's on the same continent.' Maybe sarcasm isn't wise, he reflects. 'It's in northern Tanzania.'

'Oh, aye, aye. Near that, what dae ye call it, Zimbabwe, is it?'

The man smiles a weak 'there's no point in telling you any different' smile, hopes Barney will shut up.

'You know, my friend, Ah wis readin' a book aboot Alexander the Great the other day,' says Barney, snipping casually at a loose hair he's missed on the right.

'Oh, aye, what was that?' says the man, reflecting on the fact that any barber in the world would have been able to give him this haircut, and he really needn't have subjected himself to this to get it.

'Apparently,' says Barney, electric razor poised and running in midair, ready to swoop, 'apparently he wis a complete poof. Total arse bandit, so he wis. He spent a' his time conquerin' other countries, so that he wouldnae huvtae stay at home and get married.' The razor dives down and bites hard, doing that razor thing. 'Amazin', eh?'

African Explorer mumbles something in reply. Vaguely remembers Wullie telling him this story about five years previously. He knows, however, to keep his mouth shut, and that Barney will be unlikely to go on. So he thinks.

At that moment, however, James finishes with his customer. The man rises, glumly hands over the required cash, gives a baleful look in the direction of the mirror. James turns to Bill.

'Hello, Bill. Bit out o' yer way?'

'Aye, aye, just thought Ah'd come by. Ye awright, James? Ah'm surprised ye're here.'

'Aye, well, ye know how it is. The show must go on and a' that. Wullie would've wanted it that way.'

Bill nods, thinks that's one of the most ridiculous things he's ever heard in his life. This is a barber's shop, for goodness' sake, he wants to say, not a ten-million-pound theatre production.

'Aye, well. Ah'm sorry tae hear aboot Wullie, though. That's a terrible business.'

James nods, tries hard to think about something else. There is no way he is ready to think about his eldest son being chopped and packaged. Not yet.

'Aye, well, would ye like tae step up tae the big chair, Bill?'

Bill shakes his head, smiles apologetically. 'Aye, well, if ye dinnae mind, James, Ah'm just gonnae wait for ma old mate Barney here. Heard he wis cuttin' hair like Kenny Dalglish takin' the ba' past five defenders.'

James shrugs, doesn't really mind. Barney smiles at the compliment. Assuming that it is a compliment, as he's never heard of Kenny Dalglish.

Resigning himself to his fate, he hurries through the rest of the US Marine, and sends the guy packing. Such is his relief at escaping earlier and more easily than he was expecting, Malcolm Harrison hands over an unusually large tip to Barney, almost runs out of the shop.

Barney pockets the loot, turns with something approaching trepidation to Bill. He nods at him, and Bill takes the few short steps to the doom of the barber's chair.

Barney thinks, decides he should play it cool. Innocent, but still appalled at what has gone on. Confident that Bill is unlikely to start throwing accusations at him while James sits rather forlornly, two yards away.

Swishing the cape with a matadorial flourish, he places it around Bill's neck and, resisting the temptation to throttle him with it, tucks a towel benignly in behind.

'What'll it be, then, Bill, my friend?'

Bill is staring off into some far distance, suddenly shakes his head to bring himself back. Looks at Barney in the mirror. 'Whit? Oh aye, aye. A Jimmy Stewart, please, if ye don't mind, Barney.'

'Right enough,' says Barney. 'Nae bother.' And neither will it be. The legendary 'Jimmy Stewart', a staple of any barber's repertoire for the past sixty years, is as straightforward as they come.

Bill feels a little uncomfortable. He has come because he wants to question Barney to his face. He wasn't sure what sort of set-up he had expected in the shop, or how he was going to be able to raise the subject. And now that he has found James there, he realises that there is no way he can talk about Wullie and Chris.

After he had heard that Chris too was missing, he had been on the verge of going to the police there and then, without talking to Barney first. Knew that he would be successfully put off if he did. But something had stayed his hand; had made him want to see Barney. The reports that had started appearing in the paper on Monday night were just incredible. He can't believe that of Chris, but then neither can he believe it of Barney, who is the person he set out to suspect from the first.

But then perhaps that's always the case with serial killers. It's not as if they necessarily wear their chainsaw on their sleeve. Presumably, whoever it turns out to be, there will be people who will be shocked by their identity, having thought them all along to be normal citizens. At least, not the type to go hacking up fellow humans and packing them precisely into freezer bags.

A shiver runs down his spine at the touch of cold steel on his neck.

'Game o' dominoes the night, Barney?'

Barney hesitates. What to do? Doesn't want to get into any conversations about what has happened, which he obviously will if they go to the pub; but then, he has to find out if Bill suspects him of anything, and whether or not he intends going to the police.

He is about to accept when another thought strikes him. It might be better if he agrees to meet him alone, down some dark alley somewhere. A dark and dangerous rendezvous. Perfect. Dismisses the thought straight away. Idiot. How can he arrange that now when there are three other people sitting in the shop?

The thought that he could kill all of them flits fleetingly through his head, but he manages to dismiss it before he sets out on the road of giving it serious consideration.

No, it's going to have to be dominoes in a crowded pub, and if he doesn't like what Bill says, he can take it from there. The Domino Killer. That's got a ring to it.

'Aye, aye, Bill, why not? See if Ah can make up for last week, eh?' he says, then laughs.

'No' much chance of that,' says Bill, smiling, and to anyone watching it might seem like there is nothing amiss.

Chapter 25

'The Queen of Diamonds'

Holdall sits in his office, feet on his desk. Idly tosses cards at the bin which lies three yards away. The floor is covered in them, while a solitary card sits in the centre of the wicker basket. The queen of diamonds; and if he isn't mistaken, she's laughing at him.

It is Wednesday evening, and the day has dragged interminably, as have the two which preceded it. It is far enough into the evening for him to have gone home long before, but he is too busy trying to decide how he can sort out the mess of a case in which he is involved. He has his ideas of where they should be going, and most of them lead in the direction of Barney Thomson. He's been trying to make a few discreet inquiries regarding the man, but it is proving difficult to find anyone who knows anything about him. Barney Thomson, the barber with no personality. The task is made ever harder by Robertson sticking his nose in, making sure he constantly has trivial and useless tasks to take care of. Robertson; bastard.

He isn't fooling himself. Knows full well that Robertson doesn't want him coming up with anything which might lead to the crime being solved. He is a credit freak, needs it all to himself. If it means that they spend their time going after the wrong man, well, that's that.

What they need to do is find the body of Chris Porter. If all his years of detective work have given him any nose for a crime, the whole fridge business at Porter's flat was a set-up, and a lousy set-up at that. But where exactly are they supposed to start searching for Porter's body? His idea is to keep a strict watch on Barney Thomson, the only lead they have, but that would involve plenty of man-hours, and that would require Robertson's agreement. He knows there's no way he's going to get it. Bloody-mindedly doesn't want it.

The two of spades thuds off the back wall, plummets into the basket. He holds his arms aloft in mock appreciation of the crowd's applause, is still accepting their plaudits when MacPherson walks into the room.

'Just had a cohesive thought, sir,' says MacPherson, smiling.

'Sod off, Sergeant.' Lowers his hands, resumes aimlessly chucking the cards across the office. The five of clubs whizzes past the bin, flies in a wild arc, lands about four yards off target. 'Still here, Sergeant? Won't Mrs MacPherson be looking for you?'

'Late-night shoppin' at Marks and Spencer's.'

'Thought that was Thursday nights just before Christmas?'

'And Wednesday nights just before the middle o' March 'n a', so it seems.'

Holdall grunts, narrowly misses with the two of diamonds. 'I wondered why I couldn't get hold of Jean when I tried earlier.' The king of clubs doubles back on itself, lands beside his chair.

'Ah've got somethin' which might interest ye, sir,' says MacPherson.

'Oh, aye? Rangers managed to sign that big German full back, have they?'

'Naw, sir. It's about Barney Thomson's mother.'

Holdall stops, the three of hearts poised at his fingertips. 'What? The Rangers have signed Barney Thomson's mother?'

'No, sir. She's dead.'

Holdall releases the card and it dips narrowly short of the target. 'They definitely don't want to sign her, then. Maybe the Celtic might want her. They need a full back.'

The five of clubs veers dangerously to the left, and had it been sharper of edge would have had the head off an hibiscus.

'Chief Inspector . . .'

Holdall stops in mid-toss, looks at MacPherson, lays his cards on the table – although not in any metaphorical sense.

'Very well, Sergeant, what is it you're trying to tell me?'

'Well, it seems that Mrs Cemolina Thomson died last . . .'

'Cemolina?'

'Aye, sir, Ah know. Anyway, she died last week. Thursday night, tae be precise. Buried her on Monday. It sounded a bit far-fetched, but Jenkins did say that the packages had been handled by an old woman. So Ah did some checkin'.'

Holdall has a stab of guilt. MacPherson works while he tosses cards into a bucket.

'And?'

'It a' ties up. Ah spoke tae her doctor. Says she was long down the road tae senility, but he thought her harmless enough, so he didnae have a problem wi' her staying at home. Attentive son, and a' that. She stayed in a flat in Springburn.'

Holdall purses his lips, turns away from MacPherson. The ace of hearts leaves his fingers and flies straight towards the centre of the bin. Veers wildly at the last second, misses by several feet. His cards exhausted, he turns back to MacPherson.

'So what are we saying here? That this Cemolina Thomson . . . I can't believe that anyone is called Cemolina . . . that this woman is the mass murderer? She dies, and so the son, Barney, has to dispose of the bodies?'

'There's more.'

'Oh, aye. Looking for promotion, Sergeant?'

'Ah wish. Checked out a few things. Seems she'd been placing an advert in a lonely hearts column. Mature wummin, mid-eighties, a' that shite.'

'You're kidding?'

'Naw. Straight up.'

'Was she a looker?'

MacPherson grimaces. 'She wis eighty-five.'

'Aye, fine.'

'Anyway, checked her PO box – there were a couple of replies in there. Could be that's how she got her men back to her flat.'

'Jesus. There are some sick people out there.'

'Wanting tae sleep wi' an eighty-five-year-old bird isnae as sick as lopping someone's napper aff and mailing it tae their mother.'

'Aye, fair point. What about the girl, though? Louise MacDonald.'

MacPherson shrugs.

'Who knows? It's a strange world. Maybe she answered the advert 'n all.'

Holdall looks at the carpet, loses his thoughts in its plain weave. A young lesbian with a desire for an eighty-five-year-old woman. Outrageous thirty years ago perhaps, but now? Was it so strange any more in these times of Gothic darkness?

He looks up as MacPherson starts speaking again, for he is not finished.

'And Ah also found out she's a member o' some auld wimmin's group. Ye know these things where they bugger off around the country tae look at monuments, and eat scones and jam in tea shops.'

'And?'

'So far this year they've visited the salmon ladder at Pitlochry, Edinburgh Castle, a distillery in Kingussie' – he raises an eyebrow – 'Largs, for whatever it is auld folk dae in Largs, some gardens in Aberdeen, and Ayr.'

Holdall lets out a low whistle. The towns where the body parts were posted from.

'Bloody hell, MacPherson. You're full of surprises. How long'd it take you to find all this out?'

'Couple o' hours.'

Holdall stares. What had he done for the last couple of hours? Had a cup of tea and a Mars bar; shuffled some paper; checked that night's TV schedule; tossed cards at a bin. It was time he got his hunger back. He'd been an enthusiastic detective sergeant once. A long time ago, when he thought he could make a difference.

'Good work, Sergeant,' he says. Means it.

'Thank you, sir.'

185

'Right. So what have we got? This old woman attracts young blokes back to her flat. Kills them somehow, chops up the bodies. Goes off on one of her day trips, and mails a well-wrapped part of the body back to the family. Sounds plausible. But where do Wullie Henderson and Chris Porter come into it? They died, assuming that Porter is dead, either side of the mother, if she died on the Thursday night.'

MacPherson stares at the floor. Has already wondered about that.

'Maybe Thomson killed Henderson completely independently o' his mother . . .'

'But Jenkins said that the old woman had left traces of whatever the hell it was on Henderson's body parts as well.'

'Then maybe she just happened tae kill Henderson as her next victim, and never got around tae sendin' a bit o' him off in the post. Whatever, one or other o' them did for Henderson, and then Porter finds out about it, and Thomson has tae see him off 'n a'. And then he hatched the plan tae incriminate Porter. Or maybe he just bumped off Porter in order tae incriminate him, in case we were gonnae start sniffing around. Let's face it, sir, if that's it, it's worked like a dancer. Robertson's fallen for it like shit off a stick.'

Holdall sits back and rubs his hand across his chin. He likes it. It is all circumstantial, but it has a good feel to it. An honest feel to it, which Chris Porter running off to London leaving a hand cooking in a pot doesn't have.

'Sergeant, I'm impressed. I like this, and we've got to go with it, regardless of what that eejit Robertson says. We need to do some more checking on this mother, although it seems like you might already have done enough. And I think we should have another word with Mr Thomson in the next day or two.'

'Aye, sir.'

MacPherson smiles determinedly, walks out of the office. Holdall gets off his chair to pick up the cards. Thank God for that. They have something to go on, at last, and a decent working hypothesis. No point in taking it to M yet, because he's as bad as Robertson, but in a couple of days they might have made enough inroads into the thing to be able to go public. Or they might have made complete idiots of themselves. He winces at the thought, sits back in his seat and watches as the ace of spades flies straight into the centre of the bin. Then bounces out and lands four feet away in the base of a plant.

Bill and Barney are involved in another life-and-death struggle on the dominoes pitch. They have both been putting so much concentration into it because neither man wants to talk about what they are both there to talk about. So apart from a brief argument about who should buy the first round, hardly a word has been exchanged.

Finally, after a few intricate stratagems involving double fours and threes, Bill has wrapped up his third game in a row, and after Barney has done his best to make like the good loser, it is time to talk.

They sip solemnly on their beers, wait for the other to start off. Barney has no wish to encourage him; Bill – the Great Diplomat – once again has no idea where to begin.

'So, Barney,' he says eventually, the art of subtlety still a mystery to him, 'any idea whit's happened tae Chris?'

Barney takes a long draw from his pint this time, sets it down firmly on the table.

'Naw, Ah don't, Bill. As much as you, at any rate, given what Ah've read in the papers. And if ye're here tae imply anythin' else, then ye might as well get on wi' it.'

Bill holds up his hands in conciliation. He has no desire to get straight into any argument, but at the same time he sees no reason to be delicate. It is just over a week since they sat in the same bar, and Barney told him how much he hated Wullie and Chris. The memory fortifies him, and he takes a strength-giving pull from his pint.

'Ye really think that Chris killed Wullie, Barney? They were mates, were they no'? Chris couldnae a killed anybody.'

'And Ah could, is that whit ye're implyin'?'

Bill shakes his head, wonders again about Barney being so aggressively defensive. Knows what they tell you in women's magazines about that.

'Ah'm nae implyin' nuthin', Barney. Keep yer heid on, will ye no'? Whatever happened, it's obvious that

187

someone killed Wullie, an' Ah'm just sayin' that it's right odd that it should be Chris of a' people. Such a nice lad, and the two o' them gettin' on sae well, and a' that.'

It gives Barney pause. Perhaps he has been overdoing it a little. He nods, bows his head towards his pint. He is going to have to get into the persona of someone who hasn't killed his two work colleagues and disposed of six other bodies; be convincing about it. The police have left him alone for the moment, but it doesn't mean they won't be back. And if he can't convince Bill, he certainly isn't going to be able to convince that bastard MacPherson.

'Aye, aye, ye're right, Bill. Ah know ye're no' accusing me o' nothin'. It's just been an awfy hard week, what wi' they two dyin' an my mother 'n a'.'

Bill nods. Is feeling guilty enough about accusing Barney that the words don't really register. This man is his oldest friend, after all. He has to stop so lightly accusing him of murder. Or worse. It goes a lot further than just murder, if the papers are anything to go by. There is some psychopath on the loose, and whoever it is, it surely isn't going to be his old dominoes partner. But then surely it isn't going to be Chris either.

What was it he'd just said there that had been peculiar?

'The new lad's quite a nice chap,' says Barney, breaking his chain of thought.

'Oh, aye, aye,' says Bill. 'Who is he exactly?'

'Friend o' James's. Just moved o'er fi' Uddingston.'

'Oh, right. The south.'

'Aye. Just started yesterday. A steady hand, by the looks of things.'

'Smashin'. That'll be just whit ye'se are needin'.'

'Aye, aye.'

'Aye, aye, that's right enough.'

'Fancy another game o' the blocks? It's time Ah kicked yer arse for ye.'

'Rack 'em up.'

They settle down to another dour and tense struggle on the dominoes table. It isn't until they are into their second hand that it suddenly strikes Bill that Barney had said that both Chris and Wullie had died. There is a mild flicker on his face, but he manages to contain it within the lugubrious whole. Perhaps it was just a slip of the tongue. Or perhaps Barney knows something that he doesn't.

Chapter 26

The Byzantine Triple Weave

Barney has had a good day in the shop. He likes Thursdays, always has for some reason. It is just some gut barbetorial instinct, but he feels as if he always does good work on those days, and today has been no exception. Whether it is as a result of some fine work he has done earlier in the week, or whether it is because the customers don't like the look of the other two, he isn't sure, but he has never had so many people ask for him to cut their hair. And he has responded magnificently, customer after customer leaving the shop with dream hair. He was not even daunted when one man asked him for a Byzantine Triple Weave, generally regarded as the toughest haircut in the world. He executed it with knightly splendour, his scissors swooping to cut like a majestic, unfettered eagle, his blow-dryer exercising consummate control over the intricate thatched patterns; his comb could have been forged in the elven forests of Middle Earth, so smoothly was it wielded in his hands. When he finished, he almost expected the rest of the shop to rise in calamitous applause, but instead there was just the usual rustle of paper, the soft plop of hair to the ground. The man stuck an extra fifty pence into his hand and left; the meagre gift the gods receive. Perhaps he wouldn't be mentioned in the birthday Honours list for that haircut, but at least he had the satisfaction of a job well done. Indeed, magnificently done.

And so the day has gone on. One dream haircut after another, all swiftly done and beautifully presented. Never before has a barber been so busy, and he rises to the challenge with a magnificence which clearly amazes his colleagues. And he is finding that the longer it is since the police have last been to see him, the more relaxed he becomes about it. It is only four days, but it's enough to give him some breathing space, allow him to think they are off his trail.

And what's more, there had been a wonderful item on the news the night before, when some buffoon of a policeman had said that there had been a possible sighting of Chris in London. Heaven! They had obviously completely fallen for it. If he had known the police were this stupid, he would have turned to crime years ago. He might let all this die down, and then try something else. Not grotesque murder, of course; something more financially rewarding.

He'd had a few worries with Bill the night before, and he isn't sure that he'd handled it all that well, but in the end he thinks he's got away with it. It is one thing for Bill to have his little suspicions, another altogether for him to go trundling along to the police. And anyway, will they listen, now that they are so consumed with the search for Chris? No, he isn't out of the woods yet, but he is standing at the edge of them, looking at a beautiful green field with glorious snow-capped mountains in the distance.

Mentally free of his troubles, he has relaxed into the routine of majestic haircutting, and on occasion exercising his new-found confidence with trivia.

His last customer of the day has asked for, surprisingly, an Argentina '78. It is the first one of those he has had to do in over fifteen years, and normally it might have given him cause for trepidation. But not today, however, now that he is exercising all his new wiles and confidence to their fullest extent.

'Whit? You're sayin' that Tyson would huv beaten Rocky Marciano? Ye've goat tae be jokin'. That great puddin'! All right, so he dominated boxin' before he went

191

intae prison, and maybe he'll dominate it again if he can stop bitin' bastards' ears aff, but ye've goat tae look at the quality o' the opposition. Marciano wis fightin' against some o' the greats, and he never lost tae ony o' them. Look who Tyson's beaten. A bunch o' useless wankers, that's who. My mother could sort oot maist o' these guys.'

Barney nods at the chap as he goes into the closing routine of the haircut – the sewing back up, as it were. He is a little out of his depth here, he has to admit. He has just made the bold statement that Tyson would have floored Marciano, when he has no idea who Marciano was. That's not to say that he isn't just as likely to find someone who would have agreed with him, but when you're talking about boxing you usually have to count on an argument.

'Ah suppose ye'll be saying next that Tyson could've beaten Ali.'

Barney thinks about this for a second or two; has no idea who Argentina '78 is talking about, realises once again the folly of reading the sports pages for three days, then trying to discuss them. It is obvious from the way it has been phrased, however, what he's supposed to say.

'Ali! Christ, naw, Ah widnae go that far. It's just Tyson can punch, ye know, and when ye can punch like him ye can gie onybody a go at it.'

'So whit? Are ye sayin' that Ali couldnae take a punch, is that it? Is that the crap ye're comin' oot wi', 'cause if it is, ye're talkin' shite. Ye no' remember the Rumble in the Jungle, Wee Man? Did Ali no' take everythin' that Foreman could gie him, yon night, 'cause he did. Ah suppose ye'll be sayin' next that Foreman couldnae punch, 'cause that's aboot the level o' everythin' else ye've been coming oot wi'. Ah'm tellin' you that Foreman could bloody punch, but, an' a damn sight harder than ony o' these namby-pambys that ye get fightin' these days. Christ, the very fact that that auld puddin' was still takin' them a' on, even though he wis in his sixties, surely tae shite shows ye whit the talent's like these days in the heavy-weight division. So whit does it mean if Tyson can beat maist o' them? It disnae mean dick, so it disnae, especially when he cannae beat Holyfield, an' remember that yon eejit's nae even a proper heavyweight.'

Barney nods a few times, grateful that the man has turned the argument into an aggressive monologue, for in precluding Barney from the conversation he prevents him from saying anything else monumentally stupid. He badly wants to change the subject, but doesn't know how to just step into the middle of the flow and start talking about the weather. Still, he is going to have to do it before he moves off into territory even more unbeknown to him.

The telephone out the back of the shop rings and James, who is in the middle of a tricky Lennie Bennett '91, looks at the other two.

'Aw, Arnie, could ye no' get that, please? Probably just some eejit tryin' tae make an appointment.'

Arnie has been doing a straightforward 'Groomed Oor Wullie' on an eight-year-old, nods and goes out to the back of the shop. Whoever it is, Barney doesn't care, but at least it stops the boxing fan's flow, and he doesn't immediately start up again. Best not talk about anything at all, Barney reflects, in case he wants to get into some other impenetrable sport.

'It's for you, Barney,' says Arnie, coming out of the back. 'Didn't say who it was.'

Barney creases his forehead, makes his apologies to Argentina '78. No one ever phones him at work. He has no idea why, but suddenly he begins to feel nervous; a shiver runs down his back, hairs on his neck rise; his body tingles.

He closes the door behind him, lifts the phone. He pauses for a second. Knows he isn't going to like this.

'Hello?' His voice is quiet, almost unintelligible. There is no reply. 'Hello?' he says a little louder.

'Barney Thomson?'

It is a man, a little younger than himself probably. Nothing much else to read into it. He remains hesitant.

'Aye.'

The voice comes out at him, low and ominous. 'Perhaps you'd better check on that body you disposed of at the weekend.'

Silence.

Barney feels the shock of the words like a train thumping into his chest, crushing his bones.

'What?' His voice is weak, a child crying. 'What did ye say?'

There is silence at the other end of the phone, and Barney's mouth goes dry, the sweat starts to bead on his face. He shouts 'Hello' down the phone another couple of times, but the line is empty. Then it clicks off, and he is holding nothing in his hands; alone in the small back room with his guilt and his fear.

He sits down in the seat, runs his fingers through his hair.

'Christ almighty, who the hell was that? Someone knows aboot Chris. Someone knows Ah got rid o' Chris's body. Jesus Christ, did someone see me?'

He stares wildly around him, as if expecting the person to be in the room with him. Looks morosely at the floor. The police, it must be the police. But then, what are they doing calling up and leaving cryptic messages? If they know he's done it, surely they will just come for him and kick the shit out of him, like they usually do. It must be someone else. Must be. His mind races.

And what did the Voice mean, you had better check on the body? Is it not there any more? How exactly is he supposed to check on a body which is at the bottom of a bloody deep loch? But then, maybe the loch isn't so deep. He has just assumed it would be. It could be that he ineptly tied it all together and it's come apart. He sees the body floating on the surface, floating ashore. Christ, it doesn't make sense. Why would anyone call him up if that's happened? Surely they'd just phone the police.

The fear grows within him – there is some higher force at work. Whose voice had that been? Should he have recognised it? Maybe it was Chris or Wullie? He begins the descent into the throes of panic. Doesn't believe in any ghosts, supernatural forces, but maybe that's what's going on. God, he handled eight corpses over the previous weekend. Can he be surprised if some weird things start happening?

So what was the voice? Was it good or bad? It's given him a warning, but is it doing it to look out for him? Christ, if that's the case, then he has no idea who it might have been. Check on the body? God, he will have to go back out to the loch. What else can he do? He has to listen to it, whoever it was.

The door opens and James sticks his head in, looks at him.

'Ye awright there, Barney? Ye've been in here ages.'

Barney tries not to display the turmoil he is in, coughs roughly to straighten his voice out before he speaks.

'Aye, aye, Ah'm fine. It wis just Agnes aboot something, that's a'. Ah'll be through in a minute.'

James looks at him a little curiously, returns to the shop. Barney starts rubbing his forehead with his fingers, tries to think. He has to go out to the loch, but then, what is the point in that? What does he expect to find?

Thinks of the Voice. 'Christ, Ah'm gettin' strange bloody phone calls, but Ah cannae ignore it. What'll happen if Ah dae?' he mutters to himself. Wonders if there'll be someone waiting for him when he goes out there. Chris, Wullie, anybody. A Satanic Host of the Undead; avenging angels. Whoever is going to be there, he has to face it.

Gets up slowly, walks back into the shop, half expecting everyone to turn and stare at him, pointing, shouting 'Killer!' There are a couple of half-hearted glances, but no one really pays any attention. Argentina '78 is reading the *Evening Times*, nods at Barney as he returns.

'Sorry aboot that, mate. Ye get these calls, ye know.'

'Aye, mate, don't worry aboot it.'

Fortunately he doesn't put down the paper, and Barney is able to concentrate on putting the finishing touches to what he considers to be the worst hairstyle of all time, even though, in a moment of weakness, he had one himself at one time. Every time he finishes one of these he feels horrifically embarrassed, is always amazed when the recipient expresses satisfaction. And despite his shaking hand, sweaty palm, his mind being on another planet, this turns out to be no different.

MacPherson opens the car door, gets in beside Holdall. Just as he does so, the light rain increases, becomes a torrential downpour. Shuts the door behind him, stares ahead as Holdall drums his fingers on the steering wheel.

'Well, Sergeant, did he fall for it?'

MacPherson thinks about it for a second or two, turns, looks Holdall in the eye.

'He absolutely crapped his load, sir.'

Holdall smiles grimly, clutches the steering wheel.

'And what would you say, Sergeant? Did he sound like he didn't know what the hell you were talking about, or did he sound as if he had to get rid of a corpse last weekend?'

MacPherson considers this, chooses his words carefully.

'Bloody right. He sounded as if he'd disposed of about fifteen corpses last weekend.'

Holdall purses his lips, looks out into the torrential rain.

'So, we've got the bastard, then?'

MacPherson nods, looks at his boss.

'Aye, Ah'd say we did,' he says.

And so the two men settle back and wait for Barney to emerge from the shop.

Chapter 27

E for Brigadoon

Barney heads out on the motorway to Stirling, with Holdall and MacPherson keeping a safe distance behind. Holdall is driving with a grim smile on his face, which he hasn't been able to remove since MacPherson's phone call.

They had a moment or two of doubt when Barney returned home after work, but they waited him out, and half an hour later he emerged. Looking extremely nervous, he stared wildly up and down the street to see if anyone was watching him; something he did particularly badly as the two policemen were sitting twenty yards away and he didn't notice them.

'What's the plan, sir?' asks MacPherson, as they drive past Stirling, the castle majestic through the rain on their right.

Holdall has to drag himself away from the worst excesses of his imagination. In his mind, he already has Barney Thomson arrested and convicted, and he is receiving huge plaudits. Meanwhile, Robertson has been demoted to constable and is working nights in the worst area in Los Angeles. He has never been one to go in for brownie points and success on cases for personal gain, but in this instance, since it will get right up Robertson's nose, he is going to relish it.

'The plan?' He stares ahead into the murk towards Barney's car, thinks about it for the first time. 'I don't really think we can have a plan, Sergeant, do you? Just have to wait and see what happens when we get there. If we're lucky, if we're very, very lucky, he'll have buried the body somewhere, and he'll be so stupid that he'll dig it up again for us, just to check it's still there. That is, of course, as I said, if we're very, very lucky. At which point, we move in and make the arrest. After that, I don't know about you, but I'm going to go and find Robertson and piss on his shoes.'

MacPherson nods. 'Stoatir. Think Ah'll join you. Ah might crap on them, though.' Is about to continue with what he's going to do to Robertson when he sees Barney turning off. 'Look, sir, he's taking the Callander road.'

Holdall starts to slow, not wanting to take the turn-off too close behind him. 'Callander, eh? I tell you, Sergeant, it's always the same with these quiet little Brigadoons out in the sticks. Shortcake and knitwear shops on the outside, bloodied and chopped corpses on the in.'

'Ah don't think Callander's quite Brigadoon, sir. Ah've got a mate works out here. They've got the usual problems, ye know. Drugs, the rest o' it.'

'Aye, well, Sergeant, that's the modern Brigadoon for you. The next time the damn place crops up, there'll be someone round selling them E, or whatever it is the weans are popping these days, McDonald's will be wanting to set up a franchise, and at least five of the villagers will subscribe to satellite TV.'

'Ye never know. Ecstasy might help Cyd Charisse wi' her Scottish accent.'

'But I wouldn't count on it.'

And so they wind on, through the twisty country roads towards Callander. Most of the time they lose Barney in the bends, and if he were to pull off at some point, quickly dimming his lights, they might easily miss him. Can't risk getting too close, although Barney has not spotted anything. Just as they have not spotted the car behind them.

They get a good sight of him again as he goes onto the straight road through Callander itself, but soon he is past it and back onto the twists and turns of the road on the other side.

'So it turns out that Callander isn't the graveyard of horror after all. Better look out, Sergeant. I can't believe he'll be going too much further than this. Keep a sharp lookout for his car pulled into the side of the road.'

But as it is, when it happens they are on a long, straight section of the road, running alongside a loch; Barney is well within their sights. They watch him pull in, then they drive past him, around the next corner. Park the car, dim the lights.

'This is it, Sergeant. Time to get our killer. Don't disturb him until we see the whites of the eyes of the corpse.'

'Aye, right, nae bother.'

They get out of the car, let the doors quietly click shut. The rain has stopped, but the air is cold and heavy with moisture. They creep along the side of the road beside the bushes, come around the corner where they left Barney. He has parked in a large clearing set aside for tourists; wooden benches and litter bins.

For the first time Holdall has doubts about what he is going to find. If Barney has buried the body, why on earth would he do it in such a public place? And then, as they crouch down in the bushes on the edge of the clearing, they see him. He stands at the edge of the loch, running his hands through his hair, constantly glancing over his shoulder. Even from twenty yards away they can see how nervous he is. Waiting for the Voice.

He begins pacing up and down the edge of the loch, looking out over the water. Suddenly it strikes Holdall what he's doing.

'Shitbags! Bloody shitbags!' he says under his breath.

'What?' whispers MacPherson.

'He hasn't buried the bloody body at all. He's dumped it in the bloody loch. Christ, we'll never get it now.'

He stops as Barney looks over his shoulder in their direction. They hold their breath, but there is no need. It's just part of another anxious look around, and quickly his eyes move on around the rest of the clearing, then back out to the loch.

'Why did the bloody eejit listen to us? Christ, if he's dumped the bloody body into the water, how on earth would he be able to come and check it? What a fucking idiot. Christ, I tell you, Sergeant, I've got a good mind to go down there and kick his head in. What an arse.'

'Don't give up yet. He's obviously scared, and he's going to do something stupid.'

Barney casts another quick look around him, gives a little jump as he imagines he hears something. Starts pacing up and down again, his head constantly on the move.

'Very obviously. So, Sergeant, what are we going to do?'

'Ah havenae the faintest idea, sir.'

'No, neither do I. Shitbags. Absolute bloody shitbags.'

Barney stands at the edge of the water, wonders why he is there. What was he expecting to find, exactly, and who the hell is it that has brought him to this place again? In the cold, damp, silent night air he is constantly having to fight his imagination, forever throwing his eyes over his shoulder looking for the Voice. However, there is nothing in the murk.

It suddenly struck him as he drove down that he might be being set up, that someone might be following him. Barber Walks into Trap Like Complete Idiot – Arrested for Multiple Murders. As far as he can tell, however, he was alone most of the way. Certainly, there was the odd car or two behind him, but always far enough back for him not to worry.

And even if there is someone there, what are they hoping to find? No more than he has been able to find by coming here himself again. He knows he made a good job of doing up the body. Perhaps it won't survive down there until the end of time, but it will surely be good for a long while, not just two or three days.

Despite the cold he is in a sweat, such is the beating of his heart and his anxiety. His head is filled with a hundred ghosts, every one of them chattering away, every one stepping on stones and twigs, brushing through the bushes. Whispering.

And then, suddenly, to his dread fear, to his heart-stopping horror, he hears footsteps on the stones behind him. Real footsteps; not some frantic delusion of his imagination. And more than one set, by the sound of it – four slow, heavy footfalls are approaching him from behind. He freezes, a whimper rises in his throat. Nausea – vomit not far behind, the fear is so strong.

They stop three or four yards behind him, but he can't turn round, not this time when he knows that there's really going to be someone there. Once again the mad desire to panic, to just lose control of every sense and every grasp on normal behaviour, is sweeping over him.

He tries to calm himself – think logically, Barney, for God's sake! Swallows. There are two possibilities. Either they are ghosts, in which case he is going to absolutely cream his underwear; or they are real people, very possibly police officers. In which case he is going to absolutely cream his underwear. Either way, he really doesn't want to have to turn round.

Whoever it is, they are just waiting for him, waiting for him to look over his shoulder. If it is the police, presumably it is going to be those two who have been to see him a couple of times already. Holdall and MacPherson, he thinks their names are. If they are ghosts, then it's going to be Wullie and Chris.

He starts to hope that it's going to be the police. Wullie and Chris will be really pissed off at him.

And then one of the footsteps scrunches along the stones a little nearer to him, and he can feel the arm being stretched out, the finger tapping him on the shoulder.

He knows it is coming, but at the touch a shudder racks his body, his insides are tangibly gripped by fear; he almost has difficulty in standing up straight. Slowly, slowly, he turns, an impossible thing to do, so consumed with fear and dread is he. His eyes are almost closed as finally he is able to look behind him and see the two men who wait upon him.

Suddenly there is a strange lifting in his heart. He doesn't recognise either of them. He may be standing in the pitch dark beside a loch on a cold and miserable March evening, confronted by two strange men in raincoats whom he's never seen before, but at least they're not ghosts, and at least they're not the two policemen whom he'd been expecting to see.

He is almost relieved.

Chapter 28

Stramash

The man who has tapped Barney on the shoulder steps back beside the other; the three men face each other in the gloom, as the rain once again begins to fall; a few drops and then instant torrent. Water bounces off stones.

While he is relieved at not facing a ghost or the police, Barney knows this isn't going to be a good thing. Perhaps it'll be about the rowing boat he borrowed the other night, not left where he found it. Maybe these are the Loch Police about to arrest him for dumping something into the water, even though they don't know what. Nuclear waste for all they know.

'Mr Barney Thomson?' asks the older one of the two, fishing inside his coat pocket.

Barney nods. Has no idea what is coming, knows that it's going to be bad. Barney Thomson, barber, this is your sodding life. It might as well be. The man produces an identity card from his coat, holds it up towards Barney.

'Chief Inspector Robertson, CID. This is Detective Sergeant Jobson. We're here to arrest you for the murders of Mr Christopher Porter and Mr William Henderson . . .'

Barney closes his eyes. Christ, of course he recognises him. This is the idiot who was on television the night before. Lying.

Robertson continues, but Barney doesn't hear him. So they've found him out. All his precautions haven't been good enough, and they've drawn him with this sucker punch out to where he dumped the body. All right, so he can deny it if he wants. They're not going to be able to discover the body that quickly, if at all. It might be a bloody deep loch. But he's no master criminal, just a barber; that's all. Lying will come no easier to him than disposing of bodies, or talking about football. They'll catch him out, and bloody quickly too. They've suckered him into this, and now they've got him by the balls. But whatever he does, and he's already thought about this, he has to keep his mother's name out of it if he can.

'This is where you dumped the body of Porter?' says Robertson.

Barney nods, his eyes rooted to the wet stones.

'What on earth made you come back out here? That was hardly the act of a master criminal. All you bloody eejits are the same. Thick as shit, the lot of you. Couldn't commit a decent crime to save yourselves.'

Barney looks up at him as the rain begins to fall with greater intensity. Will it never stop? he thinks – has more to worry about than the weather. Realises for the first time just how cold it is; shivers and rubs his hands on his arms. Master criminal! There's a joke. If they're talking like that, you could almost imagine that they've got the wrong man. Except they don't.

'The phone call,' says Barney. 'Wasn't it you that phoned?'

Robertson looks quizzically at him, then at Detective Sergeant Jobson. 'I didn't phone anyone. What about you, Jobson?'

Jobson shakes his head, looks stupid.

'That's because it was us that phoned, you bastard.'

Holdall and MacPherson stride out of the bushes. Batman and Robin. They have watched incredulous as Robertson and Jobson appeared from the other side of the clearing to grab Barney. And they're pissed off.

'Ah, Holdall, just in time to be too late to make an arrest. How the hell did you get here?' says Robertson.

'I could ask you the same thing.'

'We've just been keeping tabs on our man, you know,

following him around, waiting for him to do something idiotic. You didn't really think that I believed the Porter story, did you?'

'I don't see why not. You're stupid enough.'

'You can make all the insults you like, dog-breath, but I was here first, and I've got the arrest, so you can go and piss in a poke.'

Holdall seethes. Grits his teeth. Blood boils.

'You bloody bastard. The only reason he's out here is because we phoned him and tricked him into it.'

Robertson nods his understanding, smiles. 'Ah, so that's why he did it. It was you who were following him out here, just in front of us. Well, well, Holdall, you're not as thick as you look. You never know, I might mention it in the report, but then again, I probably won't. It's not as if anyone is going to believe that you used your initiative anyway.'

Turns away from Holdall, looks at Barney. Triumph! He has beaten Holdall to something for the first time in fifteen years, is absolutely delighted. That Holdall has actually turned up to witness it is all the more magnificent.

'Right you,' he says to Barney, 'are you going to come quietly or am I going to have to kick the shit out of you?'

Barney lowers his head, takes a couple of paces forward. Of course he's going to go quietly. What else is there for him to do? He's no more a criminal than he is a giant banana, chopped up and mashed with cream. Topped with a cherry.

Robertson and Jobson stand either side of him, take hold of his arms. Know there's little point in handcuffs. Both of them are privately doubting that they have the right man. Surely no mad killer this, despite what Bill Taylor told them that afternoon on the phone.

Robertson stops, looks at Holdall. The delight of victory continues doing cartwheels around his face.

'Thanks for all your help, Holdall,' he says. Voice wet with sarcasm; dripping. 'I'll try and remember you when I'm superintendent. Maybe find some more old people's homes for you and your monkey to visit. If you're up to it.'

An insult too far.

Surprisingly, when it happens, it is MacPherson who cracks, albeit only marginally before Holdall is about to.

He has heard enough. Takes three steps forward and head-butts Robertson with superb mathematical precision. Has a vague feeling as he does it that it won't do his career much good, but that's more than subdued by the delicious, hedonistic pleasure of retribution. His forehead meets the bridge of Robertson's nose with a sumptuous crack, then Robertson falls, clutching his face, the blood already spurting and running through his fingers.

A gorilla in the mist, Jobson springs to Robertson's defence, swinging his fist viciously at MacPherson, catching him full on the side of the head. Sends him reeling. As he falls back, MacPherson still reflects that even though he's just been thumped on the head, and that he'll probably be sacked, it's worth it.

Jobson has no time to enjoy his pugilistic triumph before Holdall is on top of him, fists flailing, boots lashing out. Jobson reels back, stumbles to the ground under the onslaught as Holdall assails his head and body.

Barney stands back and watches. Amazed. Strangely, has no desire to try to flee the scene. What's the point? They know where they can get him, and if he doesn't go home, where exactly is he going to go? A life on the run isn't for him. A brief vision of Brazil flashes into his head, beaches full of exotic women, but he knows it's fantasy. Prison, and a lot of it – that is what lies in front of him.

Barney starts suddenly, takes another two steps back, almost stepping into the loch. Robertson has produced a gun, and slowly Holdall and MacPherson, who have been beating massive lumps out of Jobson, become aware of him. They straighten up, stare at Robertson, leave Jobson bruised and bloodied on the floor. But through the badly beaten face, he still smiles, picks himself off the ground, and he too produces a gun from inside his coat.

Holdall and MacPherson stare them down, undaunted.

'You're finished after that, you bastards,' says Robertson. 'What the hell do you think you're doing? Do you think you can get away with assaulting fellow police officers?' He laughs suddenly. Mocking, derisive. A laugh that threatens to take away the warm glow which MacPherson still feels. Perhaps the glory will be more fleeting than he imagined.

Robertson takes a pair of handcuffs from his coat pocket, throws them at Jobson. 'Cuff them, Sergeant, and make sure they're too tight.'

They do it slowly when they do it, daring Robertson to shoot, but almost in slow motion Holdall and MacPherson bring guns out from inside their coats, lift them, aim at the others. They flinch, but hold steady.

Jobson and MacPherson aim at each other, as do Robertson and Holdall. A neat division between ranks. No one aims at Barney. Barney might as well not be there.

'What the hell are you doing with guns, Holdall? You're in so much shit for this, you useless bastard. And here was me saying that you weren't as stupid as you looked.'

'We were chasing after a known mass killer, so we had guns for the same reasons that you've got guns, scumbag. Quite within our rights, and we signed them out.'

'Well, why didn't I know about it, when I was in charge of the investigation? I should have been told.'

'I wouldn't tell you if your dick was on fire, Robertson.'

Angry words die away; the four men are left standing at gunpoint. The rain streams steadily down upon them, bouncing off the stones, thudding into the water of the loch. Slowly, slight wisps of steam begin to rise from the four bodies, curious formations dispersed under the weight of the torrential downpour. The heat of battle. Tension.

The guns remain steady, none of them willing to be the first to lower their weapon. Barney takes another pace or two back into the water. None of them are interested in him – which is odd because he's the criminal – but he doesn't want to get shot accidentally. Can't believe anyone will be stupid enough to shoot in the circumstances.

Robertson's nerve is first to wither; he makes the initial attempt at reconciliation.

'Look, Holdall, this is stupid. We're supposed to be on the same side.'

Holdall doesn't move, waits to hear what else he is going to say. He is absolutely right, of course, and it isn't as if he has any desire to shoot anybody. No matter how much he despises the man at whom he is aiming.

'We'll forget about all this, all right, Holdall? Just put the guns down, and we'll forget about any assault charges.'

Jobson winces, as he has already begun to look forward to those. The other two stand in doubtful silence. Robertson is not a man to trust.

'What about the arrest report?' says Holdall, not entirely interested. He wants to keep Robertson going while he thinks about how best to get out of the hole they have dug for themselves. Damage limitation. 'How's that going to work out?'

'I don't know, Holdall. Did anyone else at the station know that you were on to Thomson?'

Holdall slowly shakes his head.

Robertson smiles. Holdall knows what it means. 'Same here, actually. Couldn't afford to let you hear about it in case you got in there first. Too bad you were just too late, Holdall.'

The spark is coming back to him, as the throbbing pain in his nose increases. This is a bloody stupid situation he's in. There's no way that anyone is going to shoot anyone else, and there's certainly no way that he's going to give Holdall and his ape any credit in solving the crime.

'Look, bugger this, shithead. None of us is going to shoot anyone, so let's all just put down our guns and get the psycho into custody. Then we can argue about the report, but just think yourselves lucky if I don't mention your assaults. Don't think I'm about to start giving you credit for the whole damn thing.' Sneers, isn't finished. 'You and your monkey'll be lucky if you stay out of prison. Fucking morons, getting in the way of decent police work.'

Barney isn't sure which gun goes off first. It might be MacPherson's but he can't be certain. All he knows is that the instant one goes off, there's a loud report as several other guns are fired. He doesn't see anything, however, as he immediately covers his head with his hands, leaps back into the loch.

He lies in the freezing cold under two feet of water for a few seconds, terrified, desperate, listening to the wild beatings of his heart. Slowly and fearfully he lifts his head, looks along the shore. The noise has died quickly in the rain and mist and low cloud, and now there is nothing but the sound of the rain falling on the four bodies that lie on the wet stones.

Barney gets up out of the water, walks over towards

them, his face still contorted in horror and disbelief, clothes clinging horribly to him, the hands of the insane. Robertson has been shot in the face, his body crumpled on the ground, his head a bloody mess on the rocks. Perhaps he has become immune to this kind of thing after the previous few days, but Barney looks at it, doesn't even wince. Both MacPherson and Jobson have been shot in the chest and lie dead, their bodies thrown back with the force of the bullets.

Then he realises that Holdall is stirring, walks and stands over him. The shot which hit him was not so great, catching him on the shoulder and knocking him down; he isn't dead. He has a dazed look on his face, still doesn't take in what has happened.

The brief glimpse of freedom which Barney has been afforded vanishes in the dust. He looks at Holdall, bends to help him. Thinks: What am I doing? If he finishes off Holdall now, he can get away with it. He's just heard the two of them say it – that no one else at the station is in on their suspicions. Perhaps there might be someone who comes to talk to him after this, but no one who knows why these four were here. He can easily kill off Holdall, walk away from it all.

He searches around on the ground, sees Holdall's gun. Picks it up, weighs it in his hands for a second, uneasily points it at Holdall.

Christ, he thinks. This is a big step. Bloody huge. It's one thing accidentally killing your two work colleagues, and another clearing up after your mad, psychotic mother. This is cold-blooded murder.

He stands over Holdall, the gun in his hand, his doubts careering around inside his head. Holdall opens his eyes, looks at him. Barney steps back, immediately knows he isn't going to be able to pull the trigger. Barney's the man with the gun – and he's the one with the fear in his eyes, not Holdall.

Holdall eases himself to try to sit up, resting on his right arm, lessening the pain in his other shoulder. He looks at Barney, knows he isn't going to shoot. So does Barney; and he lowers the gun.

Holdall is already beginning to think. He looks around him at the other three bodies. Jesus, what the hell is there for him now? He's just killed a police officer. How the hell can he explain this? His career has just vanished down the toilet inside two minutes; along with the rest of his life. Christ, Mrs Holdall is going to be pissed off, he thinks.

'Looks like I'm in as much shit as you,' he says to Barney, looking up, away from the surrounding carnage.

Barney nods, lets the gun slip out of his fingers, fall to the ground. He hasn't thought about that, but aye, they will be in as much shit as each other.

Barney says, 'That wis just about the maist stupit thing Ah've ever seen in ma life.'

Holdall smiles, laughs. Bitter.

'Perhaps we can do a deal,' he says, 'although, Christ, it'll have to be one hell of a deal to get us out of this.'

Barney nods. Tries to think of something, but he doesn't have a naturally devious mind. Out of his depth.

'It was your mother, right?' says Holdall.

Barney nods again, surprise on his face. So they knew anyway.

'And what about the other two?'

'Ah know it sounds hard tae believe,' says Barney, 'but they were accidents. Baith o' them. But Ah didnae suppose anybody wis gonnae believe that.'

Holdall nods, smiles. 'You're right. I certainly don't.'

There is a small noise behind Barney. A low groan. A wraith. The two of them turn round. Jobson is leaning up on one arm, gun waving in his hand. It's difficult to tell which one of the two he is aiming at, and there is no time for anything other than the initial surprise to show on their faces; not even time to leap out of the way.

The gun goes off.

The shot catches Holdall full in the throat. He slumps back, his body a tangle of arms and legs on the rocks, finally dead.

Jobson aims unsteadily at Barney, the gun still meandering from side to side. Barney can do nothing, feet of clay. Closes his eyes.

Again, the gun goes off. The final explosion of noise in the night, and Jobson collapses back onto the stones; the final effort.

Barney opens his eyes. It was a wild shot, fired off into the cavernous darkness of night. He walks over gingerly, stands beside Jobson. Kicks at him gently, bends over to feel his pulse. He's no doctor, but he knows this. Jobson is dead.

Barney looks out over the water. It is difficult to see more than a few yards across the loch; thick mist, thick rain. He shivers in the cold, is once again aware of the clinging dampness of his clothes.

Go and check on the body you disposed of, that was what the Voice had told him on the phone. Well, he's done it. He's looked out over the loch and he knows Chris is still there. Dead and buried, and the secret has just died with the four policemen on the lochside.

He swallows, shivers again, turns towards his car. It's time to go home.

Epilogue

The cold weather has come to Glasgow earlier than usual, and although it is only the beginning of November, there is already a sprinkling of snow on the ground. However, it's unlikely it will last as the cold freshness of night has given way to a harsh and bitter wind, bringing low cloud and drizzle.

In the shop there is a comfortable warmth, the gentle sounds of hair flopping quietly to the floor, easy chatter between barber and customer. There are three chairs being worked, and five people waiting, having succumbed to their anticipatory trepidation, along the bench.

Barney is at the window chair, as he has been for eight months, cutting with his now legendary verve and panache. Next to him is Arnie Braithwaite, as steady and unspectacular as ever. Then there is an empty chair, and at the end a young lad who is the only person whom James Henderson has been able to get to replace himself. The shop has a grotesque reputation to live down after the events of the previous spring, and it has been difficult for James to find someone willing to come and work there.

In the end he settled for a twenty-one-year-old lad called Chip Ripkin, fresh from Ontario State Barber University. His hands are erratic, his style occasionally wayward. Some might say he's the Marlon Brando of the shop, but even at his best he can never achieve that level of intensity. He can be great, and he can be dreadful, but never is he magnificent, and never will he produce the hair of kings.

No, if you are looking for that in the area, there is only one barber; one man; one pair of scissors. Some say that he is giving the best haircuts in Europe – although there is always someone to point out how easy that is, as the second you cross the Channel you are accosted by limp-wristed, rubber-lipped French faggots, brandishing hair-dryers and family-sized cans of mousse. However, whatever his merits on the European stage, there is no denying that Barney Thomson is cutting hair like a dream. There are few who have tied it to the time when Wullie was murdered and Chris fled from Glasgow, but it was noticed by one or two people. Not that they mind or comment to anyone – they are all just happy to be able to get their hair cut by a man whose prowess is becoming legend. If Muhammad Ali had cut George Foreman's hair in Zaire in 1974, they say, this is how he would have done it.

Barney walked away from the scene at the loch, stunned and disbelieving. He wasn't sure that there would be no one else from the police to suspect him; spent weeks waiting for them to turn up at the shop, or at his house; but it never happened. Attention was distracted from the serial murder case by the horrific – and, as far as the press were concerned, singularly impressive – events at Loch Lubnaig. Then, as attention shifted back to catching the murderer, there were more sightings of Chris Porter in London, and even, Barney was delighted to see, in a small town near Brussels. It was all more than he could have dreamed of, and now here he is, eight months later – cutting hair like the British conquered colonies of pygmies in the eighteenth and nineteenth centuries, and in charge of the day-to-day running of the shop.

Of the five people sitting along the wall waiting to get their hair cut, he can be pretty sure that at least three of them will be waiting for him, and possibly all five.

Consequently, he now cuts hair as slowly as he can, making as much inconsequential chatter as he can manage along the way. Just because all these bastards are coming to him now doesn't mean that he's forgotten the resentment of the past twenty years. It's a small gesture, but it's all he can do to make them pay. He hurries for no man, and every man waits on him.

He catches sight of himself in the mirror, feels pleased at how good he is looking these days. There is a light in his eye that hasn't been there since he first picked up a pair of scissors.

He turns his attention back to his customer. It had been slightly tricky to start with. A young Arab lad came in, asking for an Anwar Sadat '67, a haircut of which Barney has no conception. The Anwar Sadat 'Camp David' is one of his old specialities, but this was new to him. However, it turned out to be the same haircut under a different name. Piece of cake. And now he is slowly making his way through it, taking as long as possible round the ears, even though he could do them in under twenty seconds, such is his new-found skill and confidence.

'Did ye know,' he says to the chap, deciding that although he is going slowly he isn't going quite slowly enough, 'that the average male life expectancy in Russia is fifty-nine? What dae ye make o' that, eh? Fifty-nine!'

Kazeem Al-Sahel smiles, tries to look interested. He'd read this stuff in a newspaper a few months earlier. Barney is probably going to mention the abortion rate next. 'You want an Anwar Sadat '67?' they had said to him in Cairo. 'Go to Barney Thomson. But be prepared to wait. And be bored shitless, be prepared to be bored shitless.'

'And ye know, there are twice as many recorded abortions as there are births. And that's recorded abortions, mind. Jings knows how many actual ones there are.' He shakes his head, waves the scissors about in the air a little. 'That no amazin'? Ye wouldnae huv thought it, now would ye? These folk can put people in space, after a'.'

Kazeem smiles, thinks about the weather. They had told him it would be cold, but this place is incredible.

'But Ah'll tell ye somethin'. The life expectancy might be fifty-nine and a' that, but huv ye noticed the age o' a' they senior politicians, eh? There's none o' them died at fifty-nine, that's for sure. An' ye know why, don't ye? Because they'll a' get perfectly good medical facilities,

213

won't they now. Aye, bloody right they will, while a' their people are dyin' at fifty-nine. And that's just the average, mind. Think how many must be dyin' younger than that.'

Kazeem affects a serious face, nods in agreement again. This is unbelievable; but as he studies the progress of the haircut in the mirror, he has to admit that it is worth it. With hair like this he can get the pick of the babes in all the seedy bars in Alexandria.

A seat is pushed back, and to Barney's right Chip's customer stands up, starts fishing around in his pocket for some money. He has been given a beautiful regulation, geometrically precise US Marine haircut. Barney smiles to himself, wonders if it had been requested. Assumes otherwise and that Chip has had to fall back on one of the old safety nets.

The man walks out looking reasonably unhappy, although it could be because of the rain and wind he is just about to face. Chip turns to the man at the head of the queue.

'All right, mate, you're up next.'

The man shakes his head, nods at Barney. 'That's OK, thanks, Ah'll wait for this fellow here, if that's awright?'

'Aye, sure,' says Chip, unconcerned. He moves on to the next and then the next until he has worked his way down the line. All of them are waiting for Barney. He shrugs, sits down in his chair, puts his feet up on the counter, picks up a copy of a two-month-old *Toronto Sun* which his mother has just sent to him. It seems a man in Flin Flon, Manitoba has transmogrified himself into a lizard and can't change back.

Barney looks along the array of men waiting on him, allows himself an even bigger smile. This is what he's always wanted. He recognises a few of them as blokes who would always have waited for Chris or Wullie at his expense, consciously makes the effort to slow down even more. He's made a good job of that ear he's just finished, but perhaps he should just go over it again. If he malingers properly he can take nearly forty-five minutes over this particular haircut.

He snips at an invisible hair, stands back to see how much of a difference it makes to the overall shape of the head. As he does so, he spots another few invisible hairs he still has to remove. This could indeed take a while after all, he thinks to himself.

The young man picks up a flat stone, skims it across the surface of the water. It bounces five or six times, comes to a stop, rests for a fraction of a second on the surface, sinks. He looks at it for a while, then picks up another stone, throws it at the wrong angle, watches it plunge straight into the water.

He turns, starts to wander along the shore of the loch. The hills rise up on the other side, the early winter snow beginning to show on the top of them. Around him, large branches lie on the rocky shore, evidence of the devastation caused by the bad storms of two days earlier.

He pulls his jacket collar up close around his neck against the biting wind, looks at the sky. It's going to be raining soon, judging by the great swathes of low cloud beginning to sweep across from the west.

His mind is not on the weather, however. He's too busy thinking about Amanda Bagel – the girl who's just dumped him for some big-city shopfitter from Stirling. He turned up in the bar in Callander one night with his fake Gucci watch, a sunbed tan and a couple of twenties in his wallet, and she fell for him like he'd been Brad Pitt. God, they'd made him look stupid.

He's walking his dog, an enormous smiley Labrador called Bond, attempting to tell himself that it isn't all that important – won't mean a thing in a couple of months. That's right, of course, but it's still difficult not to feel stupid and hurt. Particularly the way they had laughed at his 'Tie A Yellow Ribbon' during the karaoke.

He picks up a large stone – short of a boulder but still heavy – heaves it into the water. It hits with a satisfyingly loud splash, and he has to jump out of the way of the spray.

Away along the shore, where he has run off, Bond starts barking. He spends most of his life barking, but now it is with a little more gusto. He is pulling at a black bag, jumping around excitedly, frantically wagging his tail.

Andrew Marshall slowly walks along the shore towards him. He isn't too interested, knows that Bond would bark excitedly if he found a prostitute in Bangkok.

As he walks up, the dog sits down on the rocks beside the large, bound black plastic bags; tail going furiously, enormous grin on his face. Marshall stops beside the dog, pats him on the head.

'Good boy, Bond, what have you found here?'

He looks down at the large package, now loosely bound with thin rope. Doesn't want to touch it with his hands. Kicks at it, but it refuses to reveal its secrets. Kicks harder.

The bag opens slightly, and in slow motion an arm falls out, plops onto the stones. Blue, deteriorated skin, but it is human.

Marshall stares at it for a second or two, then steps back. Horror runs wild across his face. He isn't thinking of Amanda Bagel now. Turns away, and starts to vomit heavily onto the damp stones.

On seeing the product of his discovery – such a magnificent reaction – Bond goes into another frantic dance, bouncing around in circles, yapping loudly, his tail swirling extravagantly in the chill November air.